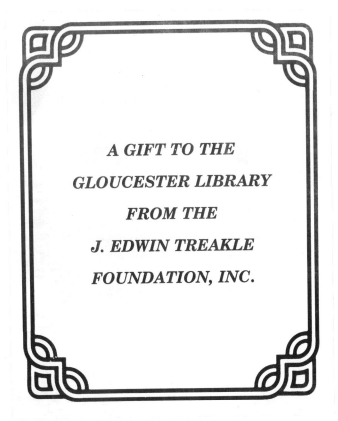

QUEEN OF BONES

ALSO BY TERESA DOVALPAGE

Death Comes in through the Kitchen

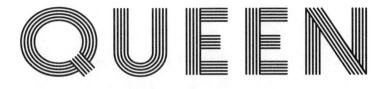

QUEEN

OF

BONES

TERESA DOVALPAGE

SOHO
CRIME

Published by
Soho Press, Inc.
227 W 17th Street
New York, NY 10011

Library of Congress Cataloging-in-Publication Data

Dovalpage, Teresa
Queen of bones / Teresa Dovalpage.

ISBN 978-1-64129-015-9
eISBN 978-1-64129-016-6

Description: New York, NY : Soho Crime, [2019]
I. Title.
PS3604.O936 Q44 2019 813'.6—dc23 2019010829

Interior design by Janine Agro

Printed in the United States of America

10 9 8 7 6 5 4 3 2 1

*To the wonderful Soho Crime team,
for making me a better writer. Muchas gracias.*

QUEEN OF BONES

PART I

OYĂ'S
FEAST
DAY

Oyá dresses in purple and dances alone, with a necklace of bones clicking around her throat. She is the keeper of the cemetery gates and welcomes refugees from life into her kingdom. She collects little sugar skulls on the Day of the Dead and offers sweets to the widows and orphans. The mother of nine stillborn children, she has a special place in her heart for women who have lost their babies, as well as children without mothers.

Owner of the seven winds, Oyá rides them and rules over storms, tornadoes and tempests. She often enters atop them brandishing her horsetail fly whisk, swirling her nine skirts.

She keeps one foot in life and the other in death. Mistress of cemeteries, the *orisha* Oyá is not to be invoked in vain.

The ceremony started in the early afternoon. That day, February the second, was devoted to the Virgin of Candlemas, associated with Oyá in the religion of Santería. (Oyá was also worshipped as Saint Thérèse of Lisieux, though even the most knowledgeable *santeros* couldn't explain her connection to the Discalced Carmelite nun.) Her devotees had gathered in an old house located in Guanabacoa, a colonial town across the bay from Old Havana. The backyard had been prepared for the ceremony. An altar stood covered in a white linen cloth and ornamented with fresh violets, candles and candy in small copper trays, as copper was Oyá's favorite metal. Eggplants—fried, steamed and raw— were served on porcelain dishes. A large print of Saint Thérèse presided over the altar.

The women who hoped to be possessed by the *orisha* wore skirts in all shades of purple. The newly initiated to Santería were dressed only in white down to their stockings and shoes, with white turbans or white kerchiefs covering their heads. Men were dressed formally, with old-fashioned, well-polished shoes and ironed shirts.

At three o'clock, the drums began to thunder. Dancers moved in a whirl and followed the rhythm that beat in synchrony with their hearts. Those who didn't dance remained in their seats eating malanga fritters, a meat and vegetable stew known as *caldosa*, and guava pastries, all of which they washed down with generous swigs of rum.

Rosita, a tall forty-year-old woman who was dressed in all purple for the occasion, felt the wind rushing in her ears. Padrino, the *babalawo* who was leading the ceremony and Rosita's Santería godfather, tapped her lightly on the head with his cane. She stood, and Oyá entered her body, whizzing through her, dancing, laughing, crying, bending over, grabbing food from people's plates and eating it right before their eyes.

"*Maferefún, Oyá!*" they greeted her.

The *orisha* blessed the guests in a grave voice laced with

contralto undertones. Oyá kept dancing until Rosita's body collapsed on the floor. Two older women took her to a bedroom and placed cologne-soaked towelettes over her forehead. After she'd recovered, Padrino came to see her.

"Oyá came in strong today," he said.

Rosita smiled and spoke in her usual high-pitched tone.

"Padrino, do you remember that boyfriend of mine who left Cuba?" she said. "Juan. The one I couldn't forget."

Padrino nodded.

"Oyá told me he would come back, like a salmon swimming upstream. Does it mean he's returning to Cuba, Padrino? Juan hasn't been back in twenty years, as far as I know."

"Maybe," Padrino said. "But do you know why salmon swim upstream, *mija*?"

"To mate?" Rosita blushed.

"And to die."

"Don't say that, Padrino," she whispered. "Juan is the man of my life. The first and the only."

1

CHANGE OF PLANS

The water was hot, but not scalding. The golden glow from the jasmine-scented candles created an ambiance that Sharon, in her real estate jargon, would have called "intimate luxury," "a private sanctuary" or something of that sort. She shifted in the hot tub and let the jets massage the tension out of her shoulders. Her acupuncturist had mentioned that she had knots underneath them. She sighed.

Yes, she was tense. Nobody had to tell her that; she already knew it. First, there was that high-end North Valley property she'd hoped to sell sooner than now. She had wooed the owners, an elderly couple, until they'd agreed to let her stage their home using everything from trendy designer friends' tips to feng shui furniture arrangement. In a year of painfully slow sales, that 1950s house, with its five bedrooms, marble countertops, and Olympic-sized pool that hadn't been used in a decade, was her small real estate company's most auspicious prospect.

An open house was scheduled for the coming Saturday, the same day her husband was flying to Havana. It would be Juan's first visit to the island in twenty years. Though he hadn't said it in so many words, Sharon had the impression that he preferred to travel alone.

She remembered their meeting with the Santa Fe–based travel agent who had helped Juan get his Cuban passport and, bizarre as it sounded, his Cuban visa as well.

"So I can buy a visa for twenty-five dollars and travel to Cuba tomorrow, while Juan, who was born there, needs to ask for *his* visa three months in advance and pay four times as much?" Sharon had asked. "That's weird."

Sonya, the Cuban travel agent, agreed that it was.

"That's Cuba for you, Señora," she said. "A little crazy, yes. But I'm here to make the paperwork easier for you."

Sharon liked her. Sonya was bright and polite. Unlike Juan, she spoke fluent English. As the only Cubaviajes representative in New Mexico, Sonya managed everything from people-to-people permits for Americans to the entry visa and passport applications for Cubans.

It took Juan five months to get all his documents ready. He needed a Cuban passport to enter the island *and* an American passport to get back to the United States. The fact that he had left Cuba on a raft in 1994 also contributed to the delay, Sonya explained. "They" had probably gone through his records to make sure he wasn't the kind who would go back to cause trouble. "They" was the ambiguous pronoun that Cubans, or at least the Cubans Sharon had met, used when talking about their government and its surveillance system. It could be the political police, La Seguridad. Or Fidel Castro himself, or his brother Raúl, or the Politburo. But things were improving, Sonya had assured Sharon. "The paperwork will get easier from now on," she had said.

Sharon looked out the picture window she had installed in front of the hot tub. She had bought this town house because of its Sandia Mountains view and the glorious sunsets it captured. She had also gotten it because Juan had fallen in love with the golf-focused gated-community gym, where a retired weightlifter offered weekly classes. Juan didn't know how to play golf, but he loved body building. He also loved the pool and Jacuzzi—and all good things in life, as he put it. Sharon wanted to think that one of the good things in his life was her.

She got out of the hot tub and glanced at her naked body in the full-length mirror. At forty-nine, she still looked good. No belly fat. Wide hips, but she had a grown daughter. Good posture. Tits nipped and tucked. For her fiftieth birthday, she would buy herself a facelift.

She opened the door to the master suite and heard Juan's voice. He was speaking Spanish. After seven years of marriage to him and several classes at a local college, Sharon wasn't totally fluent, but she understood almost everything he was saying. And he was saying this:

"I want to see you again. To make sure we're okay . . . No, no, I'm not blaming anyone! I just need to see you. That's why I'm going alone. No pressure, you know?"

Sharon waited behind the door until Juan finished his conversation. It ended with a promise to call whomever he was talking to as soon as he arrived and a muddled apology.

Sharon pursed her lips and patted herself dry. She put on a blue cardigan sweater and white pants, which she had laid out for herself on the sink before her bath, and breathed in heavily to calm herself down. When she entered the master bedroom, Juan had changed into his workout clothes.

"*Amor*, I am going to the gym," he said, pronouncing "gym" "yin."

"See ya."

As soon as he left, Sharon started looking around for Juan's cell phone, but couldn't find it. He must have taken it with him, though he usually didn't when he went to the "yin."

She willed herself not to panic. He could have been talking to a relative or an old friend. Juan had a complicated relationship with Cuba, which she had done her best to understand.

They had considered traveling together at first, but by the time Juan's paperwork was ready, the only available flights in April had fallen on the week of the open house, he'd told her. If he didn't go then, he would have to wait until June, and he was afraid "they" would revoke his visa, cancel his passport or worse before then. He had also joked that Sharon, a spoiled American, wouldn't enjoy the accommodations.

"A five-star hotel in Havana is like a Motel 6 here," he said. "I'm going to stay at the Habana Libre. It used to be a Hilton, and cockroaches live in the shower there."

"Roaches in the shower!"

"Yes, the big flying kind. Palmetto bugs, like the ones you've seen in Miami."

"What about those private homes, the *casas particulares*?" Sharon had been reading up on Cuba, scouring Yelp and TripAdvisor.

"To stay at a *casa particular*, you need to know the owners and get some references in advance. I wouldn't know where to go. I'll be fine anywhere, but you'll feel out of place. I know you'll want to leave right away."

"But it's only a week."

"A week is a long time without hot water. Or Internet. Or cell-phone service. It'll drive you crazy."

It had been clear that he didn't want company on this trip. He had to deal with too much baggage. She knew the story, or at least the bits he had shared with her. Juan and his best friend, a young man named Camilo Ceballo, had left Cuba on a raft in 1994. They'd gotten lost and drifted in the Caribbean for nine days without water or food. Camilo had died at sea, and Juan, rescued by a fishing boat, had spent two months in a Miami hospital, sunburned and delirious, while the doctors doubted he'd live. He still had the scars from severe sunburn on his back and suffered nightmares that jolted him awake at night. Then his father had been diagnosed with cancer back in Havana. Not approved for his green card yet, Juan hadn't been able to go back and see him one last time. Juan's only living relative, his grandmother, was in a nursing home and seemed to have dementia. They hadn't been able to get her on the phone in a long time. Of course he would have some unfinished business left in Havana. Sharon had tried to be understanding about what he called, only half-jokingly, his "Cuban tragedy."

It was certainly a tragedy, but why had he waited until Sharon was out of sight to make that call? And after buying a ticket for the only time he knew she couldn't accompany him? She wondered if they really would've had to wait till June. She had read that there were more flights than ever departing to Havana from Miami, Fort Lauderdale, and other major American cities.

Sharon went to the kitchen to pour herself a drink. Juan's laptop was on the counter, charging. When she'd met him, he hadn't known how to use it. She had taught him. His email was open, but besides a ton of spam, she found only a message from the travel agency confirming his ticket for April 12. He would fly from Albuquerque to Fort Lauderdale at nine in the morning, then change planes there and arrive in Havana at seven that night.

She considered ditching the open house. Her assistant, Meredith, had just gotten her real estate license. She was nice and eager to learn but lacked self-assurance. She was far too meek at times, easy to push around. No, Sharon didn't feel comfortable placing her biggest prospect of the year in Meredith's pudgy hands.

Sharon continued snooping on the laptop. Nothing in "My Documents." The only thing Juan knew how to download was the music he used in his salsa classes. She clicked on "Pictures." There was a photograph labeled "Elsa." She opened it and gazed upon a young woman with curly hair sitting on the Havana seawall with the ocean behind her. The photo had been scanned and had lines all over it, as if the original had been badly wrinkled and worn.

Sharon's phone rang.

"I'm so sorry, but we have a problem," Meredith said in the squeaky, apologetic voice that Sharon hated. She waited, tapping her fingers on the counter.

"I'm afraid we're going to have to cancel the open house," Meredith said. "Mr. Murray just called. They've gotten algae in the pool and need to shock it. They forgot to put in the chlorine you gave them. He says it looks like there are green strands of hair floating everywhere."

Sharon felt a rush of relief.

"I'm sorry," Meredith repeated.

"No big deal," Sharon said. "In fact, I'd rather wait until after Easter. The garden will look better. By the way, I need you to take over for the next week and a half. I'm going out of town. Think you can handle everything?"

"Me? Well, yes."

Sharon didn't give herself time to think it over. She punched in Cubaviajes's number. She told Sonya that she was going to travel with her husband, and could it be arranged for her to go on the same flight?

"What a great idea! Oh, he's leaving in three days! But no worries. We'll make it happen."

Sharon liked Sonya's confident, optimistic attitude. If that girl ever wanted to leave Cubaviajes, Sharon would hire her and fire Meredith in a second.

"Would you like for me to reserve a hotel room for you as well?"

"Isn't Juan staying at the Havana Hilton or whatever it's called now?"

"He hasn't made any hotel reservations with us," Sonya said. "Just the flight."

Sharon couldn't imagine Juan going online to reserve a room on his own. Maybe he'd decided not to stay at the cockroach-infested Hilton after all.

"Go ahead," she said. "A place with no palmetto bugs in the shower, please."

Sonya laughed. "Most Cuban hotels don't have those, Señora. The best one is Meliá Cohiba, a five-star high-rise in El Vedado."

Since she was still in front of Juan's laptop, Sharon did a quick Google search and found Meliá Cohiba on TripAdvisor, listed among the "Top Ten Hotels in Havana." It looked modern, upscale and bugless.

"Yes, that one will do," she said.

"It's one hundred seventy dollars a night. Shall I reserve for the full trip?"

"Yes."

Sharon put it on her credit card and hung up. She retrieved a bottle of Bacardi that Juan had bought a month before, made herself a stiff drink and plopped down on the sofa.

When Juan came in, sweaty and handsome, his muscles almost ripping his tight white T-shirt, Sharon smiled and said in the most casual tone she could muster, "I have a surprise for you, *amor*. I'm going to Cuba with you. I just called Cubaviajes and made all the arrangements."

Juan went pale. "What about your open house?"

"It got canceled."

He began pacing the floor with his arms folded. "Are you sure you want to come?"

"Yes, quite sure."

"Remember what I told you about the crappy hotels, the bugs and the lack of . . . everything? You aren't going to like it."

"It'll be an adventure," Sharon said firmly. "A new experience for me. What is it, Juan? Don't *you* want me to go?"

Without responding, he reached for the bottle of Bacardi and began to guzzle from it.

2

THE THREE MUSKETEERS

The hotel was nicer than Sharon had expected. Their room had a queen bed, a flat-screen TV, a coffee maker, noisy but functional air conditioning and a view of Malecón Avenue. It reminded her of the Cancún resort where she and Juan had spent their honeymoon. The memory made her purr contentedly. They had patched things up on the flight from Albuquerque to Fort Lauderdale.

"I hope I'm not imposing myself on you," she'd said. "I've always been curious about Cuba, but it didn't seem like you wanted me around."

"Well, I didn't at first," Juan had admitted, looking serious and sincere. "But I'm relieved you got your ticket, *mamita*. I'll need you for moral support."

He squeezed her hand and kissed it. Sharon saw layers of congealed pain in his eyes. She didn't feel like asking any more questions—for the time being, at least.

They arrived at the José Martí International Airport, passed breezily through customs and took an ordinary government-run taxi to the Meliá Cohiba. Sharon would have preferred to ride on a brightly colored *almendrón*, one of the old refurbished American cars she had seen online, but Juan had opposed.

"We don't know these drivers," he had said. "They could overcharge us or take us around for hours."

"But you know the city."

"Yes, but they don't know I do. Here, you have to walk around with four eyes."

"Walk around with four eyes" was among Juan's preferred set of quirky Cuban expressions. Sharon chuckled at the memory and left the window, where she had been enjoying a panoramic view of Havana and the Malecón seawall.

Juan was still sleeping. It was only 8 A.M., but she had rested long enough. It had taken him longer to fall asleep, which wasn't new. The guy had issues, of which she was well aware. He had finally gone to a therapist once Sharon had convinced him that he could be experiencing PTSD from what had happened at sea. After all, he had arrived in Miami dehydrated and covered in third-degree burns, with Camilo's body decomposing by his side. Though Juan had protested, saying that real men didn't need shrinks, she had insisted, and it had helped somewhat. The alprazolam helped too, when he took it. But he hated taking it, claiming it made him feel whacked out.

She sat on the bed, careful not to wake him. She studied his profile: his square jaw, his teardrop-shaped eyes inherited from a Chinese grandfather, his well-formed nose. Eight years ago, he had been so handsome that he could've been a model, she had bragged to her friends. But when they'd met, he had been a waiter at the Cooperage, a popular steakhouse in Albuquerque. He'd also had a gig on Friday nights teaching salsa classes at the restaurant. She'd signed up for one, hoping to learn how to move her hips the proper way. "Get it all loose, girl," he would encourage her. "Swing your little tail, your *colita*, not your arms!"

Three months later he declared her his best student, a claim that Sharon considered somewhat inflated, and invited her to be his partner in Salsa under the Stars, a local dancing contest. They lost, but she was sure he would have won with a better *colita*-swinging partner.

Afterward, they started to spend time together, though she wasn't interested in serious dating. Recently divorced with a teenage daughter, Sharon swore to herself she wouldn't fall into a rebound relationship. But in less than a month, she had changed her mind.

Juan made little money at the restaurant. He had done some construction work, a few gigs here and there, but his limited English didn't help. When he asked, shyly, for work doing "whatever" at her company, Sharon sent him to paint an old house and was pleasantly surprised by the results. She later bought a fixer-upper in South Valley and entrusted Juan with making it look nice. The motley crew he gathered was comprised of Mexicans, Dominicans and a handful of Cubans who, like Juan himself, had made it to Albuquerque courtesy of Catholic Charities. Despite the liberal use of expletives such as *coño, pinche cabrón* and *vaina*, they did such a good job that Sharon sold the house for almost twice what she had paid for it. From that moment on, Juan was officially on her payroll.

A good investment, all in all.

When, a year later, he suggested living together, Sharon said yes. She also said yes when he asked her to marry him in a touching, old-fashioned manner, with a diamond ring (cheap, but nice) at a candlelit dinner at the Cooperage. He had become more active in the business, his English had improved, and Kenna, Sharon's daughter, liked him. "Guess what?" Kenna would tell her friends. "My stepfather's from Cuba, and he's just a few years older than me. Mom's pretty cool, for a mom."

So what if Sharon sometimes had the nagging suspicion that Juan wasn't all that into her? After all, she was almost ten years older than him. But that could have just been her own insecurity talking, the same feeling that had made her buy her ticket to Cuba without asking him first.

"You did the right thing," Juan had told her on the plane.

"I . . . was afraid you were planning to hook up with an old girlfriend," she had admitted.

"*Ay, amor,*" he had sighed. "Don't you know you are the best thing that has ever happened to me? I wouldn't be where I am today if it wasn't for you. How could you think I am going all the way to Cuba to cheat on you? Can you imagine what my old girlfriends look like, anyway? Women in Cuba don't take such good care of themselves as Americans do."

Now her suspicions embarrassed her. But she didn't regret having accompanied him. Havana, or what little of it she had seen from the taxi, was beautiful, with its faded facades, colorful buildings, wrought-iron balconies and elaborate roofs. She had spotted Coppelia, the city's most famous ice-cream parlor, on the way to the Meliá Cohiba. They would visit it soon. Dinner the previous night at the hotel restaurant, Plaza Habana, had been excellent: chicken in garlic sauce, black bean soup and fried plantains. A Cuban band had been playing, and there had been more well-dressed and affluent-looking young locals than tourists. They all danced with abandon. Sharon felt a bit out of place—too tall, too foreign, too . . . old—but didn't mention it. She was determined to make this a fun vacation. Juan had promised to take her to the best places in the city, the ones that weren't listed on Yelp or TripAdvisor.

"That is, if I can find my way around," he had said. "I'm sure the city has changed a lot since I left."

A fly buzzed around the bed and landed on his nose. Sharon was about to swat it when Juan woke up with a start. He sat up, his face contorted in a panicked expression. It took him a few seconds to collect himself, but that was nothing new.

"We're in Havana, dear," she reminded him. "Havana," he repeated.

Juan was one of the few men who looked good before washing his face. He didn't even have morning breath, at least in Sharon's opinion. She kissed him.

"My first day here in twenty years," he mumbled, pushing her away.

After taking a shower, Juan made a call on his cell phone.

"Víctor, we arrived last night," he said. "Ah, my wife came too. Where exactly do you live now? Yes, I have the address, but—"

The call was lost. He dialed again. It didn't go through this time.

"That *hijoeputa* from Verizon told me the phone would work here," he complained, chucking it onto the bed. "He forgot to say for three minutes only!"

"If you have the address, we'll find the place," Sharon replied. "The city isn't that big."

"Yes, but I'm an Old Havana guy. I've never been familiar with this fancy-schmancy neighborhood."

"Does your friend live around here?"

"I think so."

Sharon took her purse and checked that it had everything they needed: money, sunglasses and a card with the hotel's address.

"Do you want to carry your passports?" she asked Juan. "At least the American one, just in case?"

"No. I'm afraid to lose them. It's one of my biggest fears, losing my American passport while in Cuba and not being able to get back."

She placed the three documents in the hotel room safe.

They still had to exchange dollars for CUCs, Cuban Convertible Currency, the only kind of currency accepted in the tourist stores. Juan hadn't wanted to do it at the airport, claiming that they would be overcharged. Now he wasn't sure that the hotel was a good place either.

"Aren't you being a little paranoid?" Sharon asked.

"If you had lived here for the first nineteen years of your life, you would be paranoid too," he answered curtly.

"Sorry."

Then his expression changed, and he took her into his arms.

"I'm relieved you came with me," he blurted out. "To save me from my own paranoia and *comemierdería.*"

Comemierdería, a well-used word in Cuban slang, was literally "shit eatery," but also meant "stupidity."

She put a dab of perfume behind her ears and on her wrists. Pleasures by Estée Lauder, her favorite.

"I wanted to ask you something, *amor,*" Juan said tentatively. "After we spend some time with Víctor, would you mind taking a walk and leaving us alone for a while? There are things we need to discuss privately."

The suggestion made Sharon uncomfortable. Did Juan expect her to just wander around Havana by herself while he and his friend had a tête-à-tête? But she attempted to take it in stride.

"Like what?" she asked. "I don't need to go at all, really. I trust you. But I'd like to know."

Juan walked toward the window and began to talk with his back to her, looking intently at the Malecón. He spoke Spanish, as he always did when the topic was Cuba.

"Víctor and I were best friends from the third grade on. We were accepted at the Instituto Superior de Arte, the ISA, after finishing high school. He wanted to study theater, and I hoped to become a classical musician. I'd played the guitar since I was six years old and knew a little piano as well."

"Well, I didn't know that!" Sharon said, surprised. "How come I've never heard you play?"

He turned, but still didn't look at her. He didn't appear to have even heard her. Behind his eyes, he seemed to be watching the movie of his past.

"The ISA was so far from where we lived that it took us an hour by bicycle to get there every morning. It was in the middle of the Special Period, when there was no public transportation except for eighteen-wheeler tractor trailers. There were blackouts every night—the programmed ones that were advertised in the paper and lasted from five to seven hours and the unprogrammed ones that could happen at any time and last for a whole day. Even well-off families had trouble getting food. Everything was scarce, from beans to eggs. Red meat was a luxury. We were all thin as rails, and many suffered from polyneuritis, a kind of aggressive anemia. That's why when I see people spending thousands of dollars to lose weight, I want to kick their flabby asses."

Sharon smiled. It wasn't the first time Juan had expressed his feelings about the American obsession with dieting.

"Despite all that, we had fun," he went on. "We were young and horny. Hunger makes you horny, I discovered. After class, and sometimes during it, there was a lot of *apretamiento*, hanky-panky, going on."

"I bet you had your fair share of—hanky-panky," she said, choosing not to repeat the Spanish term.

"There wasn't too much competition." Juan grinned. "Víctor and I were among the few straight males on campus, and all the girls liked us. They favored me, I must say, because Víctor was skinny and a bit awkward. Looking back, I think he might have been bisexual, though nobody used that term back then. You were either straight or *maricón*, period. But he liked girls at least. It was why we had a falling out."

"You fought over a girl?"

"It was a strange fight. Well, you know about Camilo."

Juan sat on the bed. He seemed more present now, remembering his past but not anchored in it. Sharon encouraged him softly.

"The friend you traveled with. The one who—"

"Yes. We were inseparable: Víctor, Camilo and me. People called us the Three Musketeers. *All for one, and one for all*."

"That's funny."

"So we were buddies until Camilo introduced us to Elsa. That changed everything."

Elsa. The name on the scanned picture. Sharon tried not to betray any emotion as she asked casually, "And Elsa was . . . ?"

"My girl!" Juan answered with pride.

Sharon winced. There was a twinkle in his eye she hadn't seen before.

"Lucky her," she said with an irony that Juan failed to notice.

"She *was* lucky," he said matter-of-factly. "Her father was a *pincho*."

"You mean *pinche*?" Sharon asked, thinking of the Mexican curse word.

"No, no! Here, a *pincho* is someone who is part of the government, a guy who can pull strings. He was a lieutenant general in Castro's army. Their family lived in a nice house and was 'connected.' That was why Elsa had been admitted into the school, though in truth, she had no talent for acting. Couldn't capture an audience, the instructors said."

Sharon was absurdly happy to hear that.

"We were the ISA 'it couple.' She was the prettiest girl, and . . . well, I wasn't hard on the eyes myself. When we started hooking up, Víctor and Camilo tried to be cool about it, but they were jealous. And that was the beginning of the end."

He fell silent. Sharon waited a few seconds, then prodded him.

"The end came when you left?"

"In a way. We were all sick and tired of the situation. You Know Who," Juan said, pretending to stroke an imaginary beard, the way he usually did when referring to Castro, "started talking about 'Zero Option,' where we all would live in shelters, eat in communal kitchens and cook with fire instead of electricity. Then El Maleconazo happened. People took to the streets and broke the windows of the dollar shops, stores that were reserved for foreigners, the ones Cubans weren't even allowed to enter. They threw stones at hotels like this one. You Know Who realized people were angry, so he opened the valve. He said that those who wanted to leave on rafts were free to do so. Elsa, Camilo and I decided to take our chances. Elsa didn't need to. She lacked many things, like everyone else, but her family was much better off than most. She didn't even have to bike to school every day, because her father had an old Jeep and drove her around. But she wanted to ride with me, she said."

Sharon waited. Were those tears in Juan's eyes or just the sun's reflection?

"We knew we had to act quickly because Fidel's decision wasn't going to last. We agreed on a day, and I went to see Víctor the night before. He didn't want to go, but I thought I could convince him."

Sharon tried to imagine Víctor. She pictured a skinny, gawky young man.

"Was he a Communist?" she asked.

Juan shrugged. "He sympathized with the government, but he wasn't hard-core. He said we should all stay and bear it: that the Special Period wouldn't last forever, that things were bound to improve. But I think he really refused to go because he couldn't stand the fact that Elsa was leaving with me. *For* me. We got into an argument, a stupid argument about You Know Who, and had an ugly fight. I knocked him flat and left."

Sharon looked out the window. Small waves crashed against the Malecón seawall.

"And that's the friend you're going to see today?" she asked after a moment.

"Yes, yes."

She chewed her lower lip, but before she could find the appropriate response, Juan said, "Elsa was going to take her father's Jeep and drive me and Camilo to Brisas del Mar, a secluded area on the coast where we had stored the raft. She had also promised to get antidehydration fluids in the black market. If the bitch had at least done that, maybe Camilo wouldn't have died."

The bitch. Sharon smiled again.

"She was supposed to pick up Camilo first. I waited in my apartment until he arrived on his own, all sweaty, with the few supplies he had gathered and a couple of big tires we used to reinforce the raft, which later saved our lives. When it became clear she wasn't coming, my dad paid five hundred pesos to a neighbor with an old Chevy to take us to Brisas del Mar. He hugged us before we left. 'May the Virgin accompany you, *hijo*,' he told me. That was the last time I saw him."

He had begun to sob quietly as he spoke. Sharon put a hand on his shoulder.

"I'm so sorry, my love," she said. "That must have been awful. How did your dad feel about you leaving?"

"He wasn't happy, but he knew there was nothing for me in Cuba. The music scene here was dead."

He wiped the tears from his eyes and then acted as if he hadn't cried at all, speaking in a macho overtone when he went on.

"That's it," he said. "I just need to clear the air with Víctor. I bet he's sorry now that he didn't follow us."

He stood. Sharon couldn't help but ask, "What happened to Elsa?"

Juan hesitated.

"I heard she got married," he said finally.

"Not to your friend, I hope."

"Ah, no. A Spaniard, an old guy."

Being sort of an old girl herself, Sharon felt a sting at his dismissive comment.

"I don't know much more. I found out through other people

because Dad wouldn't talk about Elsa. He always thought she wasn't the right girl for me. So did Abuela."

"Nobody in your family liked her? Why was that?"

He shrugged. "They said she was too independent and wouldn't defer to her elders. She was like an American."

"Did she ever contact you?"

"No. I guess she was ashamed, or maybe she'd never really been in love with me. In the end, it doesn't matter. I'm not here for her."

"That's a sad story," Sharon said slowly. "But why *are* you here, then?"

"I told you, to see Víctor!" he answered impatiently. "When Dad got sick, Víctor took care of him. He went to his apartment, bathed him, cooked for him. They were still neighbors. When I wanted to talk to him, I called Víctor's apartment, and though he didn't speak to me, he would go and fetch my father."

"I don't understand. Why did you call him at your friend's house? Why not at his own place?"

Juan sighed. Sharon wished she hadn't asked.

"Because he didn't have a phone, *mi vida*," he said. "We never did. At that time, I could send Dad some money, but not much, just enough to buy food. It was before you and I met. Víctor would find him milk, meat and other stuff on the black market. He was there when Dad died."

"I see," Sharon said. "All right then, you should go see your friend."

Juan rubbed his belly. "Let's go eat something first. I'm starving."

He always was.

"*Limpieza!*" A woman opened the door and entered, pushing a housekeeping cart. "I need to clean the room," she announced.

"Yes, we are just leaving," Juan said.

Sharon thought that was strange. Shouldn't the cleaning lady have asked if it was okay to come in? Or at least knocked first? But Juan hadn't complained, so Sharon didn't dare to either. Maybe it was a Cuban thing. She didn't want to be the ugly American. It would embarrass her husband and make her seem even more out of place here than she already was.

FOLLOWING JUAN

hey had breakfast at Cobijo Real, a small café on the first floor of the Meliá Cohiba. Sharon had a fruit salad and a tall glass of *café con leche*—Cuban-style coffee with milk. Juan ordered three fried eggs, two sausages, an orange juice and two shots of espresso. He ate quickly, not taking the time to chew his food. Sharon couldn't help feeling a bit disgusted by his table manners, or lack thereof.

She finished a juicy pineapple chunk and made a final decision not to go with Juan. It seemed intrusive after everything he had told her. She attempted to check her email on her cell phone, which, of course, didn't work, but the hotel did have wired Internet service at its business center.

"Why don't I stay here and catch up on work while you go talk things over with your friend?" she suggested.

Juan looked disappointed. "But I told Víctor you were coming."

"We could take him out to dinner tonight. After you . . . clear the air."

"If that is what you want."

Juan licked his fork and gulped down the last sip of his espresso.

"I'm nervous now," he whispered. "I wish we hadn't come. I don't feel safe here."

"Come on!" Sharon gestured toward the other tables, most of which were occupied by harmless-looking tourists in Hawaiian shirts, and the pretty Cuban waitresses walking around in black-and-white uniforms. "This is your country, your people. What could possibly happen to you?"

"I don't know. Something bad. My father used to say, 'Something bad is always happening to someone, somewhere, all the time.'"

"That's silly," Sharon said, laughing it off. "As long as it doesn't happen to you, you shouldn't worry. Havana is ten times safer than downtown Albuquerque. You'll be fine. Now go visit your friend. You'll feel better afterward."

When breakfast was over—and charged to their room, as they didn't have any convertible currency yet—Juan kissed Sharon goodbye and went to the front desk for a map. A young woman was the only employee in sight.

"Five CUCs," she said, showing him a small map of Havana. "If you only have dollars, I can exchange them for you."

Reluctantly, he gave her $200 and received 174 CUCs in return.

"There's a ten percent penalty because you are changing American currency," she explained, noticing Juan's shock as he counted the bills. "And a three percent transaction charge."

Juan left with the map and a sense of having been "got at" by her. He felt himself regressing to his old life in Cuba and resenting the hell out of it. This was how it had always been—the consumer at the mercy of the provider, whether the provider was a store clerk, a waiter or a doctor. Why had he allowed the cleaning lady to boss them around that morning? They were paying in US dollars, for God's sake! He was no longer an ordinary Cuban, but a tourist. He couldn't forget that.

Sharon located the business center, but the Internet connection there (at three CUCs per minute!) was so slow that she couldn't even sign in to her Gmail account. Her cell phone appeared to be working now, though. She was able to call Albuquerque, where a very sleepy Meredith assured her in her squeakiest, least convincing voice that she had everything under control. Sharon then realized it was seven-thirty in the morning in New Mexico.

Not wanting to spend three hours by herself at the hotel, she settled for Coppelia. It had mixed reviews in Yelp, but Cuban ice cream was worth a shot. When she returned to the lobby, Juan was on his way out. Sharon called out to him to let him know her plans. If he came back too soon and didn't find her, he would probably panic. But Juan didn't hear her. He left, and she ran after him.

Sharon couldn't tell when she began to deliberately follow him. But as he walked away and she kept on his tail, she realized what she was doing. And it was too late to go back. She wanted to know where his friend lived. She needed to see this man, to make sure that what Juan had told her was true. Then she would take an *almendrón* to Coppelia. Juan didn't need to know anything about it.

She tried to convince herself that it was a game, that she was just playing detective. She was also making sure Juan was okay, since he seemed so worried about his safety. But deep down, she knew these weren't the real reasons she was tailing her husband. She didn't trust him. Not enough, not even after their conversation. His bringing up Elsa hadn't helped. She cringed as she recalled the way he had said "my girl." The pride in his eyes. The sparks. She remembered a Cuban saying that he liked: *"Donde hubo fuego, cenizas quedan."* Old flames die hard, indeed.

At first, the walk was pleasant enough. The houses around the hotel were big, with well-kept front yards and lush gardens. The sidewalks were clean, the streets lined with trees. She saw not only *almendrones* but also new VWs, Renaults and the occasional Mercedes as they flew past fancy private restaurants named La Cocina Cubana and Tu Paladar. A soft, salty breeze came from the ocean.

After twenty minutes, however, she found herself in a less appealing neighborhood. The single houses had been replaced by blocks of apartment buildings separated by narrow alleyways. Garbage spilled out of the dumpsters, and the traffic had slowed. There were fewer cars and more buses with people hanging off their doors. Instead of the ocean breeze, her lungs filled with exhaust fumes. They were leaving behind the Malecón area, which she assumed was the tourist zone, and entering real Havana.

A man catcalled her, but she kept her gaze straight ahead and ignored him.

A police car drove up and down the street, and Sharon wondered if this was a place where one had to "walk around with four eyes." It wasn't run-down or dirt poor, but still a long way from Meliá Cohiba's spotless neighborhood. She was tired too. It had been months since she had walked this much, and at ten-fifteen, it was already getting hot.

Juan consulted the map often and, to Sharon's surprise, asked a woman for directions. He would never have done that in Albuquerque. Sharon was afraid he would notice her presence, but he didn't look back even once. Finally, he stopped in front of a three-story building, the kind she would have described as "family friendly" and "vintage." The open balconies of the second-floor apartments allowed an unobstructed, voyeuristic look into their dwellers' lives.

Sharon crossed the street. There was a park shaded by two big leafy *flamboyán* trees right in front of the building. She hid behind a flowering *flamboyán* and looked up. Music came from the apartment on the right. In the living room, a young man played the drums aggressively while another sang, repeating the same words over and over: *"Ana ana bana."* A third musician shook a pair of maracas.

A couple danced on the balcony. The woman moved her hips in perfect synchrony with the drums and maracas, following the beat. Ah, Sharon thought, that one knew how to move her *colita*!

Juan stood in front of the building's main door, which was closed, and rang a bell.

In the other apartment, the one on the left, a tall woman sat alone near the balcony. Sharon couldn't make out her face, but noted she was a skinny blonde in a red dress. There was a Marilyn Monroe poster on the wall behind her.

The woman stood and left Sharon's sight. Juan pushed open the door and closed it behind him.

A moment later, the door opened again, and a young man left the building. He wore a backward baseball cap, and his left arm was covered in tattoos. He walked through the park, passing so close to Sharon that she could smell the strong sandalwood cologne he was wearing.

She waited, holding her breath, and imagined Juan going upstairs. Was the blonde waiting for him? *Not necessarily*, she thought. *Víctor could be one of the musicians.* And there were two more floors. She couldn't see what was happening in the apartments higher up. But she wasn't surprised when she saw Juan against the background of the Marilyn poster.

The blonde came into Sharon's line of vision again, then closed the balcony door with what sounded like the firing of a single loud shot.

GHOSTS ON THE STAIR

It took Juan every ounce of energy he had to go upstairs—one chipped, stained step at a time. His legs suddenly weighed a ton. His head buzzed, but at least the uncomfortable feeling of being watched had vanished. He had noticed it for the first time after leaving the hotel but hadn't looked back. It was his past returning to haunt him, he thought. That past had faces, voices, smells. They began to reveal themselves to him as he climbed the stairs.

He saw his father before him. El Chino Oscar, who looked more Chinese than Juan did, with his dark eyes and straight black hair. His father in the one-bedroom apartment they had shared until Juan left Cuba. His father, asking him, "Do you have to do it? Are you sure it's what you want?" His face, prematurely wrinkled, so different from the face of the smiling young man in his wedding picture with an arm protectively wrapped around his wife's shoulders. Juan used to study his mother's features in the faded portrait: long brown hair, arched eyebrows, small mouth. He would scrutinize the white dress, the veil, the bouquet, and imagine what it would have been like to grow up with her. To have a mother, like everyone else.

Even a stepmother would've been fine. Most of his friends had had one—or two. Or more, depending on their fathers' habits. These women weren't perfect; some were downright bitches, but they were better than no mom at all. After his wife's sudden death when Juan was two, El Chino had sunk into a depression so deep he'd never totally recovered. He'd never even dated again, as far as Juan knew. He'd spent his life sitting under that wedding picture, pining for the woman he'd lost, until he'd finally been reunited with her. His first and only, Juan's paternal grandmother used to say.

Abuela. There she was, standing tall on the next step, still a striking presence at sixty-nine, the age she'd been last time Juan had seen her. He couldn't wait to hug her again. But Abuela had good days and bad days, Víctor had told him. She suffered from acute *chochería*, an almost-affectionate term in the Cuban vernacular for Alzheimer's. Would she recognize him? Juan hoped so.

Abuela had taken, as best she could, his mother's place. She would often bring Juan to her home on Zanja Street in the heart of Havana's Chinatown. The old house had been full of Chinese dolls and lanterns; yellowish copies of the *Kwong Wah Po*, a weekly paper published in Chinese; and a floral smell that he wouldn't know until many years later as opium. She was a Santería believer, a devotee of Oyá, and would leave offerings of fried eggplant and dark chocolate in the corners of the house or in the garden for the *orisha*. She also worshipped San Fancón, a syncretic deity of Chinese origin. The house now belonged to the Daughters of the Immaculate Heart, the nuns who had taken Abuela in. What had happened to the furniture, the family pictures, the knickknacks she had collected? Had they thrown it all away?

Juan's grandfather Choy Chiong was a native of the Zengcheng Village in Guangdong. He had come to Cuba in the early 1940s; opened a *tren de lavado*, a laundry business; changed his name to Ezequiel; and married María Antonia Muñoz, a tall, big-hipped, long-legged Cuban girl who had moved to Havana from the countryside a few years before. They'd had only one child, Oscar, who would become Juan's father.

Ezequiel had died when Juan was seven years old, but he still had a vivid memory of his grandfather: a small wrinkled, bright-eyed man who had looked even shorter next to his statuesque wife. Their silent devotion, Juan recalled, had at times resembled complicity. What secrets had they shared? Abuela was almost illiterate, but she had managed to learn a few phrases in Chinese to please her husband. He had never lost his accent and, when he got mad, which didn't happen often, would unleash long tirades in broken Spanish. Abuela was more temperamental and never bit her tongue. Ah, the things she had said about Elsa! She had loathed her, and she had let it be known.

The parade of imaginary ghosts went on. Now it was Elsa who stood in front of Juan, smiling, but with her pretty face turned the other way. She hadn't been fond of Abuela either. It had pained Juan that the two most important women in his life couldn't stand each other. Impulsive and opinionated, Elsa had once told Abuela that believing in the *orishas* was a thing of the past, a ridiculous superstition. After that, Abuela wouldn't even talk to her.

Elsa blocked Juan's way, refusing to let him climb to the next step. Her eyes were deep set and green. Cat eyes, her friends had called them. They had always been shining with happiness or glee. Her curly hair, which she had cut a few weeks before he left, framed her face like a frizzy halo. "Mom used to complain that my hair clogged the shower drain," she had said. "But now that I've cut it, she asks, 'What are you clogging it with now?'" She had laughed that very Elsa laugh, carefree with a hint of sarcasm.

And she had been bigmouthed. Unlike other girls, Elsa had had no qualms about using the word *pinga*, the vulgar term for penis. She had loved the fact that Juan's had three black spots on the shaft. "It's handmade," she used to say, to his embarrassment.

She had tended to get physical at times, for good and for bad. Juan remembered when she had insisted on making love in her own backyard, though her parents were home and could easily have caught them. She had been full of fire. Another time, because he had shown up late to a date—he had been with Rosita, his other girlfriend—she had pushed him against a wall with such force that he'd ended up with a concussion. She wasn't above tangling with other girls either. In the tenth grade, she had been expelled from the Lenin Vocational School, an elite boarding school, after infamously beating the daylights out of a general's daughter. After every fight, Elsa retreated into another realm, could barely breathe and forgot, or at least pretended to forget, what she had done.

Juan thought again of his last night in Cuba. Why had his Elsa gone back on her promise to follow him? She had seemed so excited to go that time . . . He and Camilo had worked for twelve hours straight, putting the finishing touches on the raft. They hadn't returned to the ISA. Juan had called Elsa's house several times, but no one had answered. Still, he had assumed that everything was fine. If she had changed her mind about it, as she had before, she would have told him, wouldn't she?

After the three of them had initially agreed to leave, she had stalled their plans several times. First because she was afraid of an upcoming hurricane. Later because she felt dizzy and tired. (She was always feeling tired in those days, even though she didn't need to pedal everywhere like most of their classmates.) The last time, her mother had gotten sick. The delays had made Camilo nervous. He feared that the Cuban government would stop the flow of rafters sooner than later, which indeed happened a week after they left. Still, sometimes Juan wished he had stayed that night. Unlike Camilo, he hadn't been crazy about leaving the country. He had been crazy about Elsa, and he had lost her.

Juan pushed her ghost out of the way. But he immediately wished he hadn't, because Rosita, his second girlfriend, was waiting for him just past Elsa, looking hurt and dejected. She was caressing her big belly, though he didn't know for sure if she had actually been pregnant, as she had assured him, or ever had his baby. If that *was* his baby. What did he really know?

Like Víctor and Elsa, Rosita had been a theater student. Quiet and taller and thinner than the other girls, she had been saddled with a cruel nickname—the Bride of Frankenstein. She was an oddity in a class full of loud, proud, curvy divas in training. What was she doing there? Juan hadn't paid much attention to her at school, so he couldn't tell if she had "it" or not. ISA folks talked constantly about having "it," whatever "it" was: talent, charisma, technique. Elsa lacked it, they all agreed, but she made up for it with looks and *sandunga*. Víctor had "it." (Juan fully expected to hear that he was taking part in some big Cuban film, maybe a remake of *Fresa y Chocolate*.) He hadn't asked Víctor what had happened to Rosita during their short phone conversations, but he would today.

Poor Rosita, the girl who had smelled of mint and desperation. Juan had slept with her because she had insisted—throwing herself at him, chasing him all over campus, letting everyone know that she wanted him. What else was he supposed to do? He was a man. But they had met only three or four times at her house and a motel she had paid for. He had never said he would leave Elsa for her, and she had known he was spoken for.

Abuela had liked Rosita because she was also a Santería believer, or rather had turned into one, probably to suck up to Abuela. But Juan had felt only pity for his on-the-side girlfriend and tried his best to keep her away from his home life. Besides, he hadn't wanted Elsa finding out about her, and he had been clear about that. When Rosita had claimed to be pregnant with his child, he had demanded that she have an abortion and stopped seeing her. He had later felt guilty and wanted to apologize. He had been too harsh. But she was trying to trick him into marrying her, and that wasn't going to happen.

He remembered Rosita's face, her pale skin and freckled nose—quite unusual in Cuba—and it suddenly occurred to him that she looked a little like Sharon. They were both thin and had auburn eyes, though Sharon was much prettier. It should have been the other way around—upon his meeting Sharon, she should have reminded him of Rosita. But he didn't think of Rosita often. Her features appeared blurred, and she soon dissolved into the air, leaving no trace behind.

Juan wondered briefly if he would see his mother, even though he knew these "ghosts" were only figments of his imagination. When he was a child, he used to repeat his mother's name, Lila, softly, invoking her presence, hoping to receive a sign that her spirit was around him. He never got one, though.

He didn't get one this time either. Instead, there was Víctor, his best friend since childhood. Slightly built, blue-eyed and smart-mouthed, a charmer and sometimes a pest. His sidekick. You could always count on him for everything. That was why, when Camilo had proposed that they all leave together, Víctor's tepid response had surprised Juan. He had been worse off than any of them economically and hadn't gotten along with his family.

"You think it's so easy," Víctor had said. "You think you'll get to Miami, and a Hollywood agent will be waiting to sign you. You're delusional! There are thousands of people like you, or better than you, waiting for a chance. We have less competition here."

"Ah, cut the crap," Camilo had answered. "There are no opportunities here. Making a movie in Cuba and shit are one and the same thing."

"No, they're not," Víctor said. "Cuban movies win tons of international awards."

"Please. Since *Fresa y Chocolate*, nobody has paid any attention to us."

"And you think someone will pay attention to you there? You all dream too big, with your obsessions with Al Pacino or that Almodóvar guy in Spain. Good luck. I'm happy to work with Gutiérrez Alea."

They had discussed it for several days. In the end, Juan, Camilo and Elsa had made up their minds to go. Víctor could stay behind if he wished to do so. He would one day regret it. But it was a friendly agreement. They were like family, after all. Juan still didn't understand why he and Víctor had had that absurd argument or how it had escalated to a fistfight that had ended with Víctor on the floor, clutching his throat.

It had surprised Juan that Víctor had taken such good care of

El Chino when cancer had struck. For free, because El Chino had had no money and Juan hadn't been able to send much. He had assumed his former friend would no longer want anything to do with him or his family. But Víctor had been with Juan's father until the end, after Abuela, bedridden and in a nursing home, was no longer able to help her son. Juan owed him big. A true friend to him, even after their angry parting.

He climbed another step and faced Camilo Ceballo, the third musketeer. Camilo and his wild locks. ("Who do you think you are, an American rock-and-roll singer?" an ISA instructor had once growled at him.) It was Camilo who had instigated the trip on which he would lose his life. "It's now or never," he had said when the government first announced that rafters were free to go. "This is cyclical. In the 1980s, they let people go out through the Mariel boatlift. Before that, in the sixties, there was Camarioca. When the pressure gets too high, Fidel opens El Malecón, lets some dissenters escape and carries on. If we don't take our chance now, we'll have to wait another twenty years, and then we'll be too old." Juan was tired of scarcities and dreamed of a different life, maybe as a singer in Las Vegas. Elsa wanted to go to Hollywood and work with Steven Spielberg or, at the very least, with Argentinean director Eliseo Subiela. Everything was possible in America, wasn't it?

It was a pity that Camilo had never gotten to live his dream. Juan heard again his friend's last whispered words: "Forgive me, Juan. I love you."

Forgive him for what? They were in dire straits, adrift on a small raft, but they'd both known how dangerous the trip was. They had discussed it many times and agreed that Miami was worth the risk. And yes, they cared for each other. They were best friends, but Cuban men never used the word "love" when talking to each other, no matter how close they were. He thought again of *The Three Musketeers*. All for one, and one for all. Now he was living out its sequel, *Twenty Years After*. And one of them was gone.

Juan welcomed the distraction that came in the shape of a flesh-and-blood young man. Rushing down the stairs, he rapped to the staccato rhythm of a *guaguancó*. It was a song older than he was, older than Juan too, maybe a century old:

> *Anabaná, el Asilo de Torrens*
> *fue la escuela de mi vida.*
> *Aprendí que no existía*
> *la palabra amigo fiel.*

Why did people still remember it? The lyrics weren't particularly uplifting: "The Torrens Orphanage was the school of my life. There, I learned that the words 'loyal friend' didn't exist."

"*A la mariconga, la mariconga va!*" the young man yelled.

Juan glared at him. What the hell was a *mariconga*? Or had Juan just been called a *maricón*?

The guy exited, and Juan hurried upstairs. He found himself in front of two doors. One was open, and he saw a set of three drums, a big plasma TV and a plump woman watching it. A sweaty man was holding a pair of maracas and saying to another guy, "This Pepito, always leaving in the middle of things!"

The woman replied, her eyes still glued to the screen: "Now, don't start that. He's a busy kid. Cut him some slack!"

Juan knocked on the other door.

"Come in!" The voice was at once familiar and unknown. Juan took a deep breath before going in.

5

VICTORIA SUNRISE

A woman waited in the living room, sitting on a faded green leather sofa. She smelled of Oscar de la Renta and had cantaloupe-sized breasts that looked fake. Her hair was thick and platinum blonde. She wore golden eye shadow, dark mascara and red lipstick. Juan hesitated. Had Víctor gotten married? Did he have a girlfriend? Why hadn't he mentioned it?

"Hi," Juan said.

The woman stood. She was almost as tall as Juan.

"Is Víctor here?" he asked, her silence making him uncomfortable. "We talked this morning. I told him—"

Instead of answering, the woman walked to the balcony and closed the door. She turned to face Juan and looked at him without a word. It was then that Juan recognized in her heavily rimmed eyes the beady blue irises of his best friend.

The room instantly shrank, becoming dark, almost oppressive. Juan gulped and stared at a Marilyn Monroe poster on the wall, then back at the woman. How could Víctor—goofy, skinny Víctor—be the one hiding under all that makeup?

"Is—is that you?" Juan stuttered.

She nodded.

Juan took a step back. "Why are you doing this, Víctor? What kind of game are you playing?"

"This isn't for your benefit," the woman replied. Her voice was still Víctor's, just an octave higher. "This is me. The real me, Victoria Sunrise."

Juan was grateful that Sharon hadn't come along.

"Sit," Victoria said with a sly smile. "You're going to fall on your ass."

Instead of sitting down, Juan walked toward Victoria and hugged her. He felt his friend's arms draw him in closer. Her Oscar de la Renta fragrance enveloped him.

"Twenty years, *cabrón*," Victoria muttered. "It has been twenty years since you left. I've counted every one."

They sat in two rocking chairs polished by time and use in front of the sofa.

"I miss rocking chairs," Juan said. "Americans don't like them. Or they have these hard, uncomfortable ones."

He stopped midsentence.

"Sorry," he said, fumbling for words. "I didn't come all the way from New Mexico to talk about furniture."

"You can talk about whatever you want. We have a lot to discuss. Who goes first?"

"You, please. What's this all about, Víctor? Why are you dressed like that?"

"You can't wait to find out, eh?" Victoria answered with a teasing grin. "And people say we *maricones* are the gossipy ones."

"You *maricones*?"

"Gays, *mijo*. Isn't that the politically correct term in La Yuma?"

La Yuma. Juan had almost forgotten the way Cubans referred to the United States. Practically speaking, he was now a Yuma too.

"Are you gay?" he asked.

"No, I'm just wearing this crap to make myself more appealing to you." Victoria laughed. "Of course I am, *comemierda*! I always was. I came out ten years ago."

To disguise his unease, Juan pretended to look around the room. Under the Marilyn Monroe poster was an oval table with two red candles, a silver handheld mirror, a vase with four roses and an old flip cell phone.

"My little sanctuary," Victoria said. "Do you like it?"

Juan turned his attention back to her.

"You can go outside like that?" he whispered. "And the cops don't bother you?"

"They don't care. Things have changed. I told you they would, remember? I even have my own show now."

Juan felt an ill-timed need to use the restroom. All that orange juice at breakfast! A flowered curtain separated the living room from a bedroom. Was there a bathroom inside?

"A TV show?" he asked.

"Almost as good. A *grand* show at Café Arabia, the best night-club in town. You should visit, see me in action." She became serious. "But enough about me. You want to know about your dad, right?"

Juan looked through the shutters and saw a small park across from the building. He was glad that the balcony door was closed. His disconcerting feeling of being spied on had returned.

"Well, that too," he said. "Last time I talked to Abuela, she said you had been taking care of him, and that you visited her often. I wanted to thank you."

"You don't have to. El Chino Oscar was like a father to me. Better than my own. Remember how my dad used to beat me?"

It all came back. Víctor running away from his apartment, hiding inside Juan's bedroom. El Chino lying to the big hairy guy next door. No, they hadn't seen Víctor, had no idea where he was. The swollen blue eyes. Víctor with an arm in a sling, muttering that he'd fallen from a tree.

"Did Dad know about your . . . transformation?" Juan asked.

"No, I never told him. Abuela did, though." Victoria winked.

"How is she doing?" Juan asked. "I called the nursing home last week, but the nun who answered said she was too sick to leave her bed."

Music came from the apartment next door. Not rumba or salsa but . . . what were they calling that new stuff? Reggaeton?

"It depends on the day," Victoria said. "Sometimes she's razor-sharp. She knew, by the way. About me. Ages before I came out. She told me it was fine with her. She was—is—a wise woman."

Juan swallowed hard. His mouth was dry, and his urge to pee hadn't gone away.

"I want to see her," he said. "And Dad's grave."

"I'll take you there. Do you want any coffee?"

"Cafe Cubita?"

Victoria cackled. "*Qué Cubita ni un carajo?* The one you buy with the ration card. Mixed with chicory, *mierda* and *café*."

"The ration card." Juan shook his head. "That still exists?"

"Some things never change."

Victoria walked into the kitchen, which was adjacent to the living room, and Juan peeked in. It didn't surprise him to find a four-burner iron stove and a round-edged refrigerator, an old Frigidaire. On the counter he saw a contraption to make coffee—a metal stand with a cloth filter called a *teta*—a granite mortar and pestle, a huge copper pot and an iron skillet. The kitchen was painted a light blue, like the rest of the apartment.

"I always tell my foreign friends to bring good coffee from La Yuma or wherever they live," Victoria said, starting to boil water. "Unless they're staying in a swank hotel like Meliá Cohiba, where they get only the best. Remember the tourism industry slogan: 'CUBALSE, Cuba at the service of the foreigners'? And the Cubans? *Ah, que se jodan.* Let them eat shit."

"Now you're talking like a *gusano*," Juan joked. "A counter-revolutionary."

A second later, he wanted to slap himself. What was he thinking, bringing up politics? It was just nerves. His mouth running faster than his brain. But Victoria hadn't heard him or, if she had, didn't mind the comment.

She poured the boiling water over the ground coffee in the *teta* and let it drip. Then she served it in two demitasses, offering one to Juan. Her fingernails were painted the same shade of red as her lipstick.

"Good coffee," Juan said eagerly, though it was only so-so. "Tastes just like home."

He was thinking of Abuela's coffee. She would "cut" it with a bit of condensed milk to make a *cortadito*. But the best *café con leche* he'd ever had was at Elsa's house, where you could always find fresh milk from the dollar store. Juan was poised to ask about his former girlfriend when Victoria spoke.

"Now, for *really* good coffee, go to the homes of the nouveau riche. They don't want for anything."

"You mean businesspeople? Like the *casa particular* owners and the *almendrón* drivers?"

"No, those are small fish. The big sharks are the foreign investors. They're making a killing. Elsa is probably one of the richest women in Cuba today."

Juan flinched. "Elsa, as in my Elsa?"

"What other Elsa would I be talking about?"

Juan placed his demitasse on the table, not wanting Victoria to see his hands shake.

"I heard she got married," he said.

"Yes. Her husband's a shrewd Spaniard who started dealing with Cuba when everybody else was too afraid to. Now they're well positioned—ahead of the Yumas, the other Europeans and everybody else."

"Do you still keep in touch with her?"

"We talk once in a while. She's helped me through a couple of hard times. She's a *capitalista* now, with real money. And me . . . well, an artist's life is feast or famine."

Juan began to sip his coffee again.

"I always assumed you had a crush on her," he admitted. "I thought you hated me because she had chosen me over you."

Victoria laughed out loud.

"You were so naïve! We hated *her* because you chose her over *us*."

Juan's face turned red.

"Don't blush," Victoria said with an exaggerated flourish of her manicured hands. "I'm not hitting on you. I'm engaged now." She giggled. "His name is Lázaro. And he—"

"Wait a minute," Juan said. "What do you mean, '*We* hated her'? Who's 'we'?"

"Camilo and I, silly."

Camilo. His decomposing body. His last words.

"Camilo?" Juan asked.

Victoria sighed. "We had to mention him, didn't we? Tell me about it."

"Not now. Maybe later."

"Did he suffer?"

"He—yes."

She looked at him expectantly, and though he didn't feel like it, Juan continued.

"The day we left . . . when we got tired of waiting for Elsa, he brought some food. Canned hot dogs, Spam, two loaves of bread. But we lost it when the waves overturned the raft. The tires that he brought were a godsend, though. I believe they're the only reason I'm still here. We grabbed on to them when the biggest waves came."

They remained silent for a few seconds. Juan couldn't help recalling that last night again. Though he would have waited until the next day, Camilo had insisted on leaving right away.

"Either the Americans will get tired of it and refuse to receive more people, or Fidel will stop it for fear of being left alone on the island. We can't waste time."

"What if Elsa is sick?"

"She doesn't want to go, man! Hasn't she changed her mind ten times before? Elsa is a spoiled girl, the daughter of a pincho. *What's more, she has no talent. And she knows it. She knows that outside of Cuba, she'd end up working in a factory. Where's she going to go where she's worth more?"*

"Did Elsa ever tell you why she didn't come with us?" Juan asked. His shoulders sagged as he uttered the words. "Not that it matters anymore, but I'd like to know."

"She never talks about it," Victoria answered. "At first, I

thought it was because she was pissed off at you. She didn't even want to hear your name."

Juan straightened, glowering.

"Pissed off at *me*?" he said. "When she was the one who left us high and dry?"

"Yeah. It didn't make sense to me either. But after we found out what had happened, Camilo's death and all that . . . she got really depressed. Dropped out of college and married the Spaniard a month later."

Juan swallowed hard. The aftertaste of coffee sat on his tongue, mixed with chicory and God knew what else.

"Good cure for depression," he said.

"And a smart move. She's a Spanish citizen now. Dual citizenship, you know—travels all the time. Things turned out all right for her. But poor Rosita . . ."

Ay, Rosita. That small house where she'd lived with her mother in the Marianao area. Her father lived in another province, she had told him. She had taken Juan to her bedroom, a *barbacoa*— a tiny makeshift attic—and he'd felt obligated to make love to her. He remembered the stifling, windowless space, the way the plywood floor had creaked and moved, his fear that it would give, and they would come crashing, bed and all, into the middle of the living room. Then his surprise when he found out she was still a virgin at twenty-one.

"Rosi, why didn't you tell me this was your first time?"

"I didn't want to scare you away."

He looked down and tensed a little. "What happened to her? Did she have a baby?"

Victoria shook her head. "A baby? What she had was a nervous breakdown. Tried to kill herself. Someone found her in the ISA bathroom just after she'd slit her wrists. I still remember it; there was blood everywhere—it looked like a murder scene."

Juan gasped. "Was she okay?"

"Obviously not. I mean, she survived, but that girl was messed up. She dropped out of college too. It was like a soap opera, all Juan's girls going away."

Juan felt guilty, then angry for feeling guilty.

"You know what, Víctor, *coño*?" he blurted out.

"Victoria, please. And *coña*."

"Victoria, whatever. In this 'soap opera,' as you call it, all the women get depressed and have nervous breakdowns. They're the victims, *las pobrecitas*. And what about me? I spent nine days at sea with no food. I saw Camilo *die* and almost died myself. I don't have to feel sorry for these bitches, okay?"

He wanted to cry, but couldn't do it in front of his oldest friend. His best friend, who was a woman now. No.

"May I use your bathroom?" he asked when Victoria didn't respond.

"Sure, my dear. Come this way."

The bathroom could be accessed through a bedroom furnished with a queen bed, a dresser and a three-door armoire. All the pieces were old but had been carefully restored. There were two vintage Avon fragrance bottles on the dresser, a couple of hats and a long-haired red wig. A mahogany bookshelf displayed books that Juan recognized from his childhood: *Cuentos y estampas*, *Ivanhoe*, a Spanish-English dictionary and a collection of Agatha Christie's novels published in translation by Ediciones Huracán. Víctor had been a nerdy, introverted kid who'd loved to read.

The bathroom floor was slippery and wet. There was a leak at the bottom of the bowl. The water trickled toward a drain in a corner. A naked shower rod hung over an old claw-foot bathtub, next to which two blue towels and a roll of toilet paper sat on a worn-out wicker chair. A heavy metal wall-mounted cabinet over a yellowish sink had a mirror glued on to its door.

Juan took care of his business as quickly as he could. As he washed his hands, he glanced in the mirror and noticed that his face was a deep red. After splashing some water on it, he returned to the living room.

"I've feared all these years that I left a son behind," he said. "It's a relief to know Rosita didn't—"

Victoria cleared her throat.

"You don't have children?" she asked. "No Yuma kids for you?"

"I wish! But when I married Sharon, she was a little old for that."

Victoria looked like she was about to say something but bit her tongue.

"Where's your wife?" she asked after a short silence. "I thought she was coming with you."

"She was tired from the flight here," Juan said, skipping the dinner invitation. There were a few things he'd have to explain to Sharon first.

"What happened to Rosita?" he asked. "Did she get married too?"

"No. She lives alone in her old house. Her mother died several years ago. Rosita's a makeup artist, a good one. We hire her at Café Arabia for big shows. That's how she makes ends meet."

Victoria waited, but Juan didn't ask anything else. She went on anyway.

"She works at the cemetery. We may run into her when we go to visit your dad's grave. She keeps it impeccable."

Silence fell over the room again, as if old ghosts occupied the space around them, making their presence felt.

"I'm surprised you didn't end up in the film industry," Juan said, changing the subject. "You were so talented."

"Well, thank you. I tried, but unless you have friends in high places . . ." Victoria shrugged. "I did have some minor roles working for Fernando Pérez and Humberto Solás. You can find me in a couple of scenes in *Madrigal* and *Barrio Cuba* if you don't blink." She laughed. "It was too hard. I didn't have the patience or the connections and got tired of waiting for my big break. Besides, I've gotten too old."

Juan had once held out for his own big break too, hoping to become a famous *trovador* like Silvio Rodríguez. He had played the guitar in several Miami clubs, both alone and with a band called Los Caribeños. But his career had never taken off. The city had been full of musicians, all better than he was. Los Caribeños dissolved in less than a year, having never made a name for themselves. By the time he relocated to Albuquerque, he had given up. The day he moved in with Sharon, he got rid of his guitar, an old Breedlove, bitterly thinking that things could have been different had he stayed in Cuba. But maybe not, especially if Víctor, who everybody had said had "it," hadn't succeeded either.

"I needed a steady income, so I carved a nice niche for myself at Café Arabia," Victoria concluded.

"What exactly is that?"

"A nightclub. The hottest in Havana! We're quite well ranked on TripAdvisor, I'm told. I sing. I act. I dance. I do everything. Three times a week. Boy, do I have a following! I've built an audience quicker than any other performer."

"Good for you."

"But I'd still like to work with Almodóvar's film production company, El Deseo," Victoria admitted, blushing. "That's my dream."

"Working with Almodóvar?" Juan laughed. "Weren't you the one who once criticized us for dreaming too big?"

Victoria stared blankly into space.

"I was wrong," she muttered. "I'm sorry I was such a smartass. I thought I knew everything."

"No, you were right. I don't know of any Cuban making it big in Hollywood."

"Andy García!"

"But he's Cuban American. It's different when you grow up there."

"Anyway, Almodóvar . . . he's my hero." Victoria's eyes grew distant. "He portrays us as we are. If I could just meet him, or if he could see me act, we'd click. He'd give me a role in one of his movies, just like that." She snapped her fingers.

Juan doubted it, but didn't dare to laugh or voice his thoughts.

"But tell me about *you*." Victoria started sipping her coffee. "Where did you say you lived?"

"Albuquerque, New Mexico."

She arched her penciled eyebrows. "Wait, did you *leave* La Yuma?"

"It's *New* Mexico, not Mexico."

"What kind of name is Albuquerque? It doesn't even sound American."

Juan wasn't ready to go through the geopolitical explanation. He shrugged, but Victoria wasn't done yet.

"Do people speak Spanish there?"

"Some do, but less than in Miami."

"Do you miss Cuba?"

"Sometimes."

Victoria grinned. "What do you miss about it? Besides me."

"I miss the good times we all used to have together. You know, as the Three Musketeers," Juan said slowly. "I haven't made many friends in La Yuma."

"I can't believe that! Everybody always liked you."

"People there are cold and guarded. They don't joke around like we do. Or maybe they just don't joke with me. I still feel like a foreigner there, even after twenty years."

Victoria twirled a blonde curl around her finger.

"That's too bad, Juan. Are you still into music?"

Juan wished she hadn't brought that up. "Not really. I tried in Miami but couldn't compete with the pros. I mean, I was only in college for a year. Now I do construction work and help my wife with her business." He took a card out of his wallet and handed it to Victoria.

"What else?" she asked, placing the card under the silver mirror.

"That's it. I repair old houses so she can sell them for more than what she paid for them. Ah, and sometimes I teach a salsa class at a restaurant." He scratched his chin. "Sorry I'm not the kind who comes back bragging about how successful he is. What you see is what you get."

"I see a happy, well-fed man."

"Too well fed, I'm afraid. But I refuse to go on a diet like those silly Americans. After I went hungry for so long? *No jodas!*"

"You don't have to. You're still a handsome musketeer."

Juan smiled briefly, then went serious and said, "Let me tell you something, Víctor—Victoria. I want to apologize. Even when we were struggling to survive out at sea, I kept thinking about that fight. I don't know why it got so out of hand. We were talking politics. I criticized Fidel, and you defended him so angrily. I didn't know you cared so much about the revolution."

"I didn't. Not *that* much anyway, but it was so frustrating that you were leaving your country, your chance to get an education and, well, *me*, to follow a girl. It was my fault as well. I . . . I loved you, and I knew I was about to lose you. I was furious."

Juan stood stock-still, feeling himself blush again. Victoria's eyes sparkled as she smiled slightly.

"Like I said, it's all water under the bridge," she reassured him. "We're just old friends now."

Juan let out a sigh of relief.

"I swear I never thought that you and Camilo . . ." he said, shaking his head. "How did I miss the signs?"

"You were too busy with your women to read the cues."

"But why didn't you guys ever tell me straight up?"

"Come on. Would you still have hung out with us if you'd known?"

Probably not. He would have been self-conscious, afraid of what people would say. *Birds of a feather flock together.* In Cuba, "birds" meant gays.

The chorus to *"La vie en rose"* cut the conversation short, saving him from answering. Victoria retrieved her cell phone from the table.

"Yes, honey," she purred. "Are you going to the *mariconga*? No? Sorry to hear. Well, I can't miss it. No, no! I'll go by myself! Bye, my king."

She blew a kiss and closed the phone.

"That was Lázaro," she said. "He's so jealous. If he finds out you were here, he'll have a fit. He's too possessive, but I love him. We'll be getting married soon."

Juan looked discreetly at Victoria's breasts. He doubted they were real but didn't dare to ask.

"I didn't know gay marriage was legal here," he said.

"It isn't quite yet, but they're getting the process started to change the law. That's one of the things we're celebrating with the *mariconga*."

"What's that?"

"The gay pride parade. See, *'maricón'* and 'conga'? But it's also a play on Mariela's name."

"Mariela who?"

Victoria threw her hands in the air. "Mariela Castro! Haven't you heard what she's done for us?"

"I have no idea. I don't really keep up with Cuban news," Juan admitted.

He didn't actually keep up with any kind of news.

"She opened the National Center for Sex Education, the CENESEX," Victoria gushed. "She gave us free gender reassignment surgeries and protection from the police. She's our queen! The *mariconga* is a way of kissing her ass too. It'll be a fun party, though. Do you want to come?"

The phone rang again. This time, Victoria glanced at it but didn't answer.

"That's the club owner," she said. "He's trying to get me to work today, but I already told him no. I understand that business is important, but money isn't everything. Down with man's exploitation of man!"

She laughed at Juan's puzzled expression.

"Yes, I can still quote old Marx," she said. "So, are you coming to the *mariconga* or not?"

Juan thought about it. He had never been part of a pride march. What if people misinterpreted his presence there? But then he realized that the chances of someone recognizing him after so many years were nearly zero. Besides, he didn't care what anyone here thought of him. And he didn't want to offend Victoria by refusing to go; it was obviously important to her. He also wanted to spend more time with her. There were a few things about Elsa he needed to find out.

"Sure," he said.

"Fabulous! Give me one second."

Victoria pranced to her bedroom and came back wearing a white hat. The brim was covered in blue feathers. A tiny red bird made of silk sat atop it.

"I need protection from the sun," she explained. "I'm using a treatment to shrink my pores, and the sun's rays will give me dark spots."

The hat smelled faintly of hair spray.

"Let's go," Juan said.

6

THE *MARICONGA*

Sharon, who was still in the park, saw Juan come out of the building in the company of the tall blonde who had closed the balcony door an hour before. Now she was wearing a hat with—goodness, was that a hummingbird on top? Sharon would have laughed, had she been in the mood for it. She waited behind the *flamboyán* that exploded in a cascade of bright red flowers. The tree, over a hundred years old, provided her with safe refuge behind its flaming foliage.

What had happened in the apartment during that hour? Nothing good, Sharon assumed. At least, nothing good for her, her relationship with Juan, her wounded self-esteem. She followed the couple at a respectful distance—not that it mattered, since they were too engulfed in their chat to pay attention to the world around them.

Sharon berated herself for having trusted Juan—not only that day, but all the years they had been together. He'd played her like a fiddle. *Oh, I'm going to see an old friend . . . I beat the shit out of him once and have to apologize.*

"Qué cabrón!"

She had become so used to her husband's slang that it came to her mind when she least expected it.

"No, *I'm* the *cabrona*," she muttered, remembering that *cabrona* also meant "cheated wife."

Juan and his companion walked fast. Having a good sense of orientation, Sharon knew they were going toward downtown, the heart of the city, where the ice-cream parlor was. Her shoes were bothering her, and her feet hurt, but she kept going.

The conversation between Juan and the blonde was punctuated by gestures. Their hands moved at high speed. So did their legs. Sharon was panting by the time they reached Línea Street.

Just when she had resolved it was time to end her chase and confront them, a man dressed in blue overalls came out of nowhere and blocked the couple's way. Sharon realized that he had been following them as well.

The man was angry. When he spoke to the blonde, he put his face one inch from hers, shaking his finger in the air. The woman answered in a soothing tone and didn't seem concerned. Juan kept his distance from both. But the other guy's voice was loud enough to carry over the fifty yards or so that separated Sharon from them.

"You are a *puta*!" he yelled at the blonde. "If you keep this up, I'll kill you!"

The man, who was younger and taller than Juan, had a few choice words for him too. Juan, Sharon noted with contempt, didn't try to defend himself or his companion. He simply stood apart, as if the confrontation had nothing to do with him. Just as the discussion became more heated, a yellow '58 Chevy drove by. The blonde flagged it. The car stopped, and she pushed Juan toward the back door and got into the passenger seat herself. The car sped off. The other guy shook his fist at the vanishing *almendrón*.

Sharon waited a few more minutes until another *almendrón* came by. She waved it down and asked to be taken to the Meliá Cohiba hotel.

The *almendrón* driver charged her fifteen dollars for the five-minute ride.

The Chevy stopped one block away from Coppelia. Victoria smoothed her hair, fixed her hat and paid the driver five CUCs.

"Don't mind Lázaro," she told Juan, taking him by the arm. "He's always making a scene."

Juan coughed. "I hope he understands that I am just . . . a friend."

"Oh, he knows I'm not a loose girl." Victoria winked. "But he likes to show off. It's a Cuban macho thing."

"Macho?"

The sculpture of a naked Don Quijote riding on Rocinante appeared in the distance. The piece, created by Sergio Martínez, had been a point of reference for Habaneros since 1980.

"Lázaro is the macho," Victoria said, swatting at Juan playfully. "He's a *bugarrón*, the one on top. Officially, he's Victoria Sunrise's man."

"Why Sunrise, if you don't mind my asking?"

"You know my two last names: Pérez and Díaz. So vulgar, so lacking in sophistication. I had a boyfriend who used to call me his *amanecer*, so I just translated that and came up with Sunrise. It befits a sensuous woman, a lady with cachet."

"You talk so openly about . . . all this," Juan said.

"It's been a long time, and like I told you, things here have changed. You'll see it at the *mariconga*."

They passed by El Quijote Park, where the two-ton wire sculpture of the man of La Mancha stood.

"Nice park," Juan said. "I had almost forgotten it."

"Now people call it Parque del Suicida," Victoria said. "A young man shot himself in the head here three years ago. He left a note saying it was because of a love affair gone wrong. Very romantic."

Juan shuddered. "I don't think it's romantic. Poor guy."

"It happens all the time." Victoria's laser-like eyes flashed under the hat. "Women set themselves aflame; men jump off bridges or shoot themselves—when they can find a gun, which isn't easy here. The case was strange because the police never found the weapon. People think that whoever discovered the body first took it and went away without a word. The story I heard was that he put the gun inside his mouth and pulled the trigger."

The conversation was making Juan uncomfortable. He had avoided military service because he suffered from scoliosis, but he also had an aversion to guns and violence in general.

A woman rushed past them. She was wearing a strong perfume, so thick that Juan thought he could almost see it, like an aura around her. It was a foreign scent, Opium or Shalimar. Back in his youth, Cuban women had worn Russian perfumes. Elsa's favorite had been Red Moscow. Elsa. He couldn't stop thinking about her. He had to find a tactful way to ask where she lived now and if there was a chance of getting in touch with her.

They soon met the first *mariconga* attendees. The scene reminded Juan of the gay pride events he had seen in Albuquerque and Santa Fe, but with Cuban flavor, a Caribbean touch of rum, conga and unabashed fun. Three transwomen in matching red halter tops and Lycra miniskirts proudly exhibited their hairy armpits. Two young men with close-shaven heads walked hand in hand, and a girl in military boots and khaki pants with a rose painted on her left cheek was carrying a white miniature poodle around. Two older men with conga drums around their necks twirled their drumsticks. One carried a bottle of Havana Club. A small crowd waving rainbow flags followed them and cheered when another musician barged in with a Chinese trumpet.

"Is she here yet?" the girl with the poodle asked.

"She's coming!" a man answered. "She'll be here in half an hour."

The drummers started to play louder.

"They're waiting for Mariela," Victoria explained.

"Is she Fidel's daughter?" Juan asked. "I thought he only had the one, Alina, who lives in Miami now."

"No, she is Raúl's daughter."

"Ah." Fidel's niece then.

Victoria chortled, but her laugh had bitter undertones.

"All in the family," she said. "But it's a good thing. An outsider couldn't have accomplished this much. Mariela has a heart of gold. If it weren't for her, we would still be invisible, hiding."

Two young, clean-shaven men in guayaberas were giving away Cuban flags.

"Those are *segurosos*," Victoria whispered. "People who work for the secret police, in case you've forgotten what that means. They want to make sure this doesn't look like a counterrevolutionary march, one of those human rights things."

Juan, who didn't even know how there were "human rights

things" in Cuba nowadays, realized how disconnected he was from his country. When he'd lived in Miami, the island was at the center of every conversation: exiles breathed in Cuba, ate Cuban food and talked Cuban politics at the restaurant Versailles. All the papers had columns about Cuba. The island was an omnipresent absence in Calle Ocho. But Albuquerque was different. The Cubans there were younger and didn't care about politics. They preferred to call themselves emigrants, not exiles.

By this point, more people had joined the parade. A dozen teenagers in their high school uniforms came and picked up Cuban flags. Most then ran off right away. Only two girls with short hair and serious expressions stayed.

"They're coming down Malecón Avenue!" shouted a diva of a redhead in front, over six feet in her mountainous heels. "Let's go meet them!"

The crowd followed her. They took a lateral street that ended at the seawall avenue. Victoria and Juan joined them.

"This looks cool," Juan said as they passed by a cafeteria with signs that advertised hot dogs, ham sandwiches, ice cream and beer, all sold in CUC. The place was packed. "If I'm not mistaken, wasn't this a dingy store where they only sold Soviet clothing and Hungarian ceramics before? It was always empty."

"All that is gone. Everything in this area is prime real estate now. It's full of offices belonging to foreign companies." Victoria pointed to a building nearby. "Elsa's is over there."

Juan stopped hearing the trumpet and drums. He kept walking, but felt his feet moving to the pulsing beat of his own heart.

"The company her husband owns?" he asked, committing the address to memory. It was a two-story Art Deco building with massive double doors.

"Don't kid yourself. She co-owns it," Victoria clarified. "The woman has power. She finally got 'it.'"

Despite his best efforts to put up a mask of indifference, Juan knew he was failing at it. His hands began to sweat.

"What do you mean?"

"The Spanish geezer's too old to take care of the business anymore. Last time I saw him he looked like a raisin, all wrinkled and shrimpy. He must be close to eighty now. Elsa's the boss. She just opened another branch in Villa Clara."

Juan glanced again at the building, which reminded him of an oversized wedding cake. "What kind of business is it?"

"Something related to computers."

A few bystanders stopped and looked at the marchers, seeming more curious than hostile. Victoria elbowed Juan.

"See?" she said. "People are getting used to us. It may take a while, but it's happening. Thanks to Mariela!"

She blew a kiss to a man who was watching them intently. The man smiled and waved. She elbowed Juan again, but his mind was somewhere else.

"What could Elsa know about computers?" he asked. "She sucked at math."

"She manages the business. Nothing to do with the technical stuff. That's done in Spain. She just brings computers here and sells them to the state."

A *seguroso* came over and offered Juan a Cuban flag. He accepted it and thanked him, trying to sound as Cuban as he had twenty years before. His clothes had likely attracted the man's attention, marking Juan as a foreigner. Victoria, who was left flagless, smirked.

"Cuba, always catering to the foreigner," she hissed. "It's CUBALSE all over again."

"How old was the Spaniard when they got married?" Juan asked, barely registering Victoria's comment.

"I guess sixty, maybe fiftysomething—not a bad-looking guy then. But twenty years is something, no matter what the song says. Remember? *Veinte años no es nada.*" Victoria took a tango dancer's stance. "*Volver, con la frente marchita, las nieves del tiempo platearon mi sien.*"

Juan couldn't help but laugh at the performance.

"Do you agree?" Victoria asked with a smile. "You came back after twenty years too."

"Come on. It's not like I've returned with my forehead all wrinkled or my temples turned silver," he told her. "Have they been together all these years, Elsa and the old fart?"

"Oh yes. A perfect couple! But he stays in Spain now because of health issues. Had a heart attack two years ago. Elsa divides her time between Havana and Seville, with a few trips to Cambridge in between. Their son is studying there."

"Their son?"

The crowd erupted in loud cheers.

"Hurry up!" Victoria said. "The *mariconga*'s about to start. I'll tell you more about Elsa later. Man, you sure *weren't* interested in her!"

More live music came from Malecón Avenue. People were shouting, "Mariela, Mariela!" as they ran to the main avenue.

"Wait, did you say Cambridge? In England or the United States?" said Juan, chasing after Victoria.

"La Yuma. The kid's at one of their big-ass universities in Massachusetts. Ah, there she is!"

Juan caught a glimpse of Mariela Castro, a middle-aged woman in a straw hat who was marching in the middle of the crowd.

People waved Cuban and rainbow flags. On a stage, a band played the national anthem.

"Homophobia no, socialism yes!" people shouted.

Victoria shouted with them, jumping up and down. She grabbed the flag from Juan's hand and joined the crowd, leaving him behind.

7

THE EXECUTIVE AT HOME

lsa Dieguez was looking for Emilio's ring when she found the gun.

She had just finished putting together a care package for her son, who, when she had visited him in Cambridge three days earlier, had requested five cans of Cafe Cubita. Cafe Cubita, of all things! When he could buy Bustelo or La Llave or one of the many kinds of espresso available in the United States! But no. It had to be Cuban. The American brands didn't taste as good, Emilito claimed. What was he, spoiled? He had also asked for a white guayabera, a framed picture of his favorite baseball team, Industriales, to hang in his dorm room and his father's old brass ring, which he thought was "cool." The package was on the dresser, ready to be sent. Elsa planned to ask a friend who worked at the Spanish embassy to mail it when he left for Madrid in a week. She didn't trust the Cuban postal service.

While looking for her husband's ring, Elsa had come across the gun that Emilio had bought in Spain, back when he was still living most of each year in Havana. The weapon was small and sleek—a

Kahr CW9, with a silencer and everything. He had insisted on buying it for "security reasons," while Elsa had privately laughed at him. He didn't even know how to load a gun, much less shoot one. But *she* did.

She remembered her father coming home drunk and firing shots into the ceiling, threatening his wife. He could really be a violent bastard at times. A veteran of the Angolan war, he'd taught Elsa how to handle not just a gun but a military-grade Russian AKM. "Don't let anyone mess with you, *mijita*," he'd told her. "Make them respect you, or else." Respect was important to him. He was also fond of repeating one of Fidel's most famous phrases, which had appeared for many years on the country's murals and billboards: "Every Cuban should know how to shoot, and shoot well." Elsa thought that in that sense at least, El Comandante would have been proud of her. Her father certainly was, at least now.

Despite his outbursts, she had been closer to him than to her mother, Silvana, a subdued housewife unable to control her rebellious daughter or stand up to her husband. When Elsa saw him hit her mother, she vowed to never let a man do the same to her. On occasion, Elsa's father would try to hit her too, but unlike her mother, she fought back every time. He seemed impressed by this and stopped when she defended herself. It was all part of teaching her how to earn his respect, she later understood.

She had resolved early on that if a single beating happened when she got married, she wouldn't be the one on the receiving end. She identified with her father, the one in charge, not that sad weakling that was her mother. But she still resented domineering men. She had been drawn to Juan because he was an artist, a gentle musician who spoke in soothing tones. Her father had preferred she dated military types like himself, or at least committed revolutionaries. In the end, she had married a man who, for his age and temperament, wasn't too different from *el pincho*. Fortunately, she had already known how to handle him.

And her father had accepted Savarria. The Spaniard was a necessary evil, like the swanky hotels for foreigners, the *casas particulares* and the CUC shops. Like him and his wife settling in the United States, the hated the "cradle of imperialism," because life in Cuba didn't show signs of improvement. Emilio had helped set them up there, but the former *pincho* hadn't severed ties with his country. He had become the president of an Amistad con Cuba group in Los Angeles and avoided Miami like the plague.

Elsa smiled at the memories. She would have to visit her parents next time she traveled to the United States. Then she returned her attention to the gun. She didn't want the woman who cleaned the house every week to see it. She took it to the half bathroom off the master bedroom and hid it in the linen closet, under the fancy lacy lingerie she hadn't worn in years.

Her cell phone rang. Elsa saw Victoria's number but didn't answer. After a message announced itself with a ding, Elsa called her voice mail and listened, putting on a bored expression.

"*Mi santa*, I haven't heard from you in such a long time. Are you still gallivanting? If not, would you give me a call, please? It's in your best interest—a ghost from your past has returned."

She paused. If Victoria's intention had been to intrigue her, it had worked. But Elsa didn't call back right away. She placed the Samsung back on her dresser and sat in front of the vanity, inspecting herself with a critical eye.

She had no reason to be too critical, though. Elsa didn't look older than thirty, though she had just turned forty. She was svelte but not skinny, with curves in the right places. Her hair, still a rich brown shade, was short for the first time in five years. A few weeks before, a stylist in Seville had convinced her that a bob would flatter her small oval face, but she still felt ambivalent about it. Curly bobs didn't flatter anyone's face, she mused now. Well, it would grow out quickly. If only everything in life were as easy to solve as bad hair days.

She was in excellent physical shape and proud of it. She had always been athletic, but after thirty-five, when her body had started feeling the effects of gravity, being fit had become an obsession. In Seville she had a personal trainer, Javier Mondragón, a tattooed guy with a crooked grin who had once coached Penélope Cruz. When she was there, Elsa met with him four times a week for weight-lifting sessions and resistance training. On weekends, she ran four miles in Parque Amate, a park that also had a sports center and a swimming pool.

It was harder to keep up her workout routine in Havana. The city's only safe running option was El Malecón, but the waterfront was always full of people sitting on the wall or walking around, kids on bicycles and obnoxious vendors. Though there were a few private CUC-charging gyms, Elsa didn't like them. They were too noisy and pedestrian for her taste. But she could take it easy for a couple weeks at least. Before flying to Cambridge, she had walked El Camino de Santiago and was stronger than ever. Elsa wasn't Catholic or even a believer but regarded the journey as a vacation from the company, the house and, above all, Savarria. She had walked the five hundred miles in a month and a half. Her legs felt like steel pistons. If it hadn't been raining and a bit cold, she would have shown them off in a short skirt.

That morning, she had chosen a beige suit from El Corte Inglés and an Hermès scarf she had bought on an impulse at the Houston international airport. Not many people in Cuba were able to appreciate the scarf's true value, but wearing it had an uplifting effect on her. The average Cuban's monthly salary was fifteen dollars. Knowing she could spend three hundred on a luxury item made her feel powerful. In control. And as the vice president and co-owner of Savarria and Co. and the only Cuban-born member of the Association of Spanish Entrepreneurs in Havana, Elsa had a persona to maintain. She would have put on high heels, but the few yards she had to walk from her parking space to the office would be slippery. She chose a pair of Michael Kors midheel pumps that clacked nicely as she walked.

She had just finished a leisurely breakfast. Early mornings were her private time before the pressures of work, meetings and assorted *jodiendas* of daily life started. She liked getting ready for work and dressed with the same care and attention to detail each day as if she were attending a reception. A successful executive should always look like one, she had learned in a "Project a Positive Image" seminar she had taken in San Diego two years before when she'd traveled with her son for a tour of UCSD. She had loved the city and hoped Emilito might settle in La Jolla for his college years. But then he was accepted at MIT, his first choice.

She sprayed Youth-Dew, her favorite perfume, around her wrists and neck and corrected her penciled eyebrows. She needed a touch-up of Botox. Her secretary had told her they were doing it in Cuba and even offered to recommend a good nurse, but Elsa had demurred. What if they botched the job? She didn't trust her fellow citizens.

She put on a light gray coat in case it got chilly—it had just started to rain. Now she was ready to go. In the garage waited her Lexus. It was only twenty to eight, and driving to her office would take her less than ten minutes. She went to the living room, sat down on the dark brown leather sofa that, like most of the house furniture and the car, had been brought over from Seville, replayed Victoria's message and pressed the CALL BACK button.

"*Mi santa!*" Victoria's voice was full of melody and drama. "Thank God you called back. I was thinking of you all day yesterday."

"I just got back from America," Elsa said. She wouldn't call it La Yuma; that sounded too Cuban, too folksy and unsophisticated. "What's up, Vic?"

"How are you? And your husband? And your handsome son?"

Elsa rolled her eyes. "Everybody's fine. Savarria's feeling better these days, almost recovered." She always referred to her husband by his last name. "I just visited Emilito. He's getting used to the cold."

"I've missed you, girl. We haven't talked in what, a year?"

Elsa found the remote and turned on the TV, careful to immediately mute it. One of the three Cuban channels showed scenes from the LGBT march that had taken place the day before. "A few months," she replied. "You called when you wanted an invitation to a fashion show at La Maison." She paused and then added, "You only call me when you need something, Vic."

Vic was her nickname for Victoria. Elsa couldn't get used to her new name but didn't want to offend her by using the old one. Vic was neutral and chic. They both liked it.

"My darling, this time it may be *you* who needs something from *me*," Victoria said.

"Vic, whatever it is, just say it. I've got to go to work."

"Oh, please, you're the boss. You can get there whenever the hell your ass pleases."

Elsa giggled. "Shut your big mouth!"

"Anyway, Miss Super Executive, do you know who's in Cuba right now?"

Elsa turned off the TV. Her eyes wandered around the room until they landed on a series of framed pictures of her son displayed on the entertainment center. Emilito skiing in Vail, rooting for Real Madrid at a game, swimming in Varadero . . . There was also a picture of Raúl Castro shaking hands with Emilio while Elsa stood by her husband's side.

"To my knowledge," Elsa replied, "there are over ten million people in Cuba at the moment."

"And one of them is *your* Juan."

"No me jodas."

She'd spoken the words reflexively. *No me jodas*, "don't fuck with me," was a vulgar expression she had completely banned from her vocabulary, along with expletives like *coño* and *carajo*. But sometimes they came back.

"You're messing with me, Vic."

"I am not!"

"I thought he lived in the States now."

"He does, but he's back as a tourist. It had to happen eventually." Elsa stiffened but kept quiet.

"He came by yesterday and went to the *mariconga* with me."

"What? Don't tell me he's gay now or something."

"I don't think so." Victoria laughed. "He was just curious to see it, I guess. Anyway, the first thing he did was ask about you. Elsa this and Elsa that. Your ears must have been ringing!"

Elsa took a deep breath. "What did you tell him?"

"Not much."

There was a pause.

"But he wants to see you," Victoria went on. "He knows you're a businesswoman now."

"Did you tell him . . . ?"

"No, no! But I wanted to warn you that he might stop by your office."

"How the hell does he know where my office is?"

"Oh, someone must've told him. You two have other friends in common."

Elsa felt her fingers grip the phone with more force than necessary. She tried to remember which other "friends in common" she and Juan still had, but no one popped up besides Victoria Sunrise.

"I don't want him showing up there," she said through clenched teeth. "I have to go now, Vic. Thanks for letting me know."

"Wait, *mi santa*. I just had an idea!" Victoria squealed. "Why don't you come by so we can chat about all this? I know you're busy, but I'm waiting for a *bisnero* who promised to bring me a whole pork leg to roast. I can make *arroz congrí* and a flan. A banquet! Better than any *paladar*. You know I'm a great cook."

"You are. And did you say *arroz congrí*?"

"Yes. Some white rice and black beans cooked with nice salty bacon, fresh onions and peppers. What do you think?"

It took Elsa a while to answer, but when she finally did, she felt more relaxed. "I'll be there then. I haven't had *arroz congrí* in months. It'll be nice to remember the good old bad old days when we were young and silly!"

"And beautiful!"

"Now, where can I park my car? Last time I left it in front of the building, someone scratched it. I don't know if that was on purpose."

"Come on. It's still El Vedado, even if we're not a chic neighborhood like yours! There's a private parking lot a block from here. For twenty-five pesos or one CUC, the *parqueadero* owner will take care of your precious Lexus like it's gold plated."

"Sounds good."

"Be here at noon."

When they hung up, Elsa walked over to the entertainment center and picked up the most recent picture of her son, which had been taken on the MIT campus. A young man with curly brown hair like hers and tear-shaped eyes.

"Damn it, Juan," she whispered. "You're a ghost from the past all right."

8

ROASTED PORK FOR A RAINY DAY

Victoria Sunrise gave the *bisnero* forty CUCs. The man put the money in his pocket without counting it. The clandestine food seller wore seven gold chains around his neck, perfectly ironed blue jeans and a Dallas Cowboys T-shirt.

"Thank you, Señora," he said. "Let me know when you need another."

"I can't afford to throw this sort of party very often." She smiled. "But I will let you know."

When the man had left, Victoria looked for the card Juan had given her the day before. JUAN CHIONG. CONTRACTOR, BUILDER, HANDYMAN. She fetched the Spanish-English dictionary from the bedroom and looked up the words.

"Handyman," she repeated, snickering. "I thought it meant a man who was 'handy' all the time."

She dialed the number, and Juan answered immediately.

"I've invited Elsa to lunch," Victoria said quickly, afraid she would lose the call.

"You have?" Juan sounded happy but a bit incredulous.

"I knew it was what you wanted, *cabroncito*."

"And she agreed?"

"Yep. She's as curious to see you as you are to see her."

"Thanks, *chico*!"

"*Chic*a."

"Sorry, I mean—thanks. You are a great friend. Eh . . . do you think she still cares about me?"

"You'll have to ask her. Be here at one o'clock. I'm going to fix you guys the best roasted pork leg you've ever had. Perfect for a rainy day like this one."

"Should I bring something? A bottle of wine? Some dessert?"

"Whatever you want, just not your wife."

She heard Juan chuckle.

"You bet," he said. "Not that she's in the mood for visits. I think Havana's getting on her nerves. Or maybe it's just the rain. But I warned her that—"

The line went dead. Victoria was still holding her cell phone when a knock-knock startled her. Outsiders would ring the building doorbell first, so she figured it was a member of the tribe next door. No one could tell for sure how many people lived in her neighboring apartment. There were five on the ration card: an old couple, Magdala and Alberto, and their three grown children, two daughters and a son. But the children had gotten married, had kids and brought a number of live-in partners and *their* families into the place over the years. And relatives from the Holguín province, where the family was originally from, would come to stay for weeks or even months. It wasn't unusual to find between ten and fifteen people sleeping there on any given night.

One of the people who lived there was Pepito. Victoria didn't know exactly what his relationship was with the original owners. A nephew? A godson? The best-informed neighbors maintained that he had come from the small town of Punta Blanca for a weekend three years before and never returned home.

The building residents were used to the arrangement and, as a rule, didn't get involved. But Pepito was an enthusiastic fledgling drummer, prone to practicing his instrument at any hour of the day or night and having impromptu jam sessions with his friends till dawn. When the noise became too disruptive, neighbors would yell from their balconies at them to shut up, cojones. The woman who lived directly above them would hit her floor with a broom handle. The police had even been called on a few occasions, only to become part of the party, dancing to the wild rhythm of the *guaguancós*.

Victoria had a soft spot for Pepito, an eighteen-year-old man with a quick smile and a sinewy, naturally sculpted body. The other neighbors joked that she had a crush on him. She would never admit it, but she knew he knew. He flirted with her. Though Pepito had probably heard about her past life—Havana wasn't a good place to keep secrets—he had never mentioned it. Lázaro was jealous of him, but then, Lázaro was jealous of any man who got close to Victoria Sunrise.

Victoria thought Pepito was a good kid. Perhaps a little thoughtless and too loud, but that was part of his charm. Yet he was already familiar with the local police station, El Vedado's Unidad 15. The first time for assault and battery—a minor street fight, his aunt Magdala claimed, with someone who wasn't man enough to keep his mouth shut about it. The second charge—unrelated to the first offense, as she always pointed out—was using and possession. "But nothing awful, just *maría*." He had been caught with a few ounces of marijuana, a crime that wasn't half as bad as it had been twenty years before, though people still went to jail for it.

"Times change," Magdala would say, and Victoria wholeheartedly agreed. Besides, Pepito was a musician, like her, and Victoria herself was on speaking terms with *maría*. It was a pity that most of the building's residents were so uptight about it.

Victoria straightened the blue strapless dress she had chosen that morning. Since she planned to be busy in the kitchen, surrounded by garlic and onion smells, she wasn't wearing her wig yet. Truth was, she didn't need it. Her own hair was long enough, well past her shoulders, but she liked wigs. And hats and hairclips and fascinators. Anything that covered her head gave her a sense of security, like having a safety blanket.

After another, more urgent knock, she opened the door. A smiling Pepito was at the threshold. He was wearing only a pair of shorts. The faint aura of *maría* surrounded him, and his chiseled chest and bulging arms attracted Victoria's eyes.

"*Mamita*, you look so beautiful today!" he said. "I mean, you are always beautiful, but this morning you are stellar."

Victoria beamed. "What's up, sweetheart?"

"I need to borrow a screwdriver. Do you happen to have one? One of our windows is coming apart with all this rain, and I need to adjust a few screws on the frame."

"I don't know much about tools, but come in and see if you find something to your liking."

"After you."

Victoria led him to the kitchen, swinging her hips seductively as she walked. A full pork leg still wrapped in brown paper sat on the counter. It was huge, with a long bone sticking out of it.

"What a piece!" Pepito exclaimed. "Are you going to cook that today?"

"Yes, I'm planning to roast it for some friends."

Pepito licked his lips. "Are they foreigners? I saw that well-dressed guy here yesterday."

"He's Cuban, but he lives in La Yuma now."

"You're so lucky, *mamita*, with these rich guys always after you."

Victoria gave him a coy smile.

"He isn't after me," she said demurely. "He's married and came here with his Yuma wife. Anyway, look around, and see if you can find what you need. I still have to put the leg in the oven and grind the garlic and the onion to start the *congrí*."

Pepito opened the door to the closet and said with mock irritation, "*Mamita*, this is a rat's nest! One day, I'm going to come and tidy it for you."

"You are welcome to come kill my rats anytime." She put a hand on Pepito's shoulder. "Maybe we could have dinner together tonight, if you're free."

"Just leftovers for me, eh?"

"Not leftovers. We're not going to eat even half of that leg."

Pepito eyed the leg, which weighed a good twenty pounds. "Fine. Never look a gift horse in the mouth."

"Or a gift pork. Let's plan for seven o'clock."

"Won't Lázaro mind?" Pepito asked, suddenly concerned.

"He left for Pinar del Río this morning and won't be back until tomorrow."

"Great! Will it be a romantic dinner, *mamita*? With candlelight, wine, porcelain dishes?"

"Dream on."

Before leaving with a screwdriver and a few screws, Pepito glanced enviously at Victoria's cell phone, which was lying on the coffee table.

"You have it made, *mamita*," he said. "Pork legs, cool phone, Yuma friends . . . You have an easy life, don't you?"

"Yeah, I got it like that." She gave him a little wave. "See you."

Pepito left, and Victoria closed the door behind him. She turned on the oven and put the pork leg inside. Then she started boiling water for the *arroz congrí* and thinking of the meeting she had so artfully planned. In the end, Elsa would thank her, even if she pretended to get mad at the sight of Juan. He was Elsa's real love, her one and only. Well, maybe not her "only" but for sure her true love. She'd cried so much after he'd left! Victoria was sure Elsa had never forgotten him. But if she knew her old *amor* would be at lunch too, she wouldn't come. She was too afraid of the past, and with good reason. *Because, let's face it, that kid of yours is Juan's.* The kid was the man's spitting image. Hadn't the Spaniard ever suspected anything?

Victoria put two garlic cloves, a chopped onion and a few cilantro and parsley leaves inside the mortar and started to grind. She liked this big, heavy mortar, a gift from a Café Arabia patron. The guy, who was from Mexico, called the set a *"molcajete."* She added salt and pepper to the mix and a bit of vinegar.

But there was something else. She had asked Elsa to come earlier than Juan because she wanted to have a heart-to-heart talk with her. Seeing Juan again had stirred up old dreams Victoria had thought she had forgotten, ambitions she had pushed aside. He had said she was talented. And she was. She had graduated with honors and acted in several plays when she was younger. Critics had praised her as the ISA instructors used to do. She had simply become resigned, after so many years, to being an underpaid performer in a third-class nightclub in Havana. Because that was what Café Arabia really was, no matter what she had told Juan.

She was destined for better things! And Elsa knew Pedro Almodóvar personally. He was a friend who had visited her El Vedado home. Victoria's eyes brightened. If Elsa could just get her an audition . . . It was a long shot, yes, but how did that saying go about shooting for the moon and landing among the stars? Elsa should help her. It wouldn't cost her anything, would it?

ABUELA

Juan sat on the bed, eyes fixed on the TV even though it was turned off. It was ten to nine. Sharon was staring out the window, watching the rain with her back to him. She had been acting strangely since the day before. After returning from the *mariconga*, he had invited her to go to Coppelia, but she'd flatly refused. She didn't say a word for the rest of the evening. They had a quiet dinner at another of the hotel's restaurants, Med. Juan ate an ample serving of excellent paella and drank two glasses of red wine while Sharon picked at her serrano ham and manchego cheese tapas. She looked angry, but he couldn't figure out why. Hadn't he told her Cuba wouldn't be all that fun? Was he supposed to stick around and entertain her every minute?

He had looked up the address of Abuela's nursing home. Victoria had advised him to call beforehand, but he preferred to surprise her caregivers. He wanted to see how they treated her every day, not a staged performance of that. If things were awful there—he couldn't help but picture a nightmarish old folks' home, run by malevolent nuns—he would take her back with him to Albuquerque. And if Sharon didn't like the idea, too bad. Abuela was his only living relative. He had to do everything in his power to make sure she was safe and comfortable.

He felt guilty for not having taken better care of her over the years. Yes, he had called El Asilo de los Ancianos Desamparados several times, but had been able to talk to her only a few times. The last one had been two years earlier, and she hadn't said much. He wasn't sure she still recognized his voice. After that, she had become bedridden, and the woman who answered his calls had told him that there was no way his grandmother could walk from her room to the phone. The woman, either a nun or nursing home employee, didn't seem to know about cell phones.

"I don't think she'll be able to talk, anyway," she had said.

Was Abuela's health that bad? She had been taken into the nursing home on the condition that she leave her house to the congregation. What if the nuns were just waiting for her death so they could sell the property or give it to someone else?

He would have to find out on his own. That would take his mind off Elsa and what they would say to each other after all this time and the very different directions their lives had taken. It would distract him from Camilo, whose ghost had continued to follow him since the day before. "I love you," he had said before turning ashen and somehow flattened on the raft floor, where his body would spend the next four days stewing in its juices. So it had been *that* kind of love. And his last request. "Forgive me, Juan." For being in love with him?

"I'm going to visit my grandmother," Juan announced to Sharon's back. "I don't know how long I'll be there. It depends—"

She turned to him.

"When we first talked about coming here, you told me you had made a reservation at the Hilton," she said out of the blue. "What happened to it?"

Juan had hoped to stay with Víctor if there was any chance of it.

"I was going to take a look at it first," he answered levelly. "I didn't want to spend a lot and thought I might be able to find a cheaper place."

Her face twisted at the mention of money—a not-too-subtle reminder of the fact that she was the one paying for this fancy hotel and all their meals.

"It was *your* idea to stay at the Meliá," he added defensively.

"And *you* were the one who said we shouldn't go to a *casa particular*, weren't you?" she snapped. "Where the hell were we supposed to sleep? Under a bridge?"

Yep, she was pissed. But Juan didn't have the strength for an argument right then.

"Did you even hear what I said?" he asked instead.

She didn't answer. Juan knew he should ask her what was going on, but he didn't. After all, this was his trip. She had come along for the ride, and he wasn't going to cater to her needs when he had only a few days to catch up on twenty years of lost time. Besides, if he tried to smooth things over, she might want to accompany him to see Abuela, and he intended to go directly from the nursing home to Victoria's apartment.

The taxi dropped him off in front of El Asilo de los Ancianos Desamparados. The thought of his grandmother as a "destitute elder" pained Juan. It was still raining, and he ran toward the main entrance. From the porch, the place looked like a gated community: green lawn, palm trees with benches around them, a freshly painted main house and several smaller surrounding structures. Someone was busy in the kitchen; the aromas of fried plantains and milk with cinnamon filled the air, mixing with the smells of earth and wet grass.

He remembered Abuela cooking in a wood stove that, according to her, worked better than anything powered by gas. Juan felt in his mouth the sweet taste of *arroz con leche*, rice pudding sprinkled with nutmeg and cinnamon.

"Arroz con leche se quiere casar," Abuela would sing softly. *"Con una viudita de la capital, que sepa tejer, que sepa bordar . . ."*

It was an old nursery rhyme. *Arroz con leche* was a man seeking to marry a young widow from the capital, one who knew how to knit and embroider. Juan thought of Sharon, who hated handicraft. Fat chance of finding a woman who loved the art of thread and needle nowadays, fatter chance of marrying her.

"Mijito, when are you going to marry that sweet girl?" Abuela had asked him the last time he'd seen her, a week before his one-way trip.

"Not anytime soon," he'd replied, laughing. "I'm too young for marriage."

"You're never too young to find true love," she had retorted.

"That sweet girl" was Rosita. Abuela had insisted that Rosita was the one Juan would marry, to the point that he'd stopped protesting and simply dodged the topic. Unfortunately, Abuela had also come up with a nickname for Elsa; she'd started calling her "that little whore." *"Esa putica."* "You should get rid of her. She's trouble."

Elsa had turned out to be the trouble indeed, leaving him and Camilo stranded that night. But Rosita wasn't the right one either.

She had courted Abuela as she had courted Juan, with a humble, dogged perseverance that had won the old woman's heart but put him off. He didn't like to be chased.

Well, at least she hadn't had a baby. The thought of a child of his growing up in Havana without a father had tortured Juan for years. He had even dreamt of him: a young man with Juan's dark eyes and hair. Abuela would have probably taken care of him, though. She loved children.

He evoked his grandmother's curvaceous figure, her preference for flashy dresses and bright colors, her loud laugh that exploded into a thousand arpeggios. What could age and illness have done to her?

He walked faster and came upon the main house. The young woman sitting at the reception desk didn't look like a nun. She was petite with short hair and wore a modest gray dress. He told her that he wanted to see María Antonia Muñoz.

"Ah, Tonita!" The woman smiled. "Are you her grandson?"

"Yes."

"Your sister told me that you lived in Miami."

"Well, I—"

"How wonderful that you've come to see her! I hope she's having a good day. As you probably know, she has good and bad ones. Just like with all of us, isn't it really?"

The mention of a sister puzzled Juan at first, but he realized she must have meant Victoria.

"That's right," he agreed.

She used an intercom to call an assistant. While they waited, Juan examined the room. There was a white wicker sofa, three chairs, an old credenza with a marble top, a wooden crucifix and a painting of Our Lady of Medjugorje. Everything was spotless.

The assistant was a sixtysomething woman with a no-non-sense attitude. Her uniform, a blouse and pants, was also light gray.

"Please, Rita, take this gentleman to Tonita's room," the receptionist said. "He is her grandson."

"Yes, Sister. Come with me, Señor."

So the girl was a nun after all. Juan looked at her once more before following Rita to a hallway. She avoided his eyes.

"Tonita was asleep a while ago when I brought her breakfast," Rita said. "She sleeps a lot; most of our residents do."

Sleeping was the best thing to do when you were ninety years old and had no family around. But Abuela had Víctor. *Victoria*, Juan corrected himself. He had been like family to her. *She* had. Ah, he would never get used to calling him "her." Víctor would always be Víctor, the scrawny kid Juan had played baseball with, no matter how many wigs or hats he wore.

Rita opened the door to a small room. The pungent smell of ointment wrapped itself around Juan. The room was sparsely furnished, with a single bed, a nightstand and a wheelchair parked in the corner.

A wrinkled sketch of a woman with a few strands of white hair and skeletal arms lay on the bed. Though he had been prepared for the worst, Juan had to look away. He would have never recognized her. *This* was what twenty years and Alzheimer's had done to a six-foot-tall, two-hundred-pound matriarch. He approached the bed gingerly. Abuela opened her eyes, the only part of her body that hadn't changed much: they were still bright and beady, though her eyelashes were now gone.

"Is it you, Chino?" she croaked.

His father's nickname. People had called him El Chino Oscar.

His grandfather had been Chino too. But not Juan. Abuela had always called him *mijito* or Juanito.

"Look who's here to see you, Tonita!" Rita said loudly. "Your grandson from Miami!"

Everybody assumed that he lived in Miami. As if it were the only place in America! But he didn't bother to correct Rita.

"It's me, Abuela," he whispered, touching her hand. Her skin was loose and cold.

"You're in luck, Chino," Abuela said. "You're my last client tonight."

"Your last what, Abuela?" he asked.

"The damn madam." She pointed at Rita. "She doesn't like it when I let you stay longer, but I don't care. *Carajo* with her."

Abuela had always had a foul mouth. But what was this about a madam?

"It's me," he repeated. "Juan."

"How come?" Abuela said. "You're dead."

He shivered. "I'm not Oscar, Abuela. Look at me."

"I saw you in Oyá's arms this morning." She closed her eyes. "She came with the rain. I asked her to let you go and take me instead."

Juan couldn't make out what she had said and bent over her body. They were so close he could smell her breath, slightly acidic, and that peculiar old folks' odor.

"She talks a lot," Rita explained. "But I don't always understand her. The only one who can communicate with her is your sister."

Juan wished Rita would leave. He simply nodded in her direction.

"In whose arms?" he asked in Abuela's ear.

"*Oyá, mijito,*" she said.

Then she did know it was him. She wasn't making a fuss, but she had never been the gushy type.

"Oyá laughed and said, 'No need to hurry, old woman,'" she continued. "'You're next. You had very sweet flesh, but it's all withered now. You used to have a big ass, but you've turned to skin and bones.' That's what she told me, *la cabrona*, when *she* is the Queen of Bones!"

Abuela went on muttering phrases that were more and more incoherent until the flow of words dried up. She closed her eyes and opened her mouth. A string of saliva dripped onto her chest.

"You may want to give her time to rest," Rita said. "She's more lucid after a little nap."

Juan followed Rita back to the hall. It was also squeaky-clean, with rustic benches and rocking chairs scattered around. There were images of saints in niches on the walls. Juan recognized the statuettes of Saint Thérèse of Lisieux and Saint Joseph. Abuela was a devotee of Saint Thérèse, but she also called the saint Oyá. Juan had never been interested in Santería, but now he regretted not having paid more attention to something that was so important to his grandmother.

"You can wait here," Rita said. "Would you like a cup of coffee? Water? Anything?"

"No, thanks. Do tell me, please. Is she totally gone?"

"Oh, no, no! I think she knew who you were."

Rita looked around and added in a conspiratorial tone, "Sometimes she remembers my name; others, I'm 'the madam.'" She struggled to suppress a laugh. "The worst part is when she calls Sister Yuleidi a pretty *putica*. The poor thing gets so red in the face!"

"My grandma always said whatever came to her mind," Juan

said, thinking of Elsa. "She liked to call . . . She would use the *p* word freely. Is Sister Yuleidi the girl at the reception desk?"

"Yes."

"I thought nuns had to wear habits and stuff to cover their heads, veils or something."

"Not all of them. The congregation has changed a few rules." Rita lowered her voice as she spoke. "Adapting to the new realities, like everybody else. You can't live in the fifteenth century forever."

"I guess you're not a nun yourself, Rita?"

She slapped her thigh.

"Me?" She cackled. "No, *hombre*, no! I've had three husbands. I mean, three I married with papers, a wedding and all that jazz. Altogether, I would say twenty and counting."

Juan smiled, grateful that Rita was taking care of Abuela. They probably got along well.

Abuela took a short nap, but when she woke up, it was only to ask for orange juice, which Rita brought, and then Abuela went back to sleep right away.

"What if you come back around five o'clock?" Rita suggested. "That's our social time, and sometimes she joins us."

"Where?"

"Outside. We take the residents to the front yard, play music and give them snacks. If she feels like it, I wheel her out, and boy, does she know how to have fun! Once, she even tried to dance to Buena Vista Social Club's '*El cuarto de Tula.*'"

"I'll be back," Juan said.

As soon as he'd spoken the words, the Saint Thérèse statuette against the wall fell to the floor and shattered.

10

VICTORIA'S DEATH

I t was only eleven-thirty, far too early for his lunch date with Elsa and Victoria, but Juan didn't feel like going back to the hotel and putting up with Sharon's awful mood. It was still raining. What a day! He took another taxi to El Vedado and, in spite of the steady sprinkling, walked around the block occupied by the ice-cream parlor, an area known as "El Coppelia," noticing the changes it had gone through in the past two decades. He stopped by what had once been a cheap, popular restaurant. There had always been a long line outside, and the employees were known for their unfriendliness. Now it had a different name, Sabor del Trópico, and there was no one waiting to get in. A printed menu listed more dishes than he remembered ever seeing there, from *carne ripiada*—shredded beef—to filet mignon. The least expensive item cost eighteen CUCs.

He glanced inside. A waiter lingering near the door greeted him.

"Good morning, Señor. How can I help you?"

"Just looking."

There were souvenir stalls all around Coppelia, tourist traps selling necklaces made from spoons and forks, bongo-drum key chains, leather purses and Che Guevara memorabilia. Juan dodged the smiling, eager vendors who attempted to engage him.

A boom box played an old rumba, *"Papá Montero,"* a festive homage to a dead *rumbero* who loved women, dance and rum: *A llorar a Papá Montero, zumba, canalla rumbero.* So many songs had funeral themes! Juan recalled *"Sobre una tumba una rumba,"* in which a rejected lover asked people to rejoice on a woman's grave, and *"Bodas Negras,"* a horrible bolero about a man "marrying" his dead girlfriend's skeleton. Yikes.

The ice-cream parlor still had long lines at its four entrances, around two hundred people waiting to enter the peso-paying areas. But a separate space, reserved for CUC clients, had plenty of room. Juan went in and ordered a chocolate sundae. It was smaller than he remembered, but had the same creamy texture as it had in his youth.

Ah, all the ice cream he and Elsa had eaten together! *Tres, gracias* or three big scoops, with Elsa usually ordering chocolate, vanilla and pineapple; *Copa Lolita*, two scoops of ice cream with flan in the middle; and *Pico Turquino*, two scoops with a big piece of cake . . . Elsa licking her lips, stealing chocolate syrup from his dish, playing with her long curls.

He couldn't wait to see her again. Yes, they were both married to other people now, but that didn't mean old feelings were gone. And Sharon wasn't helping her cause by acting like a spoiled American.

Close to Coppelia was the Yara movie theater, at the corner of L and Twenty-Third Street. It had been the most popular meeting place in El Vedado. Juan and his friends would usually agree to meet one another "in the Yara," since it was easier to locate someone there than at the always-crowded ice-cream parlor. He wandered around outside the theater, feeling lost and somewhat out of place among the women in tight outfits and high heels and the guys yelling to one another over the noise of car engines, motorcycle revving, loud salsa music and street vendors hawking everything from shampoo to shoes. That was new too. No public bartering had been allowed in Cuba during the nineties. Things were changing, no doubt.

A young man in a red muscle T approached him and whispered in his ear, "Want Cuban cigars, good weed, pretty girls or boys? I've got all that and more, Mister."

He spoke English, albeit with a heavy accent and a few mispronounced words.

"No, thanks," Juan answered in Spanish, and added, "I'm Cuban too."

"Oh. Sorry, bro," the man said, embarrassed. "You look Yuma. No offense."

The hustler went away. Juan smiled, amused. What exactly made him "look Yuma"? His clothes? The fact that he was healthy and, as Victoria had put it, well fed? But people around him weren't particularly ill dressed or malnourished. Maybe it was something intangible, a change in his attitude, the way he carried himself when he walked around. The air of otherness he had acquired after living so many years away.

It had finally stopped raining. At La Dulcinea—a *paladar* with a street counter featuring an assortment of delights: guava pastries, bizcochitos, meringue and chocolate cakes—Juan bought a golden-brown flan for ten CUCs. He didn't want to arrive empty-handed. He hoped Elsa wasn't on a permanent diet like Sharon and her friends. The smiling clerk put the flan in a cardboard box with the name of the *paladar* printed on top.

"Enjoy, Señor," she said.

It was twelve-fifteen when he headed to Victoria's apartment. Still early, but that would give them time to talk. He might be able to find out more details about Elsa's life before she arrived. He couldn't believe she'd had a son with the old Spaniard. Though there was nothing extraordinary about it, he told himself. She was no longer the young woman he had been in love with. And he wasn't the same young man.

He flagged a *cocotaxi*. It wasn't all that far, but he was getting tired and was carrying something perishable. The blocks stretched interminably. Hoofing the Havana pavement wasn't, he admitted, as easy as using a treadmill.

He rang the doorbell several times, but no one answered. Maybe Victoria had told him to come at one o'clock because she had to run some errands first. Maybe she had gone to get Elsa! He would sit in the park across from the building and wait for them.

A hand landed on his shoulder with enough force to make him lose his balance. Fortunately, he didn't drop the flan. He turned around and faced the guy he'd met before the *mariconga* had started. It was Lázaro, Victoria's boyfriend, still wearing blue overalls and a menacing expression.

"I'm going to cut your dick off if you keep this up!" he yelled.

Juan was scared, more so after comparing the guy's muscles to his own. Lázaro didn't have a gym-sculpted body; he had gotten his biceps honestly, probably lifting cement blocks.

"Calm down, please," Juan muttered.

"You calm down, cojones. What are you doing here?"

"I came to see Víctor," Juan said, making sure to use his friend's old name. "We've known each other since we were kids. I've been out of Cuba for over twenty years. I didn't even know about his . . . change until yesterday."

Lázaro looked at him suspiciously. "And you came all the way to Havana just to accompany her to a *mariconga*? You expect me to believe that?"

"I didn't come to accompany him anywhere. He asked me to go. I don't usually get involved in these things."

Lázaro gave him the evil eye before taking a key out of his pocket and opening the front door. Juan attempted to follow but had the door slammed in his face.

He waited a few minutes, hoping the smoke would clear before lunchtime. If not, he and Elsa would sneak out together, leaving Victoria and her partner behind. He imagined himself and Elsa sharing the flan, like in old times.

It was then that he heard the screams, so loud they hurt his ears. The words "bathroom" and "fall" came from Victoria's apartment. He waited, terrified. A woman rushed out of the building and exclaimed, "Ay, he's already dead!"

"Wh—who's dead?" Juan stuttered.

"The *maricón* next door!" she yelled.

Against his better judgment, Juan moved past the woman, who had left the front door open, and hurried upstairs.

When he got to the apartment, Lázaro held Victoria's limp body in his arms. Five people were already in the living room, discussing what to do.

"Call the hospital!"

"No, the police!"

"Don't worry. I already phoned Unidad 15."

"Why? It was an accident."

"So? A dead person's a dead person. We have to notify the authorities, just in case."

At first, Juan didn't see any wounds, but when Lázaro gingerly placed Victoria on the green leather sofa, her head fell to one side, and Juan noticed a gash in her scalp, very close to the crown. There was blood around it, and something whitish too. Brain tissue? Horrified, he headed for the kitchen, looking for a place to put the flan that he was still carrying.

The kitchen smelled like pork roast. The copper pot he had seen the day before, now filled with rice and beans, was on the stove. The *teta* for coffee and the iron skillet were still on the counter. He left the flan there too, next to a rusty screwdriver. His mouth was dry. He was going to reach for a glass of water but changed his mind. Better not to touch anything. Had Víctor really had an accident? Or had that crazy Lázaro guy . . . ?

Juan returned to the living room. Lázaro was kneeling by the sofa and caressing Victoria's hand.

"My girl," he sobbed. "The woman of my life."

The siren of a police cruiser drowned out his words.

By twelve-thirty, Sharon was tired of people watching, waiting for Juan and stewing in her own fury. She didn't believe for a minute he had gone to visit his grandmother, who could have been dead for all she knew. But she had memorized the address of his "friend" and how to get there from the hotel. She slathered on sunscreen and set out walking, her face flushed and her hands rolled into fists. She was ready to confront Juan and didn't stop cursing him, his trip and herself all the way to Victoria's place.

A small crowd had gathered in front of the building. A police car was outside with its lights flashing. Sharon stopped in the park, as she had the day before, and saw two men in handcuffs being led to the cruiser. One was the guy in overalls she had seen arguing with the blonde the day before. The other was Juan.

As she stood there in shock, a Lexus parked down the block. The driver got out and watched the scene from a distance as well. Sharon looked over and felt a shock of recognition: it was the same woman, just a few years older, who had been smiling in the scanned picture Juan kept on his laptop.

11

BROKEN AIR

E lsa's throat closed. The air seemed to change from a gas to a liquid substance, threatening to drown her.

"A ghost from your past has returned . . . Why don't you come by so we can chat about all this?"

Well, Vic hadn't lied about Juan. There he was, being ushered into a police car. Vic had said he'd visited her the day before—why had he come back?

Elsa continued to watch the building. A crowd had gathered outside, gossiping and snooping. She thought she'd better wait until they dispersed to drive back. She still wasn't breathing normally. She didn't want to risk running over some rubbernecking *comemierda*.

As she headed back to her car to catch her breath, she noticed a foreign woman staring at her. It wasn't uncommon for Elsa to attract attention, even in El Vedado. There weren't many Lexuses in Cuba for one thing. But her wealth usually provoked the resentment or curiosity of locals, not tourists. None of them knew she'd once gone around Havana on a cheap bicycle like most of her friends, rather than having her father drive her around in his Jeep, which he'd eventually had to sell during the Special Period.

She blinked away the tears that stung her eyes. How distant those ISA days seemed now! She had adored Juan. He'd never found out how much she had cried for him after he'd left with Camilo. Then there was Rosita. And Elsa's own pregnancy, which she'd discovered shortly after Juan had arrived in Miami. She had wanted to contact him, but how? Abuela hated her. Víctor and Juan had had a falling out. And then the Spaniard had appeared, as if sent by the *orishas* in which she'd never believed.

She got in the car and locked the door. Nobody, not even her parents, knew how much she had suffered during those first years in Seville, struggling to understand a new culture, please the old man and raise her son at the same time. She had given up her dreams of acting to become a mother and eventually, after Emilio's health declined so much he had to entrust Savarria and Co. to her, an entrepreneur. He couldn't complain with the way she'd expanded the business. She knew how to deal with Cubans better than he did and ruled Savarria and Co. with an iron fist—the employees called her the commander in bitch behind her back. She didn't care. The company was growing, and when the time came, when things *really* changed in a year or two or ten, they would be well positioned to take over the tech market in Cuba.

She had taken care of Emilio too. Old Savarria should have been grateful that he'd married her and not some *jinetera* who'd stolen his money and left him high and dry, as had happened to several of his friends. Still, she hadn't really ever been happy. Had marrying him been a mistake? Ah, she had made so many mistakes in her life. Why couldn't she stop?

She tried to breathe again. Sometimes she felt as if she was crazy, especially when she went into her fits of rage. Few things set her off, but even Savarria, after a couple of fights where she'd kicked and scratched him, had learned not to trigger her temper. This had made married life easier. But things didn't always turn out so well.

She felt a chill. Her coat was wet. She took it off and placed it on the passenger seat.

"Don't let anyone mess with you."

She saw her father drunk, threatening to kill whoever challenged him or stood in his way. The sickening sound of bullets going through the ceiling. A rococo crystal chandelier, which had been in the house when it was given to Elsa's family, falling, its delicate pieces exploding on the floor. *El pincho* barking threats and curses. A miracle he hadn't killed his wife or Elsa. He was a bit unhinged. She must have inherited the crazy genes.

But she wasn't crazy! Just impulsive. Juan used to say she was hotheaded and cold handed, *calentona* and *friolenta*. So many of the decisions she had made in life had been on a whim, like marrying Savarria. The marriage had provided her with so much, despite all the pain she had gone through. Emilio was a cantankerous old man. Not an ogre but not easy to live with either, always driving her crazy with his jealousy. Even now that she was forty and not the young beauty she had once been, he became agitated when she spoke to other men in his presence. An insecure old man, that was what he was, despite all his business acumen. He probably suspected she didn't love him. She was grateful to him but could never be attracted to him physically. *Thank God for that heart attack*, she thought sometimes, and then felt a wave of guilt for having the thought.

Had it been worth it, in the end? She had traveled the world with Savarria. He had provided everything for her and Emilito. They had a nice home in Seville, another in Havana and a smaller beach house in Tarragona. When Emilio died, she would inherit everything. But would she have been happier with Juan in a small Miami apartment or her parents' house in El Naútico if they had stayed in Cuba?

Well, no use thinking about that now.

The police car, with Juan and the other guy inside, sped toward Línea Street. The onlookers left one by one, and Elsa could breathe normally again, the liquid air finally dissolving around her. She started the Lexus and drove off.

DEAR JUAN

Each plant contains the virtue of a *santo*, a supernatural force.

—*El Monte*

Dear Juan,

I haven't heard from you in many years (twenty, to be exact), but I've never stopped thinking of you and wondering what was going on in your life. Abuela kept me in the loop while she could. She told me you had left Miami but didn't remember, or wouldn't tell me, where you're living now.

Sadly, you haven't cared to find out about me. But that's fine. I've been told that you are back, and I want to fill you in on my life, in the very improbable case that you are interested. Hope springs eternal, as the saying goes.

There are some things that you don't know.

Until I met you at the ISA, I was invisible, my Juan. Since high school, and even before that, I had felt like I had on Frodo and Bilbo's ring. All the time. Guys never catcalled me in the street. Boys never picked me as their partner for school projects. They didn't take me on dates. They didn't suggest we go to a movie together so they could kiss me in the dark, as my friends complained happened to them. If I wanted to see a movie, I went by myself. I spent many evenings in the Yara on my own, with happy couples snuggled all around me.

It was during a movie marathon—the Latin American Film Festival at the Yara—that I realized I could be an actor too. I was plain, but not unbearably ugly. My main issue was that I didn't have a big butt, but in fact, most actresses were skinny and butt-less. I had a good memory and was quiet, but not shy. I was taller than average, which most guys didn't like, but maybe it would be an asset on-screen. Why not give it a try?

My high school grades were excellent. (I didn't have many distractions.) But I'm sure you remember that aspiring ISA theater students needed to pass an acting test to get into the school's performing arts program. An "attitude test," it was called. I heard Elsa failed it, though she got in anyway. I'm still proud that I passed with flying colors.

I always wanted to tell you how I did it, to brag a little . . . I'd been learning about the alienation effect and the theater of the absurd. I had memorized Mother Courage and Her Children, *which people said was mandatory reading. I was going to name Brecht if they asked who my favorite playwright was. It was actually Tennessee Williams, but I wouldn't have dared to say that.*

The admissions committee was composed of Teatro Estudio actors and ISA instructors. They all looked at me as if I didn't hold much promise. "You're alone in an elevator," a Teatro Estudio woman said. "Suddenly, there's a blackout, and you find yourself trapped. Show us what you would do."

They were probably expecting hysterics, screams, the take-me-out-of-here scene. I just opened my backpack, retrieved

Mother Courage and Her Children, *sat on the floor and begin to read silently.*

I was accepted. And that was the best thing that ever happened to me. Not because I became an actress but because I met you.

This is turning into a shaggy-dog tale, and I haven't even said anything of substance yet.

Why am I doing this? Because Oyá promised. But sometimes I think I dove into Santería to perform on the only stage still available to me. A thwarted actor, playing the role of an *orisha* on the saint's feast day, wearing these psychedelic necklaces and long skirts that make me look like a more interesting version of myself.

Abuela was the one who initiated me into Santería. I met her by chance, because Juan never would have introduced me to his family. I showed up at his apartment on a Friday night to bring him my class notes (he had skipped a Scientific Communism lecture that morning), hoping against all odds that he was there. He wasn't, but his grandmother was. We hit it off. She told me right away I was a daughter of Oyá. I didn't believe in the *orishas* back then, didn't know a thing about religion, but I pretended to be interested.

"Oyá is very possessive of her daughters," Abuela said. "When she claims someone, she wants total ownership. What do you do, *mijita*?"

"I'm studying to be an actress."

Most people were impressed by that, but Abuela shook her head.

"The daughters of Oyá aren't actresses," she stated plainly.

"That's more for Oshún's girls. Oyá, queen of the cemeteries, is into deeper, darker things."

I don't remember what I answered. Most likely that I could change career paths if the *orisha* asked me to. I didn't plan on following through on this, but I wanted Abuela's approval. I asked her questions about Santería and put on such a good act that she invited me to visit her for personal instruction lessons. I accepted her offer. If we became friends, it would be easier for me to get closer to Juan. The *pobrecita* was delighted, thinking that she had found a fellow devotee.

"Kids nowadays are so rarely into religion," she would say. "Even my own grandson. I'm happy you're different."

It wasn't exactly true, but I didn't tell her. My maternal grandmother, a practicing Catholic, had taken me a few times to Iglesia del Carmen in Centro Habana. The church smelled like incense and musk and was poorly lit. When I complained once, my grandma had said sternly, "It may be dark, but Jesus can see you anyway. Your parents and I may not know where you are, but he does. So does your guardian angel." She proceeded to give me a lecture on sin and punishment that turned me off to religion for a long time. Her God struck me as harsh and vindictive. We had the Committees for the Defense of the Revolution and the Vigilance and Protection Committees watching us day and night. I didn't need the spiritual militia keeping tabs on me too.

But the *orishas*, Abuela said, were not in the business of judging humans—not most of them, at least—because they were far from perfect themselves. Changó cheated on Obá, his legitimate wife, with Oshún and Yemayá. Oshún had "as many lovers as the sand of the sea." Elegguá was a thief and a shameless liar. A rowdy crowd all in all. The most straitlaced was Oyá.

As the Santería lessons progressed, I became a frequent visitor at Abuela's Chinatown house. It was bigger and nicer than my mom's and had a spectacular backyard where Abuela grew chamomile, marjoram, cilantro, lavender and spearmint and left offerings to the deities that she called indistinctively *orishas* and *santos*. "You say *'orisha'* when you are working with the African part, the strong part. That's when you invoke Oyá and offer her a glass of wine," she explained. "You say *santo* when you are dealing with the Catholic counterpart; then you pray to Saint Thérèse of Lisieux and sprinkle holy water over your altar."

The *orishas* were African and Spanish men and women, dark and light, right and wrong and sometimes all that in one. "Oshún is the Virgin of Charity," Abuela told me. "She's sweet, but undependable. Changó is Santa Bárbara. Brave in battle, but he doesn't like to work and pimps out his women. Elegguá is El Niño de Atocha or Baby Jesus. Watch out! He's a trickster and a troublemaker, but as the owner of all roads, he can open or close the paths of life."

Abuela made all sorts of herbal teas, sweetened with honey, and had potions for every ailment. Chamomile for insomnia, peppermint for nausea, sage for memory loss, anise for menstrual cramps, valerian root for high blood pressure . . . "I cure myself with green stuff," she would say. "I don't trust doctors. I don't like being poked and pawed." What an irony that she's ended up in an old folks' home at the mercy of nurses and nuns!

She also told me that being Oyá's daughter was a mixed blessing. Oyá watched over her children, but held them to higher standards than other *orishas* did. And one had to be careful because the *orishas*, when angry, sent not only diseases, but all kinds of calamities, she warned.

"A daughter of Oyá isn't gossipy or racy," Abuela said. "She is a woman of character. In return, she's always protected, because Oyá destroys her enemies with the force of her seven winds. She is compassionate, but hates lies. See, if you are a daughter of Oshún, you can practically get away with murder. Oshún cheats on her men, flirts and steals other women's partners, so she understands when her daughters misbehave. But Oyá has no patience with liars and swindlers. She crushes those who don't honor their word."

Elsa must be a daughter of Oshún, I thought. When I asked Abuela, she refused to confirm it—she wasn't fond of Elsa, but being a daughter of Oyá herself, she didn't like to gabble.

But Elsa . . . God, how I hated her. I didn't understand why Juan was in love with that crazy, curly-haired chick everyone thought was so beautiful. She wasn't that pretty, in my opinion. All she had was a strong personality, which made her different in a mean sort of way.

Little by little, I became truly interested in the religion. One could ask these powerful *orishas* for help with earthly matters. There were spells for good luck, love, success . . . I could certainly use a few.

I began to experiment. I stole one of Juan's shirts from Abuela's home. (She had been sewing a button on it when I came in, but I could swear that she left it on a table for me to take. By then, she wanted us to be together.) I made a rag doll out of the shirt. When the moon was full, I wrote, using my menstrual blood, his name on the doll. I pricked its heart with a silver pin. I cut a strand of my hair and placed it under the cover of the music theory textbook he carried everywhere. Ah, what *didn't* I try?

I'd done something right, it seemed, because Juan asked me out. I don't know if the spells worked or if he felt that he had to prove he was a true macho—I had been telling everybody, including his best friends, Víctor and Camilo, about my crush on him. Whatever his reasons were, I said yes, and from that day on, we were an item.

A secret item, that is. *Contrabando*. He made it clear that he wasn't leaving Elsa for me. I promised not to tell anyone about our arrangement and pretended that I was fine with it. But I kept looking for that perfect love spell. I even gave him a bonding potion—I boiled my pubic hair with rose petals in the water I used to make coffee for him. But the spell was no good. At least, it didn't work for me, or I messed up somewhere along the way.

Ah, if only I could have found the book Abuela was always talking about! *El Monte*, the Santería bible, had been published in the fifties by Lydia Cabrera, a Cuban ethnographer who was an authority on the religion. It contains spells, tales of the *orishas*, a comprehensive list of plants and their healing properties, recipes and so much more in its six hundred pages. Abuela had once owned a copy, but she barely knew how to read and had given it away. She regretted not having kept it. "If you ever find that book," she said, "buy it; borrow it; even steal it if you have to. Oyá will forgive you. Bring it to me, and we'll read it together."

I never found it, not even in Havana's used bookstores. Back then, believing in Santería or any other religion was considered "ideological diversionism"; books like *El Monte* were banned and almost impossible to get. I heard not long ago that the book had been republished. What was prohibited twenty years ago will now become compulsory learning. That's how things work on this God-forgotten island.

El Monte, soon to be mandatory reading. Just you wait and see.

Speaking of which, instead of a letter to Juan that he'll never read, I should write my own book—an Oyá kind of book, shadowy and occult. *Black Pearls of Wisdom by a Mortician*, isn't that a good title? I'll take it to Letras Cubanas and have an editor I know look at it.

PART II

UNIDAD 15

L ieutenant Marlene Martínez brought a tape recorder to her office. She wanted to replay the conversations—she refused to call them "interrogations"—she'd had with the first witnesses in her new case. The recorder was an antique Sanyo. When would she upgrade to a more modern device? Oh, well. You work with what you have, as Comrade Instructor, her mentor at the Police Academy, used to say. She wondered where he was now. After retiring from the police force, he had become a *santero*. People had started calling him Padrino, but he also had an on-the-side business as a private eye. He was *en la lucha*, struggling to make ends meet like everybody else.

Before turning on the recorder, Martínez went over the notes that she had taken the day before. Lázaro Domínguez, a plumber, had found the body of his partner, Víctor Pérez Díaz, also known as Victoria Sunrise, in the bathroom of Pérez Díaz's apartment. Pérez Díaz's head had been resting on the floor, and there had been glass shards all over the sink and floor, some embedded in his skin. He had died of a blow to the head that left a small hole in the back of his skull. Conceivably, he could have hit his head against the bathroom wall-mounted metal cabinet—the mirror that had covered it had fallen and shattered. But a backward fall? Martínez didn't buy it.

Pérez Díaz had been a transvestite and had been dressed as a woman when found dead. It could have been a hate crime. Martínez had been seeing more of those in the last three years, especially after the official position against homosexuals had softened.

She pressed PLAY and listened to the first interview.

Interview One:
A MAN FROM THE HOT LAND

MY NAME IS JOSÉ Miguel García, but everybody calls me Pepito, and I'm from Oriente, from *la tierra caliente*. Yes, I was born in Punta Blanca, the hottest spot in the country, and that's why I'm like this. I make a living as a musician—a drummer—and to play *batá*, your blood has to be hot. There's no other way.

Why am I telling you all this, Officer? Right, sorry, I meant 'Lieutenant.' Just to explain the little issues, the *problemitas*, you brought up.

I've been involved in a couple of minor incidents because of . . . unfortunate circumstances, but I'm not a killer. Never will be. I'm a man who loves and enjoys life. My own and others'. I had no reason whatsoever to take Victoria's.

Okay, back to the issues. Yes, the first time I went to jail was for battery. But I didn't attack a woman or anything! It was another guy, a shit-eating Habanero who called me a Palestinian. You know that's how they call people from the Holguín province. He told me I was an illegal alien here in Havana, and why didn't I go back to where I belonged? I had no choice but to kick his ass. Instead of taking it like a man, he ran to the nearest police station and filed a report. There were plenty of witnesses because the entire neighborhood came out to see the show. I went to *el tanque* for a month, and that was that.

Ah, no, no! The *maría* issue is something different. See, I've smoked weed. I admit it. Who hasn't, in my business? I had a little bit with me because I needed it. For inspiration. You go drumming like I do, *kumbakin kin kin kumbakin*, without the weed, and it sounds like two trains crashing, but when you get high, you can make the drums follow the rhythm of the heart. That's the secret, and *maría* helps you do it the right way. Santa María, Mother of God.

But I've never sold it. I have other ways of making money. I have my music, and I'm good at it.

Yes, I might be a little high now. I don't know when I last used it. I honestly don't. Three days ago, maybe. Two days? I can't remember, sorry! I hope you're not gonna hold *that* against me.

Well, me and Victoria . . . We were friends, sort of. More like acquaintances. I respected her. That's why I don't usually get in trouble, because I respect people, provided they respect me.

Sure, I knew she was a guy. Or a transexy or whatever the hell that's called. I knew she was born with cojones, just like me. But if she wanted to be called a she and wear wigs and fake tits, that's her life. Who am I to criticize anyone? Live and let live, you know?

I saw her for the last time yesterday. We met on the stairs. I was coming down, and she was leaving the building. We said hi but didn't chat.

No, I didn't notice anything out of the ordinary.

Comrade, I don't know about any of her visitors. As I said, we were acquaintances. She didn't talk about her private life with me, and I didn't exactly linger at her place either.

Yes, she had a guy, Lázaro. They've been together forever, or at least since before I came here, but he didn't live with her.

No, no! I didn't see her today. I didn't see that other guy you're talking about either. I didn't see *anybody*. I don't make a habit of spying on my neighbors!

Interview Two:
PANDA BEAR

SORRY, COMRADE LIEUTENANT, I'M still in shock. I can't believe my girl is gone. I'd been so mad at her since yesterday! I'll never forgive myself for the way I treated her. I thought she was cheating on me. With a Yuma. But maybe she was. It's up to you to find out that, isn't it?

No, of course I didn't do it! I loved Victoria. I was jealous, yes, and I wanted to beat the crap out of her and that guy, but I would never have—

I don't know what I'm saying. It's just nerves. Yes, I'm a man, but I have feelings too, *coño*.

We've—we were together for six years. I met her at Café Arabia this one night I went to a show. She sings—sang there once or twice a week. I didn't like it, other guys looking at her half-naked on the stage, but she insisted it was her art. If she had to choose between her career and me, I came second. So I accepted it. But she respected our relationship, for the most part. Sure, she was a flirt, but aren't they all?

Well, that's something I don't want to discuss. Not here, not now. Yes, I knew all about Victoria's past. No, we didn't talk about it. She'd cut ties with her family because they didn't accept her as she was. I didn't get to know her parents. Everybody in her circle treated her as a woman and called her Victoria Sunrise. That, or they weren't in her circle anymore.

She loved me. I know that for a fact. She called me Panda Bear. Why a bear? Ah, Lieutenant, I guess you're not familiar with our terms. In our world, a bear is . . . what I am. A man's man. Not effeminate, not a *maricón*. Do I need to explain that too? Okay, sorry I brought it up.

But don't you want to know who came in and out of the building? I mean, I saw them! And I'd like to tell you about it.

I was watching the building from eight o'clock this morning. See, yesterday, Victoria and I had an argument in the street when I found her with another guy, that Cuban who lives in La Yuma now. The other one you guys arrested. They were on their way to the *mariconga*. She swore they were just friends, but I didn't believe her.

I went to the apartment and waited for her after the *mariconga*. She assured me there was nothing between them, that I was making too much of it. "We are old friends," she said. "From the times before I was me." I was sort of convinced, but not completely, so I took the day off and told her I was going to Pinar del Río. I planned to spend the day watching her building to make sure she wasn't meeting that Yuma again.

The first to arrive was a *bisnero*. He sells stuff to Victoria pretty often. Ah, you know, black market stuff: milk, pork, rice, whatever. Sure, I can give you his name and address, but I hope he doesn't get in trouble because of this. I mean, being a *bisnero* isn't a crime, at least not a serious one.

He was carrying a huge package. He left without it, and more people went in. They were Alberto, from the next-door tribe, with a bag full of groceries; a woman who lives on the second floor; and another gal I didn't know. She was carrying an umbrella, a big red one. I can't tell you for sure if she went to visit Victoria because the balcony door was closed. That's what she does when she doesn't . . . when she didn't want anybody to know what she was up to. Yes, you're right. It was raining. And the woman could have gone to visit another neighbor. She left soon after going in. But to be honest, I didn't pay much attention to her. I was more concerned about *men* going into the building.

The next one to ring the bell was that Yuma, the guy I saw yesterday. Ah, that was what I had suspected all along. Victoria had lied to me! I got so pissed, Lieutenant. I yelled at him and went upstairs, ready to slap her. Yes, I was mad, but—never enough to kill her. I was mad because I *loved* her.

I came in shouting, "*Puta*, where are you?" She didn't answer. But I knew she was still in the apartment because I hadn't seen her leave. I went to the kitchen, then to the bedroom and finally found her body in the bathroom, lying on the floor. The bathroom was wet; it always is. There's a leak I've been planning to fix forever. I thought she had slipped and fallen down.

The bathroom mirror was broken, and there was glass everywhere. A mess. She might have tried to hold on to the cabinet as she fell, and the mirror got unglued? That's the only thing I can think of.

Anything unusual? Well, she didn't have a wig on. It was right there, though. On a chair. Maybe she was combing her hair when—she looked like she had fainted, but she was . . . dead.

She was lying faceup.

Eh, now that you mention it, yes, it is a little strange to fall and land faceup. But it didn't occur to me then. I didn't suspect foul play until you guys came in.

No, I didn't notice anything out of place. The apartment looked just like it had the day before. No signs of a fight. It smelled of food, like she was cooking. And she was—I saw a big pot full of *arroz congrí* in the kitchen.

Enemies? I don't know. There were people in her little world at Café Arabia who didn't get along with her, or who she didn't get along with, but nothing serious.

I can't imagine my life without her. I just can't. I'm sorry, Lieutenant. I don't mean to cry in front of you again, but I can't help it. I've lost the only woman I've ever loved, and I haven't had the time to come to terms with it.

Interview Three:
THE MATRIARCH'S STORY (I)

MY NEPHEW IS A decent young man. He's had issues with the law, but he's cleaned up his act. He lives for his music. He has lots of friends. Some good, some bad, some so-so. The bad ones have led him astray in the past, but he doesn't see them anymore. He's cleaned up his act.

I know that because I watch him all the time. I'm responsible for that boy. If something were to happen to him, what would I tell my sister? She entrusted Pepito to me when he was fifteen. He wasn't doing anything constructive down there in Punta Blanca, the ass end of the world, so she sent him to Havana.

A famous musician, that's what he wants to be. I pray to the *orishas* that he finds his way to fame someday. And he will. He's that good, seriously. You have to hear him play. Even my godfather, Padrino, says he's never seen a *batá* drummer like him. *Siacará!*

What? Yes, I'm a Santería believer. Proud of it too. I am a daughter of Oshún. My nephew is a son of Changó, the *orisha* of war and thunder. He can be a little careless and hasty, because that's how all Changó's children are. But he has a good heart.

Victoria? Ay, Comrade! What can I tell you? Poor guy. Nah, I called him Señora and *amiga* to humor him, but in my eyes, he was a guy. I'm too old for those modernisms of trans-this and trans-that. You're born with a *pinga*, you are a man. Period. Even if you cut your *pinga* off. Which I don't think he did, by the way. But that's none of my business.

A decent person, yes. He wasn't the kind to have ten drag queens for dinner every night, shrieking and partying and bringing shame to the neighborhood. He had his boyfriend or whatever he was, that Lázaro, but they kept quiet. And the truth is, if you didn't know what they were, at first sight they looked like a regular couple.

But everybody knew.

Yes, I want to cooperate with the investigation. I have nothing to hide! Please, ask away, and I'll answer as best I can. *Siacará!*

Siacará doesn't mean anything bad, Lieutenant. It's just a Santería word I'm used to saying. Sorry, I didn't mean any disrespect. I promise it isn't a curse or anything!

The day started quietly enough. It was raining. My husband went to the grocery store, and I left the door open for him . . . Well, I always leave the door open. I like to know what's going on in the building. Around noon I saw a woman with a red umbrella on our staircase landing. I think she went into Victoria's apartment, but I'm not sure.

No, I didn't see her leave. But I was busy cooking. My husband, Pepito and I had lunch. Nothing else happened until I heard the commotion next door. Lázaro was yelling that Victoria was dead. I rushed over and saw him. He was wearing a dress, like he always did, but didn't have his wig on. He looked more like a man in death than I'd ever seen him before. I felt sorry for him, but in a way, I thought he deserved it. He sinned against God and nature, trying to make himself into a woman when the *orishas* had made him a man. That's wrong. I don't care how many *maricongas* Mariela Castro sponsors. If El Comandante were still in power, we wouldn't be seeing such things.

Interview Four:
THE *BISNERO*

AY, LIEUTENANT! YOU MEAN Victoria wasn't Victoria? That she wasn't a woman? With those tits? I would have sworn—I've been dealing with her and her man for over two years, and I never suspected it. She was always nicely dressed and very feminine. A lady past her prime, maybe, but still rocking it.

I don't know much about my clients' private lives. I mean, I don't have time for that. Yes, I am self-employed. I buy and sell different things. For a profit, yes. I have a license, but not as a *bisnero*, since it isn't an authorized profession yet. I'm licensed as a grower and seller of ornamental plants and a collector and seller of recyclables too.

This morning I sold Victoria a pork leg, the biggest one I had, for forty CUCs. She told me she was having some friends over for lunch. Yes, I delivered the haunch to her apartment. That was early. It was just starting to rain . . .

Lieutenant Martínez turned off the recorder and began to review the results of the search conducted at the victim's apartment. The most significant piece of evidence was a screwdriver found on the kitchen counter. The fingerprints on it matched those of José Miguel García, also known as Pepito. There was no blood, but he could have cleaned it. She browsed a file that contained a detailed description of his encounters with the law. He seemed too young and not like the type to plan and execute a crime like this, she thought. He didn't have a motive. Unless Pérez Díaz had tried to flirt with him, and he had panicked and attacked her. This type of thing had happened before.

He claimed he had last seen the victim the day before the murder. Hadn't he seemed nervous when he'd said it? Though Martínez was waiting for a detailed forensic report, the wound on the dead man's skull could have been made by the tip of the screwdriver. But why would García have then left the weapon in plain sight? She wasn't ready to charge him with *that* crime yet, but she would keep him locked up. She had to, anyway. He'd had marijuana in his system and had admitted to it, so there was no way he would be back on the streets anytime soon.

As for the others, two witnesses had confirmed that Lázaro Domínguez had been walking around the block watching the building all morning. Pérez Díaz had been dead for at least two hours before his partner found his body, so Domínguez wasn't technically a suspect. There was also that woman both he and Magdala had seen. Martínez wrote: *Woman with a red umbrella?*

She also wrote: *Pork leg?* A copper pot full of black beans and white rice had been found on the stove, still warm, but there had been no trace of a pork leg. And yet, the first cops who answered the call had noticed a strong smell "of something roasting." When she herself had arrived, the apartment had smelled of what could very well have been a pork roast. But the oven was empty.

Juan Chiong, the Cuban American tourist who had been at Pérez Díaz's apartment when the police arrived, said that he had planned to have lunch with Pérez Díaz, a childhood friend. It would have made sense to find a roast then. Chiong's alibi had been verified with El Asilo de los Ancianos Desamparados employees. The flan he had brought had come from La Dulcinea and been sold at the time he'd said he had bought it.

No, Chiong wasn't a suspect. But Lieutenant Martínez was still seething about the way she had been ordered to act around him. When she informed La Seguridad, the Ministry of the Interior, that there was a foreigner involved, a Cuban American, they had forbidden her to record their conversation and basically told her to treat him with kid gloves. Unless she had concrete proof against him, they'd said she'd better let him go. Messing with an American tourist could harm the now-improved USA-Cuba relationship. "First the Yankees were the enemies," she grumbled. "Now we're kissing their asses. How crazy."

Anyway, the guy had been born in Cuba. He looked Cuban enough to her. And his claiming not to have known that his friend was a transvestite before he'd come back to Cuba didn't ring true to her.

1

CHINESE WITCHCRAFT

Chinese witchcraft is so hermetic that even Calazán Herrera . . . couldn't penetrate any of its secrets or learn anything from them. He only knows that they often eat a paste of bat meat made with ground bat eyes and brains, excellent to preserve sight.—*El Monte*

Dear Juan,
I haven't heard from you in twenty years, but I've never stopped thinking of you and wondering what was going on in your life. I'm sure you haven't been as curious about mine, but I'll fill you in on the details. I never graduated from the ISA. I'm a mortician now. I chose to become a mortician the day I didn't die.

This is better. It'll hook him, like opening a movie with a sex scene. But it's not true. The day I didn't die, the last thing on my mind was a career change.

The first week he was gone was the worst. Despite all my spells, my prayers to the *orishas*, Juan had left. Not left just *me*—which was reasonably within expectation—but Cuba. On a raft, probably forever. For most *balseros*, that was a one-way trip.

But there was more. A few days before leaving, he'd told me to my face that he didn't care for me. Not one bit. He didn't want our child either. I'll never forget the shock and horror on his face when I told him, "Juan, I've been on the pill, but something went wrong. I'm pregnant, *mi amor*."

"*No jodas, Rosi!* I asked you—"

"It's not my fault! I'm sorry."

He wouldn't have suspected that I'd never been on the pill or that I'd carefully timed the few occasions we made love with the days I was ovulating. I had known he'd be upset, sure, but I had thought a child would change him. He would always be part of me, part of my life, whether he wanted to or not.

He had abandoned me, yes. But at least not with Elsa. Because of what I did? Because I told her? If I ever see him again, I'll ask for forgiveness, even if I've already been punished enough. I did it so she wouldn't follow him to La Yuma, and for all I know, it worked better than any spell I could have put on him. She slapped me hard, which I deserved, but never said a word to anyone about it. She was probably ashamed that Juan had cheated on her with *me*.

Not so long after that, she dropped out of college. What a relief, not having to see her curly hair every day in class. As if her absence (and Juan's) was all I needed to blossom, I started getting more roles, the instructors saying often that they saw the spark of "it" in me. Nobody called me the Bride of Frankenstein anymore. I made a few friends. I got to play Kattrin in *Mother Courage and Her Children*. A month passed, and I was almost happy, despite having lost Juan. Happy even in my melancholy.

I wasn't showing yet. Nobody knew I was pregnant. After I had the baby—and what a beautiful baby it would be, with Juan's eyes, hair and face, an exact copy of him—I would tell Abuela. I would ask her to be the baby's godmother. His name would be Juanito, and she would forgive me for tricking her grandson. She would invite us to live with her. "What's an old woman like me doing living here all by myself?" she had already said so many times. As someone outside the family, I had no business sharing her home. But as the mother of her only great-grandson, I would get a spacious room for me and Juanito instead of my tiny, stuffy *barbacoa* in my mother's house. El Chino, Juan's quiet, sweet father, would become a surrogate father to me as well, since Dad lived in another province and seldom called or visited me. I loved Juan's family as much as I loved him.

Abuela and I had become good friends, despite our age difference. She told me secrets that she swore not even Juan or her son had ever known. When she was a teenager, she'd had an affair with a married man, and her parents had disowned her. "I know that sounds ridiculous today, but in those times, especially in the countryside, it wasn't uncommon," she said. "My folks threw me out. I hitchhiked all the way to Havana, and without any means to support myself, I went to work in a brothel."

"What about the man? What happened to him?" I asked.

"Nothing. He stayed with his wife."

One of her clients was Ezequiel, Juan's grandfather. "Thank San Fancón and all the *orishas* he rescued me from that life," she said softly. "He even married me. He was a sweetheart who never, ever brought up my past. I was lucky, because Chinese men, *mijita*, make very good husbands. Better than Cuban guys."

Juan was part Chinese—I could be lucky too. I knew that he had made it to Miami and, after recovering from dehydration and heat stroke, found a job in a supermarket. "Yemayá, the *orisha* of the ocean, took pity on him," Abuela said. "I sacrificed two fat chickens to her, and she graciously accepted them. *Alafia* to her! But I also prayed to San Fancón and lit a lamp in his honor for seven days and nights. I called on the spirit of Ezequiel and all his ancestors who were buried in China. I fed them rice and coconut milk. They all protected him. Chinese witchcraft is as powerful as African, *mijita*, sometimes even more so."

It was then that I started praying to San Fancón, although I didn't have the slightest idea of what I was doing. It was about intentions, wasn't it?

The dream played itself out in my head. When the time came, Abuela would be so thrilled that she'd call to tell Juan immediately. I would take little Juanito to spend time with his grandfather, El Chino Oscar, who had been depressed and lonely since Juan's departure, and provide new purpose for the man. With love and patience, I could become a member of Juan's family, even if he did get married in La Yuma and have other children there. Who knew? He could one day send for me and Juanito. But in a few years, I would be a famous actress with roles in all the international telenovelas, so I would decline. Until he begged me, that is.

I continued to make offerings to Oyá, knowing she liked eggplant, chocolate, red wine and all things purple. I would cut an eggplant into nine pieces, fry them in lard and take them to the Havana Forest. I would drop chocolate chips at crossroads and scatter violets for her at the cemetery. Little did I know then that I would eventually end up working there. I bought small black coral branches at La Plaza de la Catedral (ay, they were expensive!) and offered them to her as well, because Abuela had once mentioned Oyá was fond of black coral. I spared no effort to get in Oyá's good graces again. I knew that she was mad at me, rightfully so.

Abuela's health had begun to deteriorate after Juan had left, and she often forgot to eat. Forgot to take showers. Forgot where she lived. Eventually, she forgot her son's name. She wouldn't even tend to her garden. I would make tamales for her, with crispy bits of pork roast inside, and bring them to her house. I passed along important news and messages from others in town and prepared herbal teas and potions for her. "Make the sage tea strong," she would say. "My head is like an open cage, and all the birds are flying out." I offered to spend a few days with her. She said yes, but when I showed up with a suitcase and a pot of chicken soup, she didn't let me in. She had forgotten who I was.

That was the beginning of the end. I had sinned against Oyá by revealing a secret, and she would ensure I paid for my transgression, hitting where it hurt the most. She ended up being as harsh and vindictive as the Catholic God my grandmother prayed to.

At first, it felt like a menstrual cramp. I was in the middle of an improv workshop with Corina Fernandez, a Teatro Estudio veteran; we were "playing panic." Víctor, who wasn't yet Victoria, was onstage. We were having a blast. The pain was so mild, I didn't even go to the bathroom. It passed quickly.

After the workshop ended, I walked to the dining hall. The ISA menu usually consisted of watery black beans, soy fritters and stale bread, but that day it also included a special treat, mortadella sandwiches. The cook, Tía Juana, was cutting the mortadella with a big kitchen knife. Thin slices, almost translucent. A throng of hungry students swarmed around her.

"Hey, make those slices fatter!" someone yelled.

She's probably going to take home half of that mortadella, I thought.

But at least I would get some protein. The baby needed it. I got in line.

A girl I didn't know whispered in my ear, "Aunt Flo just paid you a visit."

I didn't know the expression.

"I don't have any aunts."

"Seriously, you're bleeding," she said. "Look at your pants."

I ran to the bathroom and exposed the crime scene between my legs. I watched my hopes and dreams disappear. My future with Juan, our permanent connection, Abuela's home in Chinatown. My perfect imagined life. Gone.

There was no toilet paper, so I used my socks to make a sanitary napkin. It looked like a tamale. When I scurried back to the dining hall, the mortadella was gone, and with it all the hungry students and Tía Juana. I took the knife and returned to the bathroom, where my tiny unborn child lay spread on the floor. I wanted to join him.

I should have known that a rusty knife from a college dining hall wouldn't do the trick. Nonetheless, I was a mess when Corina Fernandez came in and found me. That was no "playing panic"; I can still hear her shrieks of honest-to-Oyá horror. There was blood on my pants, my blouse, my forearms—everywhere. Víctor and Corina took me to the hospital. They didn't know that not all the blood had come from the same place.

Mom made me see a psychiatrist, who said I was suffering from "obsessive love." Ha! I'd never even thought my feelings for Juan might have a clinical name. The shrink recommended medical leave from school. It was supposed to be temporary—only a year—but I didn't return to the ISA. I had lost my ambition, my interest in acting. I had lost "it." I came to realize that Oyá had punished me. Abuela was right—Oyá holds her daughters to a high standard, and I had failed her.

Elegguá, get off that table! Some people think that naming a cat after an *orisha* is disrespectful. But I don't see it like that. Elegguá is playful, almost childlike, and so is my cat. Besides, he has Elegguá's colors, red and black. His coat is black, and his nose is dark pink, almost red. I bought him a cute red collar to match it. I'd better feed him soon, or he'll get into the offerings. Wouldn't be the first time.

There he is, sniffing the honey. Elegguá!

TWO AND TWO EQUALS FIVE

Sharon returned to the hotel shortly after encountering Elsa and seeing her husband handcuffed and led into a police cruiser. The sight had terrified Sharon, and she hadn't dared to intervene. What if they took her too?

The comments she had heard in the park had confused her even more. Someone had been found dead, but she couldn't figure out if it was a man or a woman. Maybe it was two people? "She was a good neighbor." "He fell in the bathroom." "She wasn't breathing." Was "she" the blonde Juan had gone out with the day before? If not, why had he been arrested? What about the other guy?

Then there was Juan's former girlfriend, that Elsa. Why had she shown up just then? And where was Víctor? Did he even exist? Sharon tried to piece things together, but nothing fit. She took an alprazolam she had brought for Juan and slept for a few hours. When she awoke, a red-and-yellow sunset filled the window. The morning rain had cleaned the sky, and the day died swathed in a soft shade of purple. The Morro Castle lighthouse looked as if it were on fire.

Sharon went down to the cafeteria, ordered a sandwich and returned to her room to eat. It had occurred to her that the American embassy could help Juan if he was in trouble. *If* there was an American embassy in Cuba. She called the front desk to ask—there was still no working Internet on her phone—but the person who answered didn't know either.

"There is a US Interests Section," the receptionist said. "But I don't have their number."

Hours passed. All night long, Sharon had visions of Juan in a cell without food or water, interrogated by the Cuban police. Her resentment dissolved into tears. No matter what he had done or been accused of doing, she needed to help him get out. Yes, there was still the question of the blonde the day before, but that would have to wait. At least, she repeated to herself as a weak consolation, it hadn't been Elsa.

At 8 A.M., the hotel room phone rang.

"Ma'am, this is Lieutenant Marlene Martínez," a woman's voice said. "I'm calling about your *Cuban* husband, Juan Chiong."

Sharon froze at the mention of his nationality. He'd been an American citizen since 2010. But he had entered the island with his Cuban passport, according to the law. Cuban law.

"Yes, where is he?" Sharon asked in Spanish after a moment, reminding herself that the police had no idea she'd witnessed his arrest.

"At the police station."

She tried to sound surprised and offended. "Why would that be?"

"We'll explain that when you arrive."

The idea of setting foot inside a Cuban police station frightened Sharon, but she wrote down the address with a shaky hand.

"I'll be there as soon as possible," she said and hung up.

She made sure to take both of Juan's passports with her when she left the hotel.

The cabdriver looked perplexed when Sharon directed him to Unidad 15, but said nothing. It took only ten minutes to get to the police station. Sharon got out of the car and hurried to the unimposing two-story building. The guard who stood at the front door made no attempt to stop her. She entered a brightly lit lobby and told another uniformed young man that she had come to see Lieutenant Martínez.

"She's waiting for you."

He hadn't asked her name. She thought they might not have foreigners there often, and she was clearly not Cuban. She hoped that would work to Juan's advantage.

Lieutenant Martínez was a tall woman with a big behind, the kind of *colita* Sharon would have wanted for herself years before. Martínez led Sharon to her office, a cubicle furnished with a metal desk, two chairs and a file cabinet. She explained that Juan had been brought in to explain his relationship with Víctor Pérez Díaz, a transwoman who had been killed the day before. "He was right there when—"

"Wait a minute," Sharon said, recovering from her jaw drop. "Víctor was a transsexual?"

"Yes. That means—well, you know Spanish, don't you?"

Sharon's pulse raced. "What exactly is my husband accused of?"

"He isn't accused of anything. We just need him to cooperate with us. And he's done so, up to now. He's free to go back to the hotel, but I want him to be available while the investigation takes place."

"How long will that be?"

"I can't say." Lieutenant Martínez looked her in the eye. "We've just opened the case. But the National Revolutionary Police are very efficient. We don't have many violent crimes here, and the few we deal with are solved quickly."

Lieutenant Martínez's straightforward manner put Sharon at ease. Somewhere—had it been Yelp? Travelocity?—she'd read that the probability of being a victim of violent crime in Cuba was low. She'd read nothing about the possibility of being *involved* with a violent crime, though.

"We called you at your husband's request," Martínez said. "I also want to find out what you know about Víctor Pérez Díaz."

Sharon's first thought was to claim that she didn't know a thing, but she changed her mind. She didn't want to contradict anything that Juan might have said.

"Not much," she answered cautiously. "Just that he and my husband were longtime friends. They went to college together. He never mentioned that Víctor was trans."

As she talked, she remembered the tall blonde in the apartment, the man who had followed them and Juan's reserved, aloof attitude during their argument. The pieces were fitting together properly at last.

"I don't think he knew," she said with a sigh of relief.

But, she thought, *why didn't he tell me?*

She met Juan in the lobby of the police station, where he had been brought while she talked to Martínez. He didn't look much worse for the wear. She waited while he signed a document and picked up his driver's license, then kissed him on the cheek and walked with him outside the *unidad*.

"Thanks for coming," he muttered.

"How could I *not* come?"

"I know I have a lot of explaining to do," he said apologetically. "But I want you to know something first: I didn't kill Víctor."

Sharon caressed his hair. "*Mi amor*, I've never for a minute believed you could kill anyone."

She flagged a pink convertible *almendrón*. They got in the back seat together. As the car returned them to El Vedado's heart, with its tree-lined streets and clean sidewalks, Sharon felt her faith in mankind and her husband restored. She remembered Martínez's confident demeanor, and for a moment, Sharon also had faith that the National Revolutionary Police would handle everything.

3

THE MATRIARCH'S STORY [II]

The apartment belonging to Pepito's extended family smelled of sandalwood incense and black beans seasoned with cumin. The living room was furnished with two overstuffed blue armchairs, a plasma TV and a set of three double-headed, hourglass-shaped drums. Magdala sat in an old wicker rocking chair. At sixty-two, she was plump and heavyset, with Frida Kahlo eyebrows and smooth mocha skin. Padrino had always thought she looked like an African matriarch.

Next to her was an altar dedicated to the Virgin of Charity, Cuba's patron saint. The dark-hewn, placid-looking statue of the Virgin, linked in Santería with the *orisha* Oshún, wore a bright yellow dress with tiny rhinestones embedded in the fabric. There were nine golden bangles on her right wrist and a small copper crown on her head. Her regular outfit was a simple blue tunic, but in view of the circumstances, Magdala had attired her with the regalia usually reserved for September 8, the saint's feast day. She had also sprinkled the altar with cinnamon.

Padrino, sitting in an armchair, listened to Magdala.

"It was my fault!" she sobbed. "I should have told Pepito to borrow the screwdriver from someone else."

"Hindsight is twenty-twenty," Padrino said. "Now, what exactly did he steal from your neighbor's place?"

Magdala's face turned red.

"He didn't steal anything, Padrino!" she exclaimed. "He only took the cell phone and the pork leg because . . . well, because they were there. Like I said, when he went back to return the screwdriver, the door was open. He went in and didn't see anybody. The pork leg was in the oven, almost burnt. I could smell it all the way from here."

She stopped to adjust her Santería necklaces. They were yellow and gold, Oshún's favorite colors.

"I even said to him before he left, 'Tell your pal next door that her pork is going to turn into chicharrón if she doesn't take it out of the oven,'" she said. "Five minutes later, Pepito came back carrying the pork leg. It was enormous, with a big bone sticking out, and it was piping hot. 'Victoria's so busy with her Yuma friends that she forgot her lunch!' he said. Pepito was hungry and we didn't have anything ready, so he suggested we have at the animal. He was laughing the whole time like it was a big joke."

"Didn't he suspect that Victoria would get mad at him for taking food from her kitchen?" Padrino asked. "It's a serious matter, *mija*, and more so if she was expecting guests."

Magdala shrugged. "He said that her Yuma friends must have invited her to eat out. Anyway, he was doing her a favor. If it had been left in the oven, that roast could have burned down the entire building with all of us inside!"

"Right."

Magdala started rocking furiously. She fingered her necklaces and avoided looking at Padrino.

"Between you and me, even if Victoria had caught him red-handed, she wouldn't have been mad at Pepito," she whispered. "She had a crush on him. That's why he did it, because he knew he could get away with it."

"Does Pepito get pissed off easily?" Padrino asked. "How does he react when you tell him to stop playing the drums after midnight?"

"He always cooperates! He's a nice kid. Are you implying, Padrino, that my nephew would murder someone over a pork leg?"

Padrino shook his head. "I'm just getting the facts straight. That's what the police do."

"Well, the cops don't know a thing about the animal," Magdala whispered. "Or the cell phone. As you can imagine, this is strictly confidential."

"Tell me about the cell phone."

Magdala glanced at the Virgin of Charity statuette. The siren of an ambulance wailed in the street.

"Pepito told me that it was lying out on a table," she said slowly. "I scolded him. I said, 'Don't touch what isn't yours.' Taking food isn't that bad since there are usually—what do you call them?—extenuating circumstances."

Padrino frowned. "*Ay, mija*—"

"Understand that Pepito is still a child, Padrino," she pleaded. "He doesn't think things through sometimes."

Padrino studied his goddaughter's expression. She kept fidgeting with her necklaces and the hem of her dress.

"I'm scared," she said, lowering her voice again. "The

lieutenant, that big-assed bitch, thinks Pepito did it. I could tell by her questions that she suspected him."

Padrino's face lit up. "Lieutenant Martínez?"

"That's her name, yes."

"We used to work together."

Magdala's unibrow went up in alarm. "Please don't mention the cell phone or the pork roast to her!"

This time, it was Padrino who looked at the Virgin of Charity, asking for patience.

"Tell me everything that happened yesterday, Magdala," he said. "Don't leave anything out, even if you think it's not important."

"It all started with the rain," Magdala sighed. "My bedroom window was coming apart. There was water all over, and it was driving me crazy. My husband had gone to the grocery store, and I asked Pepito to fix the window. He went next door, borrowed the screwdriver and started tinkering. In the meantime, I saw a woman go into Victoria's apartment."

"What did she look like?"

"I don't know, but I heard her heels click-clacking up the stairs and peeked out as she went into his apartment. I didn't see her, but she hung a red umbrella outside the door, still dripping. She smelled good too. One of those foreign fragrances. Maybe it wasn't a woman, but a he-she like Victoria? When Pepito finished with the window, he returned the screwdriver and came back with the pork leg and the phone." She paused. "He wasn't at Victoria's apartment more than five minutes, barely enough time to get the roast out of the oven. We had lunch. A little later, I heard Lázaro screaming that Victoria had had an accident in the bathroom. I hurried to find out—"

"'A little later'—what does that mean, Magdala? Ten minutes? Half an hour?"

"Half an hour, perhaps. I don't remember. I was busy putting away the leftovers. I would have given them back to Victoria if she'd asked for them."

Padrino took a cigar out of his pocket and lit it. After inhaling deeply, he said, "Your neighbor might have already been dead when Pepito went to return the screwdriver. If the body was in the bathroom and he didn't go there, he had no way of knowing . . ."

Magdala paused again to think. Padrino watched her. Was she really considering that as a possibility for the first time or just pretending to do so? She nodded quietly.

"Did he really leave the screwdriver there?" Padrino went on. "I'm assuming his fingerprints are all over it."

Magdala threw her arms in the air.

"Yes, he did. See, that shows you he didn't have bad intentions. If he had, he would have cleaned the screwdriver or just kept it. We've watched enough *CSI* episodes to know that!"

Padrino smiled. *CSI: Havana*, he thought.

"It was a little joke, Padrino," she whispered. "Stupid, yes. Criminal, no."

Padrino put his hand on hers. "Let's hope so, *mija*. Where was Lázaro when you came in?"

"In the living room crying."

"What about the damn screwdriver? Was it around?"

"I don't know! I didn't even think about it until the cops came back and started snooping around and asking questions. I imagine Pepito left it in the kitchen, then retrieved the pork leg from the oven and brought it here. But I haven't had the chance to ask him about it."

Padrino stood.

"I'll try to help your nephew, Magdala," he said. "But no promises."

"I'm sure you'll do fine. I trust you! And I'm not trying to cover up for Pepito. If I thought he had killed Victoria—if it even crossed my mind that he had, I would tell you. I wouldn't tell that big-assed lieutenant, but I wouldn't be sitting here lying to you with a straight face."

"I believe you," Padrino said, though he didn't. Not totally. "Now, where is that cell phone?"

Magdala stood. The rocking chair continued to move. She hurried to stop it.

"*Siacará!*" she cried out. "I don't want any bad spirits sitting here and getting ideas."

"Of course."

She went to the bedroom and came back with Victoria's phone.

"Did Pepito call anybody?" Padrino asked.

"I don't think he even knows how to use that thing. I don't, for sure."

Padrino pocketed the phone. "Call me if you hear from the police."

"Do you think they'll release Pepito soon?" Magdala asked, holding her breath.

"Who knows, *mija*?" Padrino answered, but added in a low voice, "Probably not."

4

RADIO BEMBA

After leaving his goddaughter's apartment, Padrino went straight to Los Tres Perros, a bar three blocks away. He needed a *cañangazo*, and this was the best place for a cheap, stiff drink. The bar was low-end, with gray walls covered in stained posters of Los Van Van and Irakere, bands that had been popular in the eighties. A mural depicting three spotted dogs gave the establishment its name. The place smelled of the lard used to make fish fritters and croquettes. There was music—reggaeton, of course—but at a tolerable level. There were only five patrons there, quietly sipping their drinks.

Padrino sat down at the counter and ordered a *doble*. When the bartender brought him a glass full of rum, he gulped it down. He was nervous and somewhat out of sorts. For the first time in his life, he was sorry he had taken a case. He had done it for the money, no question about that. Though Magdala was his Santería goddaughter, religion was one thing and business another. She had asked him to help her nephew using his skills as a detective, not his *babalawo* gifts. They had agreed on 200 CUCs as payment for his services. To shop at the parallel-market stores, the only outlets that carried products like deodorant, electronics, milk and red meat, he needed CUCs. Summer was quickly approaching, and the electric fan that Padrino and his wife owned, a venerable 1959 Montgomery Ward, had finally died. Electric fans retailed for 60 CUCs at the Plaza Carlos III Mall.

Padrino didn't charge for his Santería work. He accepted what people gave him, but also worked with those who couldn't pay. His godchildren brought him fruit, bags of rice and homemade treats. He never went hungry, because his wife raised chickens and pigs, and they had a vegetable garden, but so many indispensable items were only in that damn "convertible currency" now! His monthly pension was 600 Cuban pesos, which amounted to 24 CUCs. He had worked with some Americans and Europeans who had gotten in trouble with the police and paid in dollars, but those gigs were scarce.

Padrino knew other *santeros* who demanded *only* dollars or CUCs for payment. They advertised on specialized classifieds websites popular among Cubans with Internet access and disposable income. But he just couldn't do it. He wouldn't risk enraging the *orishas* for a few dirty bills. His Angolan godfather had forbidden any monetary transaction the day he'd consecrated him to Yemayá, the goddess of the sea.

Time fell away. The bar and its surroundings receded. Padrino remembered his first encounter with the *orisha* in 1987. He hadn't been Padrino yet but Sergeant Leonel Fábregas. Young and idealistic, he had gone to Angola to support the MPLA, the ruling party, against the UNITA, the rebel forces led by Jonas Savimbi. Leonel didn't believe in Santería then, or in anything that wasn't backed by Marx. Unlike many of his comrades-in-arms, he wasn't a career soldier or conscript but a volunteer, having signed up for the Angola adventure in a fit of patriotic fervor inspired by El Comandante's five-hour speech on May 1 of 1986. Cubans were actually Latin African, Castro had stated that day, because most of their ancestors had come from Africa. It was their duty to help the Angolans. Leonel, a descendant of African slaves, agreed.

Once in Angola, despite his best intentions, Leonel was often left confused and angry at the very people he thought that he had come to help. Some supported the government but struggled with ethnic loyalties: Savimbi was Ovimbundu, and many Angolans were related to him by tribal links. But no one explained that to the Cubans. They didn't understand the local language or internal alliances, the current affairs or ancient resentments. Years later, Padrino concluded that they had acted like Martians landing in the middle of World War II.

The day Leonel died, his platoon had been marching through the bush, breathing in the stench of dung, wetness and rotten carcasses, surrounded by the constant buzzing of insects. They had traveled from Cuito Cuanavale to a town called Mavinga to attack a UNITA camp. Padrino saw himself again, a skinny guy with grubby fatigues and heavy combat boots that made him drag his aching feet. He was developing ulcers in his legs due to infected wounds, and his toenails had turned black.

The UNITA camp was quiet and everyone inside hopefully asleep. There were three Olifant MBTs, the South African Army's pride and joy, monster tanks that the Cubans jokingly called "elephants" and planned to capture that day. The sixty-ton machines *did* resemble the huge animals that Leonel had caught sight of a few times. The platoon hid in the bush, waiting for their officer to give the order to attack. But then the main gun of the closest tank turned toward them. Leonel couldn't see anyone in the hull but understood, in the few seconds that lapsed before the gunner opened fire, that they had been led into a trap, that the UNITA guys had known they were coming, that they didn't have a chance.

He heard shots and felt a pang in his chest. A popping noise, then nothing. Silence and darkness engulfed him as he lost consciousness. The next thing he knew, he was staring at his own body, which lay on the ground in fatigues drenched in blood and with eyes closed. He looked down from above, peering over the branches of a tree he had floated into unbeknownst to him. He didn't feel pain or fear, just awe at his newly acquired ability to fly.

His comrades were corpses all around him. He realized he was also dead. He hovered over his body, recalling the stories he had heard about wandering ghosts and lost souls. Was he one of them now? Later, in Cuba, he would talk to others who had also left their bodies and returned to tell the tale. Most recalled feelings of peace, love and becoming one with the universe. Many had seen a tunnel, a bright light . . . but they'd had their experiences in hospital rooms, not on a battlefield. All Leonel had felt was pure hatred for those who had killed him.

A tall, imposing black woman dressed in all blue came out of nowhere. She knelt by Leonel's body and touched his forehead. He heard another pop and was sucked back to life, right when an MPLA chopper landed nearby to rescue what was left of the platoon.

He was taken to a hospital and made friends with his nurse, an older, motherly Ovimbundu woman named Balbina. She spoke Spanish and not only helped him heal but gave him a crash course in Angolan history. *"Usted no sabe en lo que se está metiendo,"* she would say, tousling his hair. No, he certainly didn't know what he had gotten into! When Leonel told her about his experience in Mavinga, Balbina said that the *orisha* Yemayá had chosen him for her personal service and he needed to be initiated. She introduced him to her godfather, Okeke, who refused to deal with Leonel at first because he didn't trust foreigners, particularly Cubans, whom he called intrusive, busybodies and worse. But after a few weeks, the old man relented. Okeke took Leonel under his wing and agreed to teach him about Santería. They ended up communicating in an invented language, Portuñol, because Okeke didn't speak Spanish and Leonel didn't understand Portuguese.

It wasn't an easy process. Leonel had rigid ideas about what religion meant and a degree in dialectical materialism from the University of Havana. He was a staunch atheist, and everything that Okeke said was against the beliefs Leonel had held up to then. In Marx's book, there was no room for the experience he had had. His known world had turned inside out—war and the *orishas* did that to you, he would later say.

Finally, he was initiated. Okeke told him in no uncertain terms that he now belonged to Yemayá. He was her instrument for healing and guiding people, and he was to do it for free. Balbina and Okeke remained in Angola, but Santería followed Leonel back to Cuba. He retired from the police service and became a *babalawo*. Now, almost thirty years later, he knew he still couldn't charge for his Santería work when he thought Yemayá was looking the other way. The *orisha* didn't have a sense of humor.

He was thankful that his private-eye work was different, and happy to keep it separate from his *santero* practice. After his retirement from the National Revolutionary Police, Padrino had put to good use the skills he had learned during his career. Sometimes he teamed up with his former comrades, as he planned to do with Marlene Martínez, but he often acted alone. The work was profitable and stable, as steady as crime itself, but he was getting tired. Maybe he was just getting old, he concluded. After all, he was sixty-five. Time to retire for good, if he could just afford it.

He ordered another drink. He thought again of Pepito, the dead man and the mysterious woman with the red umbrella. Somehow, he had the feeling this wasn't going to be easy.

"He had it coming," a voice said, bringing Padrino back to Los Tres Perros. "It didn't surprise me that someone dispatched him."

"Well, it surprised me," another voice answered. "In fact, I didn't even know she was a guy. She had me fooled this whole time."

"Did you ever look at his feet? Even tall women don't have feet that big. His hands were pretty muscular too. They're a dead giveaway with these people."

"I never really looked at her hands."

News about violent crime traveled fast in Havana. Padrino glanced discreetly at the two men who sat at the other end of the counter. One was wearing overalls. The other, who looked like an office worker, had a button-down shirt and black pants.

"I know it straight from the horse's mouth. I used to work with Lázaro," the guy in overalls said. "At first, he talked nonstop about his girlfriend. It was 'Victoria this' and 'Victoria that.' One day, 'Victoria' stopped by the construction site, and we finally took a good look at her. Man oh man! Lázaro quit two weeks later, tired of getting into fights with people who called him a *maricón* to his face. The guy had hard fists and a temper to match. But it got to be too much, even for him."

"Do you think he killed her?" the office worker asked.

"No, no! He was way too in love with her—him, whatever. I bet it was that neighbor of his, the drummer. You know him?"

"Pepito?"

"Yep. I saw two cops arrest him with my own eyes!"

"But why would he kill Victoria?"

The guy in overalls lowered his voice. Padrino strained to hear. "Because 'Victoria' had a thing for him, that's why. I bet he got too frisky with the kid, and Pepito . . . well, he had to put him in his place, and got carried away. Not that I blame him, eh. I would have done the same."

There was a brief silence as the bartender brought them a couple of beers.

"I heard it was an accident," the office worker said.

"Accident? They found the guy with his throat slashed open!"

"Who said that?"

"Radio Bemba."

Radio Bemba, the grapevine, was responsible for the wildest rumors and the most twisted truths. Nobody trusted Radio Bemba, yet everyone listened to it. It was the voice of the street, both wise and unreliable, Central Station of slander. Padrino listened intently, pretending to be brooding over his drink.

"No way," the office worker said. "I can't see Pepito doing that. Just a couple years ago, he was a kid playing baseball in the street!"

"Most killers were once sweet little kiddos, man."

The bureaucrat shook his head. "Do you know the French phrase '*Cherchez la femme*'? There must be a woman in it somewhere."

"Forget the French. These folks don't need any women; they just act like them."

Padrino scratched his chin. Magdala had mentioned that Victoria had had a crush on Pepito. Maybe the guy in the overalls was right. But then there was that slashed-throat detail, a total fib. As for *"Cherchez la femme,"* he needed to find out who the woman with the red umbrella was. He fought the temptation to have another drink. It was time to go home and start working the case.

5

WOMAN WITH A RED UMBRELLA

ell phones had become more popular and affordable (though still available only in CUC) in the last five years, but were still a novelty. After he got home, Padrino inspected Victoria's. Many of the calls had been made to the same number, marked as "Café Arabia" in the address book. Padrino focused on the last two, placed the morning of her death. One recipient was labeled "Elsa Dieguez." The other was a number with the area code 00 1 575.

He called the international number first, from his own cell phone. The call went directly to voice mail. "Hi, this is Juan," said a male voice in English with a heavy Cuban accent. Padrino waited a few minutes and called again. He left a brief message and then dialed Elsa Dieguez's number. A woman answered right away.

"May I speak to Elsa?"

"Who is this?" She sounded surprised.

"I'm working on a criminal case involving Víctor Pérez Díaz, also known as Victoria Sunrise." Padrino didn't add that he was working on his own. "Did you know him?"

There was a short silence.

"Barely," the woman said.

"I'd like to talk to you about him."

"Are you a cop?" she asked.

"Not exactly."

"I don't have time to talk now," she said. "I haven't seen Victoria in ages. I don't really know her. And as a Spanish citizen, I want a lawyer and a representative from the embassy to be present in any communications I have with the police."

She hung up. Padrino stared at the phone, speechless. He wasn't used to this kind of treatment. And was she really Spanish? She'd sounded Cuban to him.

He turned on his computer and Googled her name. He found a Facebook account, which he couldn't access, and a write-up in the Cuban newspaper *Granma*: SAVARRIA AND CO. SIGNS CONTRACT TO SELL FIVE HUNDRED COMPUTERS TO THE SCHOOL OF MEDICINE IN JANUARY. *"We're looking forward to a bilateral cooperation," said Savarria and Co. vice president Elsa Dieguez, a member of the Association of Spanish Entrepreneurs in Cuba.*

Savarria and Co. was headquartered in Seville, Spain. The Cuban branch was at 555 Línea Street. Padrino got into his car, a battered VW Beetle, and drove to Unidad 15 in El Vedado. He wanted to talk to Marlene Martínez before he did anything else.

Padrino parked outside the police station and walked through its doors for the first time in years. He and Marlene Martínez had worked together on several cases but hadn't been in touch since she'd been transferred from Unidad 13 in Centro Habana to Unidad 15 in El Vedado. Padrino didn't exactly know what to expect when he asked the young clerk to tell Martínez he was there. He was pleasantly surprised when she came out of her small office right away.

"Comrade Instructor, I was just thinking of you!" she said, shaking his hand. "Come on in. We haven't seen each other in . . . what, two years?"

"Around that long," he answered. "How are things going with you, *mija*?"

"Same old, same old. Sit down."

"I don't want to bother you if you're busy."

"No, no! In fact, I need your professional opinion. I'm dealing with a *santera* right now."

Padrino feigned surprise. "Is that so? The religion is taking over!"

"Not so much." Marlene wrinkled her nose. She'd never been a fan of Santería. "And in this case, I don't think 'the religion' looks too good, considering who's practicing it. Say, do people who practice mostly wear amulets and stuff when they have things to hide?"

Padrino laughed. "Believers wear their protective 'amulets' not only when they want to hide things but rather as a preventive measure. Which means all the time."

"Ah! Understood. So there's this old woman . . . Her nephew's a suspect in one of my murder cases. He had *marihuana* in his system too. She comes in with a medal this size"—Martínez formed a five-inch circle with her hands—"and keeps kissing it when she thinks I'm not looking. She smells like incense and keeps saying, '*Siacará*,' which she admits is a Santería word. Should I consider all that a sign of guilt?"

Padrino didn't answer immediately. Was she talking about Magdala? And why hadn't his goddaughter mentioned that

Pepito was smoking pot? After he'd asked her to tell him everything.

"She may have just been nervous," he said. "What's going on with the case?"

"Víctor Pérez Díaz, a transvestite, was found dead." Martínez retrieved several photos of the crime scene and showed them to Padrino. "In his bathroom, near a wall-mounted cabinet where there were traces of blood. A mirror that used to cover the bathroom cabinet was broken, so we *could* assume that his head hit the cabinet. But"—she pointed to a picture of the bathroom—"what are the chances of him inadvertently hitting the back of his head against a cabinet that's been there forever? It's over the sink, not in the way at all. Someone must have pushed him."

"Who found him?"

"His lover. He's not a suspect, though."

"What about the *santera*?" Padrino asked, shoulders tensing. "Is she a suspect?"

"No, just her nephew. A screwdriver with his fingerprints was on the kitchen counter. The medical examiner said a blow between the temporal and occipital bones caused Pérez Díaz's instant death. He could've been hit with the tip of the screwdriver, but then the killer tried to make it look like an accident? That *santera* acted nervous the entire time, and so did the *mariguano*. Like they were hiding something."

Padrino had been tempted to mention the stolen cell phone and the pork leg earlier, but now it would only make Pepito look even worse.

"I'm not sure the guy's guilty, to tell you the truth, but I don't totally trust his story. Or his aunt's," Martínez concluded.

"Is there any way I can help you with this case, *mija*?"

"You could talk to the *santera*, find out what she really knows. I'll give you her address. These people would rather talk to you than me!"

Padrino relaxed. "I can do that. Are there any other suspects?"

"Suspects as such, not really, but there's some woman who came into the building carrying a red umbrella. It looks like she visited Pérez Díaz, and I want to find out who she is and why she was there. It shouldn't be too difficult to ask the other neighbors, but people there are tight-lipped, at least with us."

"Anyone else?" Padrino asked.

"Well, there's also a Cuban American," Martínez wrinkled her nose. "Or rather, a Cuban who now lives in the United States. He was going to have lunch with Pérez Díaz, but when he arrived, Pérez Díaz was already dead. He isn't a suspect either."

When Padrino left Unidad 15, he had formed a plan. No matter what, Pepito would be locked up for at least a few months because of the *maría*. It was Padrino's task to find out if he could shield the boy from a worse fate, though the twerp was a *mariguano* and a petty thief. If it turned out the woman with the red umbrella was Elsa, he would have something of substance to present to Martínez.

If he was sure the boy didn't do it, Padrino corrected himself.

He would track Elsa down, visit her office, that Savarria and Co. Since he was working with the police now, albeit unofficially, she might be more inclined to cooperate. But he still had a bad feeling about this case.

6

SAVARRIA AND CO.

When they got back to their room at the Meliá Cohiba, Sharon seemed exhausted. Juan, on the other hand, felt more wired than wiped out. He had gotten some sleep at Unidad 15 and just needed to eat.

He told her the truth, or most of it. He recounted to her his meeting with Víctor, their run-in with Lázaro, his visit to the nursing home, and how he had returned to his friend's apartment for lunch only to find him dead. Basically the same story he had told the police. As he had when he talked to the police, however, he omitted a few facts. One was Víctor's admission of his old crush on Juan. After all, he reasoned, it was indeed "water under the bridge" and a private matter. He also left out that Elsa was supposed to have lunch with them that day. At Unidad 15, he'd thought he simply hadn't wanted to offer extraneous information or involve anyone else in this awful mess. Now, as he talked to his wife, he could see he'd been trying to protect Elsa all along.

"They didn't accuse me of anything," he finished. "The lieutenant didn't even give me a hard time. Guess I don't look suspicious enough? Or Cuban enough. But I don't think I can leave the country until they say so."

"At least you're free now," Sharon said. "It could have been worse."

"You're right. I still can't believe—I mean, poor Víctor," he stuttered, wavering between the relief he felt for himself and sadness about his friend's death. "If it wasn't an accident, then his lover must have killed him. But he didn't have the time, unless he went in earlier or it all happened very, very fast."

Sharon curled up in bed.

"Was he that mad at Víctor?" she asked.

"It looked like he was mad at *me*."

"It's horrible," she whispered.

Juan sat on the edge of the bed and hung his head. "If Lázaro did do it, then it was my fault for going back to the apartment. If I'd stayed away—"

"Oh, don't say that!" She took one of his hands in hers. "You only wanted to see an old friend."

An old friend who once loved me, Juan thought. He held his wife's hand tightly. His Sharon, so concerned for him, so sweet and understanding. He didn't deserve her.

"I should have told you all this yesterday," he said. "It was just such a shock when I went in asking for Víctor and found—Victoria. And that pride march was something I never expected to see in Cuba, much less take part in. It was *surreal*. But I should have explained it to you instead of clamming up."

"I understand, sweetheart. But how come you never heard about your friend's change? Your community's not exactly the best at keeping secrets."

"If I had stayed in Miami, with so many people coming and

going, I'd have found out sooner or later. But when I moved to Albuquerque, I lost contact with everyone. And Víctor and I weren't really on speaking terms until I called him to tell him I was coming."

She kissed him, her small auburn eyes full of compassion, and he was once again reminded of how much she resembled Rosita. Their bodies were quite different—in fact, Sharon looked far better at forty-nine than Rosita had in her twenties—but there was something eerily similar about their faces. It was the shape of their mouths, which lent them a sense of softness and vulnerability. Juan loved Sharon. He was sorry he had caused her so much trouble with his trip, this special Cuban vacation she had expected to be fun. But in his heart, he realized with a jolt, he still pined for Elsa.

"Why don't you try to sleep, *amor*?" he asked.

"I will. But I'm sorry about your friend. I wish I could do something."

"There's nothing we can do. I'm going to go back to the nursing home," he added. "I promised the woman who's taking care of Abuela that I would come back in a few hours, but—well, obviously, I couldn't. But she might've told Abuela about it, and I don't want to keep her waiting. Do you want to come?"

"Not now. We could take your grandmother out for dinner, though."

Almost the exact same thing she had said about Víctor. Juan didn't want to tell her that, given Abuela's condition, she wouldn't be able to leave her bedroom, much less eat at a restaurant. He didn't want to go over the bleak memory again.

"I'm going to take a nap," she said with a guilty smile. "I'm fried."

"Yes, get some rest. Thank you again for coming to get me," he said, smiling and giving her a quick kiss. "I'll take a shower to get rid of that *unidad* smell. That was the first time I've stepped inside a police station, and I hope it's the last!"

Half an hour later, after saying goodbye and tucking Sharon into bed, Juan, freshly showered and shaved, ordered a tall glass of *café con leche* and two Cuban sandwiches—ham, cheese and pickles—at Cobijo Real and devoured them. *How can I be so hungry after everything that's happened?* he berated himself. What kind of insensitive clod was he? He could still see Víctor's body in Lázaro's arms—the wound in Víctor's skull, his fingers curved as if attempting to grasp back the life that had been taken from him.

Poor Víctor, the weakest of the Three Musketeers. Juan hated to think that Lázaro had killed Víctor because he'd been jealous of him, of their friendship. How could Lázaro have misunderstood? But Juan remembered the pained, desperate expression on Lázaro's face, the way he'd kept repeating "my girl" and sobbing. No calculation or instinct to protect himself from accusation.

It could have been an accident and not a homicide. The lieutenant had acted a bit hesitant, as if she wasn't too sure herself. The idea that it might have been an accident comforted Juan, made him feel less guilty.

He took a sip of *café con leche*. What about Elsa? If she'd arrived after the police had gone into the building, seen the cruisers and heard what had happened, she'd probably left. Who could blame her? She might have been looking for him right then! That she had agreed to have lunch with him might mean she still cared for him. Or at least, enough to have a conversation.

Staring at the now-empty dish, Juan had a moment of inspiration. Elsa wouldn't know where to look for him (unless Víctor had told her Juan was staying at the Meliá Cohiba), but he knew where to find *her*. He would go by her office. He could both do that and return to the nursing home, he told himself as he flagged down a taxi outside the hotel.

Once he was on Twenty-Third Street, he avoided Coppelia and headed straight for the Art Deco building. He entered the air-conditioned lobby and read the golden nameplates on the doors: CEMEX, EMPAQUES SILVERT, ADVANCED COMMUNICATIONS. A rose-scented air freshener tickled the insides of his nose. Canned music filled the hall.

"Can I help you, Señor?" A security guard approached him.

"I'm looking for Elsa Dieguez," Juan answered, feigning an American accent.

It worked.

"Ah, yes, Savarria and Co.," the guard said. "Come this way, please."

The guy led him down a carpeted hall to the door he had been looking for, bearing the same elegant golden nameplate as the rest. Juan had started to sweat, despite the air conditioning. His hands were trembling so much that he had to hide them in his pants pockets.

The two women at the reception desk were in their early twenties. They had long hair, fake gold jewelry and theatrical makeup. The taller one bore a particularly hard expression. She sized him up the moment he came in, making him recall the hotel clerk. Young Cuban women had a certain defiance to them now, an attitude they hadn't had when he was young.

"How can I help you?" asked the shorter, younger-looking one.

Juan stuttered that he wanted to see Elsa. He forgot to use a foreign accent this time.

"Señora Dieguez isn't here now," the older receptionist answered dismissively.

The office was small but clean and well equipped. While he searched for the right words, Juan noticed a computer and a modern landline phone on the desk, along with a framed print with the Savarria and Co. logo (a laptop surrounded by sunrays) hanging on the wall.

"Is there any way I could leave her a message?" he asked.

The women exchanged bored looks.

"Do you have a card?" the older one asked.

He took one out and handed it to her. He hadn't really expected to use any business cards in Havana when he'd slipped a few inside his wallet before leaving Albuquerque. The receptionist glanced at the address, and her face relaxed.

"I'll call her personal line and let her know you stopped by," she said in a more respectful tone.

"Thank you so much," he said.

She called right away, pronouncing his name and last name carefully and reciting his phone number twice on what seemed to be a voice mail.

"Do you know when she'll be back?" he asked.

"Possibly after lunch."

There was nowhere to sit. He wasn't invited to wait either. He walked to the door, but before closing it, he overheard the taller receptionist saying, "*La señora* is in high demand today."

"And by some interesting characters." The other giggled. "Well, at least this one looks richer than the old mulatto who came by this morning!"

7

RICE DREAMS

Rice is a useful grain. The water in which it has been rinsed can destroy bad spells. White rice with *guengueré* beans is a traditional offering to Oyá.

—*El Monte*

Dear Juan,
You left a long time ago—twenty years and counting—but I've never . . .

I'm done. I'm not going to write this stupid letter to Juan. As if he's the only man in the world! There are others who actually *care* for me. Last month, my friend Carlota introduced me to her neighbor Armando Bacallao, and she's been playing matchmaker ever since.

I guess I could be interested in Armando, but still, if Juan were to come back to me, I'd take him in a heartbeat. Yet I know that won't happen. No matter what Oyá promised, it won't. And I want my life back. I don't want to spend another twenty years waiting for a guy who's probably forgotten my name by now.

Armando Bacallao is known around here as Armando del Arroz because he has a small *paladar* called La Casa del Arroz.

"House of Rice" is a fitting name—all the dishes he makes are rice based. Rice with chicken, rice pudding, fried rice, cream of rice and a dish he invented called *arroz con todo*. I'd like to try it and find out what "everything" means. Carlota says that it is like fried rice on steroids. Mmm.

Carlota also says Armando's smitten with me. Smitten, bah! But at least he isn't a *pláfata*, one of these people who ask one foot for permission to move the other. Not only has he opened a successful *paladar*, but he's also bought an old Chrysler, one of those orange ones that used to be government taxis, and is going to start taking orders to his clients' homes and workplaces. He says he got the idea from the American movies. "You always see the pizza guy doing deliveries," he told me. "Why can't I do the same here? La Casa del Arroz will be the first *paladar* with delivery service in Havana. It's gonna be a hit!"

I like his attitude. Positive energy. Maybe some of that will rub off on me. He isn't bad looking either. Ten years younger than me, but that isn't really an issue on my end. At first, I told Carlota he wasn't my type. But what exactly *is* my type? Juan? Armando doesn't look like him at all. He's short and a bit chubby, but with a handsome face and earnest eyes.

Carlota has a small business too. Bellísima, a beauty salon next to La Casa del Arroz. She handles everything from nails to hair, and now she wants me to start helping her. I could do makeup, cut hair and put acrylic nails on. Same thing, minus the acrylics, that I've been doing forever. The difference is that my current clients don't complain, I told her. "They don't tip either," she retorted. "I need a partner here. I'm tired of working by myself and having to turn people down because I don't have time to take care of them. That's money I'm losing. We both could be making it."

We'll see. I'm not sold on the beauty business, but I promised Carlota I would think about it. Frankly, I don't want to be sixty years old and still working at the cemetery. Well, at least that didn't scare Armando off. I've learned to say to most people, "I have a job with Necrological Services." But they usually keep asking and figure out what it means. It freaks them out. They always want to know how I ended up making such an "unconventional career choice."

My mentor at the funeral home was Celeste, an old woman. Or she looked old, though she was the same age then as I am now. After I had my "little problem," as Mom started calling it, at the ISA, I had to register for group therapy sessions at Calixto García Hospital. Celeste had a sister in the therapy group—a basket case who thought she was a reincarnation of Mona Lisa—and picked her up after our sessions in a beaten-up Oldsmobile. It was raining one afternoon, and Celeste offered me a ride home since Mona Lisa and I were the only patients still waiting outside the hospital. It was better than walking two blocks in the pouring rain to the bus stop, so I took her up on it.

"Do you know how to make funeral wreaths, by any chance?" she asked me. "I'd pay up to three dollars for a good one."

I didn't know, but three dollars during the Special Period was the equivalent of a hundred and fifty pesos. I said I could try. She gave me the materials—fresh flowers, ribbons, glue and discarded wire hangers—and I made a passable wreath. She ordered seven more.

Though funerals and burials were free, the wreaths had

become black-market items. Mourners paid for them in dollars, which had just become legal. I soon began working alongside Celeste, who shared with me her secrets for funeral makeup. I attended embalming workshops and learned about the business. When she retired eight years later, I inherited her job, just like that. I had apprenticed under her for long enough. And I'd had no competition. It wasn't like I was asked to take an aptitude or personality test.

Little by little, as with everything in life, my faith came back. I had cursed Oyá and all the *orishas* after losing the baby, but once I healed, I turned back to them and asked for forgiveness. Abuela had already been taken to a nursing home at that point. On one of her good days, she told me to contact Padrino, the *babalawo* who later became my godfather. He formally initiated me into Santería ten years ago.

By that time, my mother had died of cancer, and I was working at the cemetery. I was surrounded by death constantly and gave myself over to Oyá. My poor mother had been dying inside, slowly and painfully, ever since Dad left her and moved to Oriente with his new wife, who was close to my age. *La titimanía*, that's what they call the sudden urge that overcomes middle-aged men to abandon their longtime wives for younger, prettier girls. It was a national phenomenon that inspired songs and movies. My mother kept waiting for him to come back, which never happened.

Are we doomed to repeat our parents' mistakes? Now that I think of it, I'm living her life, except without a child—all alone, waiting for a man who doesn't love me anymore. But I *won't* become her! I'm going to give Armando and his rice business a chance. And give myself a chance as well.

I pray the *orishas* show me which path to take because this one . . . this one's getting old. Sometimes, I'm even tired of being the Queen of Bones' handmaid. That can get old too.

8

A FUNERAL TRANSACTION

Juan knew he should return to the Meliá Cohiba. Or at least pay another visit to his grandmother, as he'd told Sharon he would. Today might be a better day for her. He could spend a couple hours at the nursing home. It would be interesting to talk to Rita again and to see that young nun, Yuleizi or whatever her name was. Why would such a pretty girl choose to be a nun, especially nowadays? There was probably a secret behind her decision, he mused. Maybe one having to do with love. Everybody had secrets, even the people you thought you knew best. Look at Víctor. Look at Camilo! Juan had always seen himself as a what-you-see-is-what-you-get kind of guy, but he too had kept secrets, from his wife. He didn't know if he would ever be able to fully trust someone again.

As he stepped out of the Art Deco office building, a hearse drove by. The usual black limousine with tinted windows, followed by a Lada and two *almendrones*, one blue and the other red. Juan tried to imagine what his father's funeral had been like. Besides Víctor, who else had attended? El Chino Oscar hadn't had many friends. How many people would attend Víctor's funeral? He should go, shouldn't he? If he was still in Cuba when it took place, he certainly would. *Ah, the Three Musketeers! All for one, and one for all*. But now he was the only one left. How short-lived the happiness of reuniting with his old friend had been. He shouldn't have left Albuquerque for this. But *this* was more than Víctor—it was also Elsa.

He felt his skin tingle. Would she call him? But he had left his cell phone at the hotel, turned off, so as not to bother Sharon. He didn't dare to go back for it now. That could make her suspicious. He would stop by Elsa's office again in an hour or so. In the meantime, he could visit his father's grave. After all, the Colón Cemetery was only a short walk away.

It took him a good half hour to get there, when it should have been fifteen minutes. He could have traveled faster, but the places he had passed had brought back memories and faces. Elsa's above all. There was the pizzeria they'd gone to during the Latin American Film Festival, when they would watch five films a day and subsist only on pepperoni slices and Coppelia ice cream. Their favorite movie was Eliseo Subiela's *Man Facing Southeast*, in which Rantes, a psychiatric hospital patient, claims to be an alien visitor, with most people failing to believe him despite the miraculous feats he performs.

"Would you love me if I were an alien?" Juan had asked Elsa.

She had smiled. "Of course. I would love you even if you were a little green man."

Now he *was* an alien, a visitor in the foreign landscape of his own country. Would she still love him? He wished the answer didn't matter. It was like *el diablo*, the devil himself, was tempting him, making him forget all obligations to his wife. Sharon was the sweetest, most level-headed woman he had ever been with. The most mature too. In his youth, he'd been attracted to women who were a little—if not a whole lot—crazy, but he didn't need that drama in his life anymore. And yet . . .

By perverse association, thinking of Sharon reminded him of Rosita again. What had Víctor said about her working at the cemetery? Rosita, mortician. It was almost like a bad joke, and yet it seemed a more natural job for her than being an actress.

He passed a busy bus stop. How many times had he waited there with Elsa? She'd had a driver's license, but her father had seldom given her permission to use his Jeep. She needed to learn to use the brakes first, they'd joked.

"Elsa has no brakes" was something people had frequently said at the ISA due to her notoriously hotheaded, daring nature. It had been Elsa, not Juan, who had suggested they have sex only three weeks after getting together. They had sneaked out to the Almendares River, to a desolate area near El Bosque de la Habana favored by young couples who couldn't afford a hotel. Unlike Rosita, Elsa had been experienced and proud of it. Though it was implied that she had been with several guys before, Juan hadn't asked how many, feeling inadequate and nervous during the early stages of their courtship. She had taught him a few things while he was still relatively unskilled, only a brief affair with an older divorcée in his "repertoire."

In the early months, he had been unable to believe that Elsa, the prettiest girl on campus and the *pincho*'s daughter, had chosen him, a garden-variety guy from Old Havana. But she had—for a while, at least—though her father hadn't liked him. He wasn't half the man his daughter needed, he had said. "Dad says that musicians, actors and artists in general are ideologically deviated," Elsa had explained, laughing.

Juan thought of the old Spaniard and everything else: the golden nameplate, air-conditioned office and snobby receptionists. He wondered what the *pincho* thought of Elsa's husband. Was *he* man enough for her? Or was he "ideologically deviated" as well?

The Colón Cemetery's main entrance was a Romanesque triple arch. Juan had to tiptoe around a string of Santería offerings: flowers, rotten bananas, eggs with names written on them, coins, an ear of corn and even a dead chicken with a red ribbon tied around its feet, feathers strewn all over. He shook his head. The deities his grandmother worshiped had always struck him as suspicious. After being taught at school that religion was "the opium of the people" and after his early attempts to communicate with the spirit of his dead mother had failed, he had rejected Abuela's attempts to induct him in any kind of Santería ceremonies. But she had kept harping at him. "If you visit the cemetery, always leave an offering by the gate," she used to say. "A plum, a black hen, some chocolate pudding . . . anything to show respect to the Queen of Bones. You don't want Oyá angry with you." Absurdly, he thought he should have brought something, just in case. But he waved the idea away with a sweep of his hand.

He stood among the elaborate tombs and statues of angels, engulfed by an ocean of marble, blistering white in the sunlight. Though he had vague memories of visiting his mother's grave when he was a child—his paternal grandfather had been buried in the Chinese cemetery—he didn't remember where it was. But he knew it was called "the Lasalle mausoleum"—it had belonged to his mother's parents, who had died before he was born. He thought it shouldn't be too difficult to find.

An old man was going around selling gladioli, marigolds and roses. Juan asked him about the Lasalle mausoleum, and though the flower vendor didn't know where it was, he was able to direct Juan to the information office.

"Someone will help you there," he said. "Was it a recent burial, the one you're looking for?"

"No, my dad passed away fifteen years ago."

"That's *fresh*, man!" The vendor cackled. "Foreigners come here all the time asking for loved ones who died sixty or seventy years ago. I have the sorry job of telling them that those graves probably belong to someone else now."

"I'm not a foreigner."

"Fine. Just ask them to let you consult the *registros* book. The information office is left of the main entrance; you can't miss it."

Juan thanked the vendor and walked off. At the information office, a young man dressed in all black—black-blue jeans, a Grateful Dead T-shirt and an unmarked baseball cap—offered Juan the services of an English-speaking guide. "The admission fee is five CUCs, Señor. You can pay here. We also have a horse and carriage tour—"

"I'm *not* a tourist!" Juan blurted out, fed up with the constant confusion. "I just want to see my father's grave."

"Sorry. Just go to *registros*. Here, let me show you on the map."

Following Grateful Dead's instructions, Juan passed by the imposing Central Chapel and turned toward the northeastern quadrant. He walked quickly by a succession of mausoleums, iron grilles and glass windows—some intact, others broken— but didn't stop until he saw a small gray building. A faded sign on the door read *registros*. The door was half-open. He went in without knocking and found himself in a windowless room. There were two large wooden benches with a Formica table in the middle. A picture of Fidel Castro watched him from the wall. Juan had forgotten how ubiquitous El Comandante had always been in Cuba.

A faded blue curtain acted as partition between the main office and another area from which Juan could hear the murmur of voices. When he approached, he was hit by the scent of withered flowers. It wasn't a horrible smell—not rotten exactly, but reminiscent of decay. He fought the desire to run as fast as possible from the pungent aroma of death.

Once he resolved to stay (*It would be childish to flee*, he told himself), he couldn't help but eavesdrop. Two women were talking; one said, "The whole-body price, please?"

"One hundred CUCs," another voice answered. "But I'm willing to give you a discount because of your special circumstances."

"That's nice of you."

"It will be *only* eighty. Price includes a suit, shoes, tie, the whole shebang. Plus hair and makeup."

Juan stopped to listen. This couldn't be what he thought it was, could it?

"That—that's still a bit steep for me," the other woman stammered. "How much for just the hair and face? We're having a closed casket, with a small glass portion on the upper part." She cleared her throat. "His body was completely crushed."

Juan felt like vomiting and again considered leaving. But he stayed, unable to move without hearing the outcome of the negotiation.

"Just face and hair, then," the first woman said. "And what's the condition of the face?"

"Bad—very bad. Head-on collision with a truck. And he was on a bicycle. Even I had trouble identifying him."

"That means I'll have to do facial reconstruction. Let's say thirty-five. It includes eyes and a wig if needed."

There was a pause. And finally: "Okay. I'm sorry to be such a cheapskate; I just don't have much money. But I can give you this as payment too."

Juan heard the thump of a metallic object placed on a hard surface.

"Oh, that's a beautiful San Lázaro! But no, I can't accept it."

"Please, take it. It belonged to my husband. He was a devotee of Babalú Ayé."

"Wouldn't you like to keep it? I'm fine with the thirty-five CUCs, really."

"No, no. It reminds me too much of him. I must tell you, the medal and chain aren't made of gold or anything too valuable. It's some kind of alloy."

"But it's so elegant! A man's piece. Tell you what—I'll give it to my godfather and ask him to pray for your husband's soul. Now, you have to make sure they bring the body with enough time for me to do a good job. When's the burial?"

"The day after tomorrow at noon."

"Then I'd like to see him here tomorrow afternoon. Based on what you've told me, he'll need some serious work."

"I'll call the hospital and let them know. The body is still there."

A quiet sob.

"Which hospital is it?"

"Calixto García."

"Ah, you don't need to worry. I know all the guys there. I'll handle it."

"Thank you so much!"

There was another pause. Juan heard the click of a purse, then a movement of chairs. The curtain parted, and the two women entered the office. One was dressed in black and didn't even look at him. The other smiled in recognition.

"Hello, Juan."

9

CONFESSION AT THE CEMETERY

He had expected Rosita to look haggard and uglier than he remembered after so many years, but she had improved with age. Her hair was pulled back in a French twist, and a few gray streaks gave her a distinguished air. She had gained weight, making her figure more proportionate to her height. She looked poised, her smile brighter, and she had a twinkle in her eye.

"Good . . . good afternoon," he stuttered.

Rosita led the other woman to the door, closed it behind her and turned to Juan. He didn't know what to do. Hug her? Shake her hand? And why didn't she seem surprised by his visit? It was as if she'd been expecting him. Maybe Víctor had told her he was back. Yes, it had to be. Did she know Víctor was dead?

Rosita pressed her left cheek to Juan's mouth.

"Better late than never," she whispered. "I had given up on you."

Juan kissed the air around her face. The smell of decaying flowers enveloped them both.

"How—how have you been?" he asked.

It was a silly question, but he couldn't think of a better way to break twenty years of silence.

"Not as well as you," she replied. "You haven't changed a bit. Did you preserve yourself in formaldehyde?"

Juan coughed out a nervous laugh.

"Bad joke, sorry." She winked. "A mortician's joke."

Juan sneezed. He searched his pockets for a handkerchief and feigned another cough to avoid speaking.

Rosita fanned the air with her hands.

"I have to do something about the smell. We ordered a shipment of flowers, but the family never showed up with the body. They decided to cremate it at the last minute. Ah, the competition!" she said, her voice rising in mock indignation. "I left the flowers in my office in case we might be able to use them. We're big into recycling here. But they're starting to stink."

"Oh, I hardly noticed," he lied.

"It's so nice to see you again, Juan."

She spoke as if they had parted ways only a few weeks before.

"Well, the same, Rosi."

"Do you want to go out now? I'm supposed to stay here until two, but I'll leave a note. Give me one second."

She disappeared behind the curtain. Juan heard a whisper. Was she talking to someone? Praying? She came back with a piece of paper and taped it to the door. The handwritten note read, *Going out, urgent matter. Will be back.*

"Let's go," she said with a confident, happy expression that pained Juan.

"Go where?" he asked, hesitant to go anywhere at all with her.

She flipped her hair.

"Oh, wherever you want," she said breezily. "There are lots of places we could grab a bite and talk for a while. Remember when all we had was a few pizzerias? Now there are *paladares* all over. My favorite is La Dulcinea. They make great desserts."

The name sounded familiar. Juan tried to remember where he had seen it.

"They also have ice cream, homemade vanilla. And the best flan in Havana."

Oh, where he had bought the flan for Víctor. *Carajo*. No way he was going back to that place.

She took him by the arm and started walking.

"Rosi," he managed to say, "I can't. I don't—I don't have time. My wife's waiting at the hotel. I came here to visit my dad's grave." She stopped and let go of his arm. Silence floated between them, like the smell of rotten flowers.

"Fine," she said flatly at last. "I'll take you there."

They set off walking again. Juan avoided getting too close. Should he mention the past, apologize to her? He didn't want her to get any ideas—he was married, after all—but finding out what had happened with her pregnancy, or at least asking, was the right thing to do.

"I keep it clean and nice here," she said. "I bring flowers the third day of every month, because Oscar died on February the third."

Juan realized she was talking about his father's grave. She'd done that for El Chino Oscar all these years?

"Thanks," he said, trying to stave off a nauseating guilt. "I'm happy to pay you."

"Oh, you don't have to. Victoria does. I would have taken care of it anyway, but she brings me five CUCs when she can and finds makeup gigs for me at Café Arabia."

Juan decided not tell her about Víctor's death. He just wanted to pay his respects to his father and leave. Rosita was getting on his nerves already, as she always had.

They passed by the mausoleum of Juan Pedro Baró and Catalina Laso. In the early twenties, when divorce hadn't been legal in Cuba, Catalina had left her husband and fled to Europe with her lover, Juan Pedro. When the divorce law was finally passed, they had come back to Havana, but she had died a few years later. Juan Pedro built an Art Deco mausoleum for her in marble and black granite, with a crystal rose carved on top.

Juan remembered the story because Víctor and Elsa had been in a play inspired by it. Víctor had been the male protagonist, which now seemed ironic. Elsa had played a high-society lady who despised Catalina.

"Here we are," Rosita said.

The unpretentious Lasalle mausoleum was tucked on a side street, away from the main avenues. A cement vase on top contained three withered red roses. OSCAR CHIONG and 1947–1999 had been engraved next to it. Below were the names of Juan's mother and other relatives, almost weathered off the tombstone.

"Are they all buried here?" Juan asked, perplexed. Unless the grave was very deep, he couldn't fathom how they had managed to get more than four bodies in.

"Not anymore," Rosita said. "All the Lasalle folks have already been moved out."

"Mom too?"

"Yes."

Juan blinked. "You mean she isn't buried next to Dad? Why? Where is she?"

"When the body decomposes, only the skull and some of the bigger bones remain. We put them in an ossuary after a certain number of years. This makes it possible to bury other people in these spots, since space is limited."

Rosita spoke mechanically, sounding bored. She must have repeated these lines often. He thought of asking whether Catalina and Juan Pedro had been separated and their vacant spots given to others, but decided it was none of his business.

"There's still room in your mausoleum," Rosita added cheerily. "We can place up to three more bodies here."

Juan wanted to offer the space for Víctor, but didn't. He needed to leave this place. He couldn't stand Rosita's gaze—strangely self-assured, almost smug. But he still had to ask. He inhaled deeply. She looked at him and waited.

"Rosi," he started.

"Yes?"

He heaved a sigh. *Just get it over with.*

"I'm sorry for the way I treated you," he said.

"I was just your backup girlfriend."

"Ay, Rosi! I shouldn't have . . . My only excuse is that I was young and stupid. I hope I didn't cause too much trouble for you."

"What do you mean?"

She wasn't going to make it easy. He glanced at the mausoleums, which shone eerily under the sun.

"The—our child," he said. "The last time we talked, you told me you were pregnant. What happened? Did you . . . ?"

She shook her head. "Oyá punished me, and I lost the baby."

Her eyes swelled with tears. Despite himself, Juan put his arm around her shoulders.

"Don't say that," he said. "Punished for what? You didn't

do anything wrong. It was my fault too. I should've been more careful."

She sank against him.

"I *did* do something wrong," she whispered. "It's why Oyá punished me. After you left me, I went to see your girlfriend and told her about us."

Juan winced. "You told Elsa?"

"Yes."

Rosita's voice became firmer as she went on.

"I heard you were planning to leave . . . just Elsa and the Three Musketeers. It wasn't fair that I would end up here, discarded like an old rag, while you and Elsa stayed together forever in La Yuma. I told her I was nine weeks pregnant. At first, she didn't believe it was yours." She smiled wistfully. "She couldn't accept that after being with her, the girl everyone at ISA wanted, you'd waste your time with someone like me. But I offered her proof. I described your *pinga* to her, the three birthmarks on it and everything."

She seemed almost proud.

"How did she react?" Juan asked in a voice he didn't recognize as his own, hoarse and cracked.

"She slapped me." Rosita's cheeks turned red. "Twice. 'This for being a *puta* and stealing my man,' she said. 'And this one in case you're lying.' She went for my hair, but I ran."

Juan's eyes wandered over the graves surrounding them. He wished Rosita's body were in one.

"Why would you do that?" he asked. "Why, Rosi? I never told you I would leave Elsa for you. You knew I was in love with her."

"Hey, I was young and stupid too," she said defensively. "I was hurting and knocked up and had no one to turn to."

The flower vendor approached them.

"Ah, you found it!" he said to Juan. "Would you like some marigolds?" He held up a bunch. "Look, they're still fresh."

Juan ignored him. He waited until the man went away and then asked Rosita, "When did you tell her?"

"I don't remember. A few days before you left, I think."

"You have no idea how you've wrecked my life, Rosi," he hissed.

"I wrecked *your* life?" Her eyes narrowed. "You really don't care about anybody but yourself, do you?"

He imagined grabbing Rosita by the neck and strangling her. He avoided her eyes, tearful but shining with conviction and self-righteousness. He had to leave, before he did something stupid. After all, he wasn't young enough to be excused for it anymore.

He walked briskly away, and she called after him: "Why does it matter now? Juan!"

He broke into a run and fled the cemetery, chased by the smell of rotten flowers.

10

LAST IMAGES OF THE SHIPWRECK

Speaking of secrets. Speaking of trust! No, he would never trust anybody again. Not after this. But still, he had to find Elsa. More than ever. Everything had just become clear, as if someone had opened the window of a dark room filled with junk, dust and cobwebs, letting the sun shine into its dirtiest corners.

When he returned to the Art Deco building, the same security guard escorted him to the Savarria and Co. office. The two young women were still at the reception desk, gossiping and laughing. No, Señora Dieguez hadn't come in. No, she hadn't returned their calls either. And no, they definitely couldn't give him her personal number, much less her address.

"We're old friends," he argued. "We haven't seen each other in twenty years. I'm only in Cuba for a few days and need to speak to her."

"I'm sorry," the younger receptionist said, unrelenting. "Señora Dieguez has made it clear that we aren't allowed to divulge her personal information. I don't want to lose my job."

"I'll never tell her you told me!"

"She'll figure it out. I have a child to take care of, Señor."

Frustrated, Juan left the office for the second time that day.

"Wait."

He stopped. The taller, slightly older woman had followed him. He smiled, hope lighting up his eyes.

"Why do you need to talk to the boss?" she asked.

"We were sweethearts a long time ago," he disclosed. "It's been twenty years, and I don't know when I'll be able to return to Cuba again."

She smiled knowingly. "I see. Well, I can give you her address."

"Really? Thank you so much."

She chuckled. "Not so fast, *chico*. If the commander in bitch finds out, she'll fire my ass, as my friend has mentioned."

Commander in bitch. Juan couldn't hold back a nervous laugh. "I promise—"

"Promises won't feed me. What's this worth to you?"

He finally understood. "You mean money."

"*Real* money. Dollars or CUCs."

Young Cuban women had no hair on their tongues, as Abuela used to say. They never minced words. He took one hundred CUCs from his wallet and offered them to her. After counting them, she said, "It's within walking distance from here. Eight blocks down L Street, then turn left on Tenth Street, and look for a big house painted blue. I don't remember the exact number, but you can't miss it. There's a ceiba in the front yard."

Juan thanked her profusely. It wasn't until he was en route to L Street that it occurred to him that she might have given him false directions. If so, what could he do? Go back and confront her for squeezing a bunch of CUCs out of him? Bah. He would give her the benefit of the doubt for now. He said a quick, preemptive prayer to the *orishas*.

"Please, let Elsa be there. Let her listen to me. Give me the chance to explain . . ."

He walked fast, blocking out the mental image of Rosita. She was as dead to him now as the bodies in the Colón Cemetery, slowly fading to dust under the marble headstones.

The neighborhood looked and felt rich. It was even a step above El Naútico, the bourgeois district Elsa's parents had moved to in the sixties when the original homeowners had fled to Miami. Juan remembered the crystal chandeliers in the living room that had dazzled him when he first saw them. But during the Special Period that house had fallen into disrepair. In 1992, after more than thirty years without a decent paint job, with old plumbing and broken fixtures, it had still been impressive, but not the most comfortable place to live.

These El Vedado houses, though also built before the 1960s, had been carefully remodeled. Their facades had been repainted, their garages fitted with automatic doors. There were brand-new metal fences with German shepherds behind them and Mercedes and BMWs parked out front. There were green lawns and parabolic antennae on the roofs. Juan found the blue house—a single home with a coquettish picket fence and a spotless front yard where a majestic ceiba grew to the left, surrounded by shrubs. The property had probably been mapped out around the tree to avoid cutting it down, as the species was considered sacred even by nonbelievers. The garage door was open, and Juan spotted a blue Lexus, nicer and newer than the Toyota he drove in Albuquerque.

He opened the gate, crossed the front yard and stopped at the door. He then noticed a man dressed in white with red and blue Santería necklaces around his neck watching him from across the street. Juan brushed off the reflexive alarm that triggered his paranoia. The *santero* was probably looking at the ceiba, maybe praying to it.

Juan's heartbeat was rapid. He didn't know what he was going to say to Elsa, or what to do if she let him in.

He rang the bell and waited.

A familiar voice, one he'd heard many times in his dreams, replied, "Coming!"

The door opened, and there she was. Elsa, just as beautiful, with shorter hair, thick and shiny, her small mouth and deep-set green eyes. The same eyes that had looked at him so lovingly twenty years ago now glared coldly.

"What are you doing here?"

No, she wasn't happy to see him. In fact, she seemed pissed off.

"I need to talk to you," he said.

"We have nothing to talk about."

"But we were supposed to meet yesterday," he insisted.

"We were?"

"Víctor told me you wanted to have lunch with us."

Elsa seemed confused. Taking advantage of the moment, he pushed past her softly and sneaked inside the living room before she could protest.

And what a living room it was. Even after living abroad and constantly seeing the rich folks' homes that Sharon bought and sold, he was awed by the marble sculptures, the massive entertainment center, the well-preserved antique mirror with its ornate golden frame.

"Nice place," he said.

She waited by the door, raising an eyebrow.

"Elsa, please. Let's talk."

He realized that he sounded like Rosita, desperate and vulnerable. But he shrugged off this thought. True love made you unafraid to show weakness, he decided, feeling a brief pang of empathy for his backup girlfriend.

"There are some things I didn't know about until today." He approached Elsa and took her hand in both of his. It was cold. "Please, give me a chance to explain them."

She closed the door. "Fine. Follow me."

She led him through the living room and a formal dining area—he had a quick glimpse of the sleek dining set, a Persian rug and two oil paintings—to a breakfast nook furnished with a white table, two chairs and a matching hutch. It was in a kitchen full of stainless-steel appliances. A tray with three éclairs on it rested on the granite counter beside a notepad and a pen with the Savarria and Co. logo. A wall clock read one-thirty.

Elsa brought the tray to the table. "From La Dulcinea, the best *paladar* and bakery in Havana."

Juan gave a slight involuntary shudder. They sat down at the table.

"Have an éclair," she said. "They're good."

Juan hesitated but took a bite. He couldn't help thinking of the flan he had bought for Víctor. Did everybody in El Vedado go to La Dulcinea? The éclair tasted like chalk, though he suspected it was just the association with his dead best friend.

"Mmm," he mumbled for show, closing his eyes. When he opened them again, she was watching him closely. There was no love in her eyes, as he'd hoped there would be, or hate, as he'd feared, but a cold, almost calculating expression. He looked away and saw a bottle of *creolina*, a tar-based cleaning agent, sitting near the sink.

"I haven't seen *creolina* in years," he said.

"It's the only thing that leaves tile floors spotless," she answered, as if the benefits of a specific cleaning product was a normal conversation topic for former lovers seeing each other for the first time in two decades. "I've tried Pine-Sol and Clorox, but there's nothing like *creolina*. I always get it at Havana Libre."

Juan glanced out an oval window, which looked out onto a roomy backyard. There were jasmine shrubs, rosebushes and two palm trees. A three-tier fountain stood in the middle, surrounded by terra-cotta pots.

He devoured the éclair faster than he had intended out of nervousness, piled the crumbs on one corner of the table and said, "I couldn't wait to see you at Víctor's. Do you know what happened?"

"When I arrived, the neighbors were talking about it," she said as she wrung her smooth, perfectly manicured hands. "Vic had invited me to lunch, but she hadn't said you would be there."

His face fell. "I thought you wanted to see me."

"Yes, I *would* have wanted to see you," she admitted with a smile. "But I don't understand why Vic didn't tell me outright. I almost didn't go. Yesterday my secretary didn't show up, and I had a ton of things to take care of. These useless Cuban employees! Work ethic is still a foreign concept here, you know?"

Commander in bitch speaking. Juan suppressed a laugh.

"I showed up a bit late."

"Unfortunately for me, I was too early." He frowned at the memory. "Which made the cops think I knew how he died."

"How's that?"

Elsa listened as he filled her in on the details. He didn't mention Sharon, though. If only by omission, he wanted to let Elsa think he was in Cuba alone.

"I thought it was just an accident," she said when he finished. "That's what people kept saying."

"Marlene Martínez seemed to think differently," Juan said. "But even she wasn't sure."

"Who's that?"

"The lieutenant in charge of the case, a tall blonde with an ass as big as a basketball."

"You noticed her ass, huh?"

"Couldn't help it." He laughed. "You know how I am."

Elsa shifted in her chair.

"It could have been Lázaro," she said after a short silence. "He followed Vic around, controlled her and behaved like a total caveman. The worst part was that she liked it."

She giggled, then covered her mouth with a hand.

"*Ay, Dios!*" she said. "What am I saying? Poor Vic."

Juan smiled. This was his Elsa—her quick laugh, her irreverence. And Víctor was a safe topic. A good way to put off the moment he'd have to explain everything.

"Did you know, back then, at the ISA, that he was . . . ?" he asked.

"I sort of suspected it."

"Guess I was the only one out of the loop," he said. "Were you two close?"

"Not very. We saw each other occasionally. I tried to help him—her. I still mess up the pronouns sometimes, but I did come to acknowledge her as a woman."

She stood, opened a drawer under the granite counter and took out a pack of Camels. While her back was turned, Juan palmed his wedding ring and slipped it into his pocket.

"Want one?" she asked.

"I shouldn't. I quit a few years ago."

"I took it up after—"

She paused. Juan waited, his heart rate speeding up again.

"After you left," she concluded.

This was it. But Juan didn't know where to start. *Coño*, there was so much to say! He had wanted to ask why she hadn't joined them that night, demand an explanation, but now he knew Rosita *was* the explanation.

A noise startled him. It was a soft rustling, as if a wind had blown the leaves outside. But there was no wind, and the leaves were still.

"What was that?" Juan asked.

Elsa got up and surveyed the backyard, then closed the window. The kitchen looked darker, and the stainless-steel appliances seemed to have lost their shine.

"I thought El Vedado was safe," Juan said.

She shook her head. Her short bob was cute, Juan thought, but he preferred her hair as it had been before, longer and crazier.

"You've been away from Cuba for too long," she said. "There are no safe places anymore. There's scum everywhere, and we have plenty of break-ins, especially in rich neighborhoods."

"So would you say you're rich now?" He was careful not to sound resentful or envious.

"I guess so," she said casually. "By Cuban standards, at least."

"Well, you always were, right?"

She let the comment slide. "You need to walk around with

four eyes these days. My secretary called earlier to say that a suspicious-looking guy came to the office this morning asking for me."

He chuckled. "That was me! I didn't think I looked suspicious, though."

"Not you. A mulatto. And by the way, who gave you my address?"

Juan drummed nervously on the table before answering, "Víctor."

She pursed her lips. "Figures."

She had a way of holding the cigarette in her left hand that reminded Juan of the black-and-white movies they used to watch. Like Bette Davis! Back at the ISA, Elsa had worshipped her.

"All those movies we watched," she said, as if reading his mind. "Weren't they so much more interesting than reality? I wanted to live them, despite what our professors thought of my acting ability. As if they knew so much, those Teatro Estudio types! Big fish in a small pond, that's what they were."

"Pass me a cigarette."

She arched an eyebrow and grinned slightly. With her left hand, she lit one with her own and handed it to him.

"*Now, Voyager*!" Juan exclaimed.

"Paul Henreid. I was so in love with him."

Juan took a long drag of his cigarette.

"I forgot you were left-handed," he said.

"A contrarian in everything, like my dad says."

"How's he doing? And your mom?"

"Fine. They live in Los Angeles now, near Hollywood. Can you imagine?"

No, he couldn't. Weren't they *pinchos* who hated the Yankees? He wanted to ask but didn't.

"I liked American movies, but those were from our parents' times," Elsa went on. "We had Subiela. Remember *Last Images of the Shipwreck*? It was our favorite, wasn't it?"

"Yes . . . You cried every time we watched it. Funny how sorry we felt for the Argentinians who suffered under a military dictatorship when we were blind to our own suffering."

"Everybody was worse off than Cubans. Argentineans, Uruguayans, Angolans, South Africans—you name it. That's what they wanted us to believe. *Cabrones!*"

Elsa, like most children of revolutionary parents, had had the privilege to rebel, criticizing the government and rooting for perestroika. Poor kids like Víctor had been the ones who still defended communism.

She touched his arm softly, and he felt the old spark pass between them.

"I met Subiela in São Paulo," she said. "At the premiere of *The Hostage of Illusions*. I didn't have a chance to really talk to him, though. But do you know who's a friend of ours now?" she asked, her expression happy and playful.

"Who?" said Juan, flinching at the implied "us" of Elsa and her husband.

"Pedro Almodóvar!"

"You're kidding."

"An acquaintance introduced us at a reception at the Spanish embassy." She smiled, and her eyes crinkled. "He talked about filming some scenes here, in our house. He used to come to Havana every year—until he was caught in a raid at El Periquitón, a gay discotheque." She laughed. "That was long before Mariela

Castro and her *maricongas*. It was the end of his love affair with Cuba, but we've kept in touch. He knew I'd studied acting and even offered me a role once."

"Did you take it?"

"I was tempted, but no. It was only a small role, and I have a business to manage. Life's too short."

Life *was* too short. There was never enough time. Juan glanced at the clock. He had been there for almost half an hour and hadn't told her yet.

"Listen, Elsa," he said urgently, leaning forward. "I got involved with Rosita once or twice because she kept chasing me. I felt sorry for her. But I only loved you. I would have done anything for you. I was so devastated when—when you didn't show up that night."

Her face had hardened. She looked older now. A mature woman who had survived the biggest shipwreck of her life.

"Why did you leave then?" she asked coldly.

"Because—because Camilo insisted. It wasn't the first time you had backpedaled. I just found out on this trip that Rosita told you about us and thought—"

Elsa chewed lightly on her cigarette butt before tossing it away.

"*No jodas, Juan!*" she yelled. "Yes, I was furious when Rosita told me you had knocked her up, but I loved you. I was determined to go. I had collected cans of Spam, soft drinks and antidehydration fluids. Everything was ready, but someone stole two tires off Dad's Jeep that night."

An invisible hand choked Juan. A wet hand, dripping water.

"I couldn't find you! You didn't have a phone. I called Víctor, and he said you guys weren't speaking anymore. The next day, I discovered you and Camilo were gone."

"You said someone stole your tires?" His voice quavered.

"Yes, it happened all the time then. Rafters were using them to secure their balsas. Don't you remember?"

Juan heard Camilo's voice as he insisted they leave that night. "Elsa is a spoiled girl, the daughter of a *pincho* . . . Where's she going to go where she's worth more?" The raft, the waves, the tires that had saved their lives. But at what cost? He couldn't say a word, feeling as if he had taken a double dose of those whackadoodle pills that Sharon and his shrink were always pushing on him.

Elsa was still talking. "I didn't think you would leave without me! I figured you'd wait at least another day. I even thought that you and Camilo . . ."

Juan stayed silent, his arms hanging by his sides in total defeat.

"But it's true that I had changed my mind at the last minute several times already," she admitted in a softer tone. "I wanted to go because it was this big adventure and you were part of it, but I was afraid too. I still don't know if I would've had the courage—I tried to cover it up, but I was a big chicken. And I was hurt, but you did the right thing. They closed the Malecón a few days afterward."

The doorbell rang.

"Oh, Lobster Lady," Elsa said with a tired smile. "I forgot she was coming today."

"Lobster Lady?" Juan echoed, still in shock.

"There's a woman who sells lobster and shrimp in the neighborhood. Illegally, of course, but cheaper than in the dollar shops. Wait here. If she sees you, she'll get nervous since she doesn't know you."

"Why? Will she think I'm law enforcement or something?"

She sighed. "Just wait here, okay?"

Juan was left alone in the kitchen. He grabbed another éclair and devoured it. He heard Camilo's last pleading words again. So that was what had eaten at him as he lay dying of thirst under the merciless Caribbean sun. "Forgive me." But Juan never would. What a pair, Camilo and Rosita. How could the people who had claimed to love him have betrayed him in the most ruinous ways?

He would have to tell Elsa. It was awful to lay the blame on Camilo now, but she deserved to know the truth. He wondered if, once she found out, their love might have a second chance. But what about Sharon? Ah, why should he care? Did anybody care about *his* feelings?

Five minutes passed. Was Elsa still talking to Lobster Lady? He went back to the living room. The door was half-open, and he heard the two women making small talk. In a corner was a huge duffel bag he hadn't noticed before. It was unzipped and filled with soap, toothpaste, batteries, flashlights and other small items.

An umbrella hung from the hook of a standing coatrack. A funny piece, that coatrack. How many times a year did people wear coats in Cuba? Well, Elsa seemed to have done just that. There was a chic gray coat there. She had always been *friolenta*, more sensitive to cold than others. He turned his attention to the photographs on top of the entertainment center. He recognized a well-dressed couple in front of the Eiffel Tower. Elsa's parents. He thought bitterly of his own father in his small, phoneless apartment, with no money to buy milk or meat. He scowled at the other photos: Elsa with an older guy, probably her husband; Elsa, the old guy and Raúl Castro (Juan gasped at the sight); Elsa with a group of friends at the restaurant Versailles in Miami; Elsa and a young man with dark hair and tear-shaped eyes.

When Lobster Lady left, Elsa closed the door and came back with a basket wrapped in newspaper.

"I thought she would never leave!" she said. "I try not to be rude, but you don't want these people getting into your house and snooping around, then telling everybody and their sister what they see."

She passed by the open duffel bag and shook her head, embarrassed.

"Excuse the mess. I haven't had time to unpack. When I leave the country, I always bring back little gifts for my employees, stuff that's cheap outside of Cuba but you can't get here, not even at the dollar shops."

She stopped, noticing Juan's angry expression.

"What's wrong?" she asked.

He pointed at the pictures. "Is this why you married the Spaniard?"

She returned to the kitchen without a word. Juan remained in the living room, staring at the picture of the young man skiing in Vail. The kid had his eyes, his hair, his shy smile. It was like looking at himself at twenty years old. It was the son he had dreamt of all along. Not Rosita's child but Elsa's. He felt miserable and lucky at once, impotent and strong.

He finally followed her. She sat at the table, staring at the basket full of lobster tails in front of her. Her eyes brimmed with tears. Juan knelt at her side and tried to take her hand. She withdrew it.

"Why didn't you tell me?" he whispered.

"What do you mean, tell you?" She slammed the table, making the basket jump. "You had already left me by the time I realized! What was I supposed to do? I tried to have an abortion, but I couldn't. I had polyneuritis, and the doctor refused to do it. It could have killed me."

"You should have found a way to tell me! I would have sent for you both. I would have taken care of you."

"You didn't take care of Rosita, did you? You told her you were too young to have children."

"With *her*!"

Juan was bathed in the salty smell of ocean that came from the basket. Salt. Ocean. The raft buffeted by the waves. Camilo.

"I had no way of getting in touch with you," she said. "I didn't even know if you had made it to Miami. It wasn't until a month later that I heard you were in a hospital and Camilo was dead."

Juan stood.

"He was the one who stole the tires," he blurted out.

She froze. "What?"

He had never seen her face so pale, her green eyes so round.

"I didn't know they were from your dad's Jeep," he said. "He told me he had bought them. And he kept pushing, saying that if we didn't go that night, we would never have another chance."

"*Hijo de puta!*"

She pounded the table again and burst into tears. Juan tried to hold her, but she pushed him away and ran out of the kitchen. He heard a door close with a slam. A bathroom door, he thought. Why did women always cry in the bathroom? Well, he would give her time. She needed to process this. So did he. It was going to take time. But at least she knew. Things could only get better after they'd touched bottom. They would come back up for air—together, he hoped.

For ten long minutes, he was left staring at the clock with the Savarria and Co. logo. When Elsa came back, her eyes were red. She sounded sad, but calmer.

"It was fate, Juan," she said. "We weren't meant to be. Let's not blame anyone. But it's too late."

"It's not too late!" he protested. "I love you, Elsa. I've never stopped thinking of you. I only had one thing with me when I was rescued by those fishermen—a photo of you. I've kept it all these years. I had it scanned and saved on my computer before it fell apart. You were the last thing I looked at before passing out on my raft."

"Ay, Juan," she said with a heavy sigh. "That's sweet, but I'm married now. Vic told me you were too. Why destroy the lives we've built?"

"Because we only have one chance. Why did we agree to not be happy?" he asked, quoting from their favorite movie. He felt as if Subiela and his crew were around, filming them.

He leaned in and kissed her on the cheek.

"No," she said, pushing him away gently. "It's not worth it."

"But, Elsa—"

She took the basket with the lobster tails and placed it in the sink, then crumpled the pages of newspaper and threw them in the trash. Juan waited, not understanding why she was busying herself with these ridiculous ordinary tasks when they were discussing the most important decision of their life.

"You should go now," she said without looking at him. "Forget this conversation; forget me. You have a good life in America, and

I have a good life in Spain. Let's keep it that way. Maybe someday we'll meet again."

"You're crazy!" Juan yelled. "How can you just tell me to forget this? I want to meet my son. What's his name? Does he know—"

"*You're* the one who's crazy," she replied. "Of course he doesn't know, you idiot. No one does. Why the hell would you want to meet him now?"

"Because he's my son!"

Her lower lip trembled. "You're not meeting him."

"Why?"

"Can you imagine the effect it would have on him to find out his father isn't really his father? He's at an American university that Savarria is paying for. What can you offer him?"

The inadequacy Juan had felt before returned. He couldn't afford to put his son through college, much less an expensive one. He didn't even have a home of his own! Supposing that Sharon agreed to take his son in, why should the kid want to move from the East Coast to Albuquerque? He hung his head and didn't answer.

His humility seemed to soften Elsa. It always had when they'd fought. She moved closer to him, sliding her arms around his neck.

"I'm sorry, Juan. But I have to protect him. I want the best for Emilito."

"You're right, *amor*."

He was thinking that he would look for the boy on his own once he got back home. How hard could it be? The kid's name was Emilito Savarria, quite an unusual one, and he lived in Cambridge. Thank God for Google, as Sharon liked to say. Though a bit late, he was learning to scheme too.

"We'll do whatever you want, Elsita," he said soothingly. "Let's not argue now, please. We're together again, and that's what matters. Because you're my only true love."

"And you're mine."

She tilted her head up and kissed him.

It was finally happening, the thing he had always wanted. He said nothing, afraid to break the spell. She took his hand and led him into the bedroom, where there was a king-sized bed with a blue chenille bedspread that gave off a lavender fragrance. They lay there kissing until she slipped out of his arms. He thought she was about to take off her clothes, but then she walked out of the room.

"Where are you going?"

"It's a surprise," she said, smiling coyly, and disappeared into the bathroom.

He looked around, admiring the carved furniture and the porcelain ornaments on the dresser. There was a big package next to them. From the bed he made out the recipient's name, Emilio J. Savarria, and a Cambridge address. He jumped out of the bed. Elsa was still in the bathroom; he needed to act fast. He hurried to the kitchen, grabbed a piece of paper from the notepad and the pen with the Savarria logo and started writing down his son's address.

PART III

EL MONTE

Elegguá is the *orisha* of jokes, of the cruel, big, overwhelming jokes or small, irritating ironies: of the unexpected and unforeseen.
                                                                    —*El Monte*

It's over. I don't have to wait for him to come back anymore. I don't have to write him more letters, real or imaginary. I can just forget.

When I saw him in the *registros* office, I was so happy I could've screamed, but I managed to play it cool, like a true daughter of Oyá. "Hello, Juan." He was completely dumbfounded. His eyes almost popped out, as if he'd seen a ghost. I guess that's all I am to him.

But it turned out that he hadn't gone to the cemetery looking for me. Either Oyá was wrong, or Elegguá got in the middle. Ah, the trickster! Well, at least I did my part. I confessed. I did the right thing, and my conscience is clear.

I think finding the book shortly afterward was a good omen, a smoke signal that my *orisha*'s sending me from her kingdom of bones. A reward for my honesty. Because it can't be a coincidence that I simply came upon it after so many years. Just lying there on the counter, as if it was waiting for me.

After work, I passed by a souvenir stall on Línea Street. They're everywhere now. Some are owned by the government and others, the most interesting ones, by individuals. This was a *tiendita particular* overflowing with merchandise: dream catchers, postcards with prayers, Santería dolls, rosaries and books. The cover caught my eye because of the graphic designer's sophomoric idea of a Santería offering: three bananas, a whole pineapple—everybody knows you're supposed to cut it before presenting it to the *orishas*—four candles and what looked like half a coconut. I snickered and picked up the volume out of curiosity. It was *El Monte*. The Cuban edition, published by Letras Cubanas in 1993.

One might consider spending twelve CUCs for a book splurging. But I don't splurge often, and this wasn't just any book. It was *the* book, the one and only, by Lydia Cabrera, that Abuela had advised me to get at any cost. I paid for *El Monte* feeling important, almost like a foreigner, and the owner looked at me as if I were batshit crazy. After all, how many Cubans in their right mind would spend that much money on an old book?

I was planning to start reading this evening, but Carlota called and offered to do my hair for free. (In truth, she wants me to be her guinea pig for a new Brazilian treatment she just bought.) I'll try it and read later. And who knows? I may get a chance to see Armando and taste his renowned "rice with everything" tonight.

A few months ago, I would have thought it impossible to forget Juan. But considering the way he treated me, the way he still is,

I realize it's time to move on. Maybe that was the point of our encounter, the *orishas*' way of telling me that it's over. And even if Juan looks good for his age, he's still a run-of-the-mill forty-year-old guy. He isn't my "one and only." In fact, I wonder if there's really a "one and only" for anybody. Armando can be my "next one."

1

THE GREEN RAY

After sleeping for three hours, Sharon woke up hungry. She went down to the second mezzanine floor and discovered a restaurant called La Piazza, where she sat down and ordered a caprese salad and spaghetti Bolognese. The rich sauce was full of flavor and made her feel somewhat more reconciled with her Havana adventure. The walls were decorated with pictures of Cuban baseball players, which she found odd for an Italian place, but service was fast and the tablecloth clean. A glass of red wine restored her spirits.

The only off-putting thing was that the waiter had brought a dish of fried plantains—fried in lard, ugh!—though she hadn't ordered it. She took a bite, but they were too sweet and greasy and didn't go with the rest of the meal. Had it happened in her country, she would have sent back the dish immediately, but here . . . The politically incorrect ghost of the ugly American hovered over her as she stared at the lard-dripping plantains. She let it go and didn't even protest when the dish was included on the bill.

Later that afternoon, she took a dip in the hotel pool. The water was warm and crystal clear. In the gift shop, she bought two psychedelic gourd shakers for her daughter, a straw hat for Meredith, a bottle of Havana Club Siete Años to share with Juan and a glittering black coral necklace for herself. She didn't know if it was even legal to bring it back home, and she wasn't usually into flashy jewelry, but the strand of polished beads attracted her with irresistible, unexplainable force. She put it on right away and returned to the room to wait for Juan. Now that she was feeling rested, she had thought of a few questions that hadn't occurred to her at first.

Above all, she wanted to know more about Elsa. She would come clean and admit she had followed Juan the first day, then returned to Víctor's place the second. She still believed Juan's story, but some details didn't jibe. Why had he planned on lunch at Víctor's without her? Had Elsa been invited too? She wanted the full truth.

A construction crew was hanging a ten-foot banner across a section of the Malecón wall. They moved at a leisurely pace, often stopping to catcall the women who passed by and stare at the boats sailing across the bay. Sharon craned her neck from her seat on the balcony, trying to read the banner and expecting to see the "green flash."

A while back, she had watched the 1986 movie *The Green Ray* with Juan. He had loved it and often quoted the line "When you see the green ray, you can read your own feelings and others' too."

Time passed slowly as Sharon waited in the hotel room. The blue waters turned a deep indigo under the watchful eye of the Morro Castle lighthouse, and the sun, now red, sank beneath the horizon. Sharon had a brief glimpse of a lime-colored flash that could very well have been the green ray. A pity Juan wasn't there to see it. She looked at her watch and started fingering her new necklace. It was close to seven. Maybe Juan was still with his grandmother. What a long visit! But, of course, they had a lot to talk about after so many years. Sharon had no reason to fret.

The first stars appeared, but Juan still didn't return. Sharon became agitated. As another hour went by, she felt the crude, unforgiving light of the green ray piercing the darkness of her trust. Juan had lied to her. He had never really loved her, and she had been blind to reality. Was he with another woman? Elsa? Could he—oh, even the thought of it made her feel sick—could he have been involved in Víctor's death? Had he killed his friend? Was that why he hadn't wanted her to go with him?

By nine-thirty, Sharon was on the verge of a nervous breakdown. She tried calling Juan, but he didn't answer. She discovered his cell phone, turned off, on the nightstand. She turned it on and entered his password—it was a lazy one, the last four digits of his number. There were two new messages. The first voice mail was blank, and the second had been left by a man named Padrino (Had she heard that correctly? "Godfather"? Whose godfather?) urging Juan to call him back as soon as he had the chance. It was "a very important issue," he said gravely. She called the number he'd left, but nobody answered. A generic message said that the user wasn't available.

Had something happened to Juan's grandmother? Sharon wished she had asked him the name of the nursing home. But he couldn't still be there, not after more than nine hours. If something had happened to the old lady, if she'd been taken to the hospital, he would have called the hotel.

At 11 P.M., she wondered if the police might know something about where he was. What if he'd been arrested again? She got the number of Unidad 15 from the front desk and asked for Lieutenant Martínez. She wasn't there, the clerk who answered told Sharon in a sleepy voice. When Sharon asked if Juan Chiong had been taken back to the police station, the clerk said no and wanted to know who was calling and why. Sharon hung up.

What if he'd had an accident? Or had been mugged? Or hurt? But Cuba was supposed to be safe! She could only recall one recent incident of a foreigner being harmed here, a Canadian tourist who had fallen from the fourth-floor balcony of a Varadero hotel. It wasn't clear yet whether it had been intentional.

She started pacing the room. The minutes stretched interminably to midnight and spilled into the early morning. Another long, sleepless night.

At seven-thirty in the morning, when she looked outside again, the banner was finally in place. It read in bright red letters: WELCOME TO HAVANA. MY CITY IS YOUR HOUSE.

Sharon spat out the window.

The detectives arrived at ten o'clock. The front desk clerk called and asked Sharon to come down, explaining that "the authority" was there to talk to her. She hurried to the lobby, expecting to see Lieutenant Martínez again, but this time around "the authority" was a thirtysomething woman and an older gray-haired man. The woman wore a plain brown dress, and he a white guayabera and blue jeans.

"Good afternoon, Señora," the woman said. "I'm Agent Alicia, and this is Agent Pedro. We work for the Ministry of the Interior."

A government branch? Didn't they have last names? Were they cops? They weren't in uniform like Lieutenant Martínez.

"We're from La Seguridad," Agent Pedro offered, noting her bewilderment.

That wasn't much help. Wasn't La Seguridad the political police? Sharon stared blankly at them.

"Is something wrong?" She tried not to fumble her words. "What do you need from me?"

"Are you Juan Chiong's wife?" Agent Alicia asked.

"Yes, I am," Sharon answered in a weak, shaky voice that sounded too much like Meredith's.

"Do you know where he is?"

"No. I—I've been trying to call him since yesterday."

A brief, uncomfortable pause followed. Their faces, somber and excessively courteous, told Sharon what they were going to say before the words were uttered.

"A man who *could* be him was found dead," Agent Pedro said. "You need to come with us to Calixto García Hospital to identify the body."

Sharon swallowed hard, holding back tears.

"He's been missing since yesterday morning," she muttered. "What happened to him? Did you say that he might be—dead?"

"We aren't sure it's him," Agent Pedro said.

She felt dizzy. Everything from that moment on happened in slow motion: the walk to the car—an unmarked Lada waiting outside the hotel; the short ride through a city that had suddenly become menacing; the explanations offered by the Seguridad people that didn't make any sense to her.

Agent Alicia sat with Sharon in the back seat and spoke in a hushed manner while Agent Pedro drove. That day, at six in the morning, a man had been found dead in El Quijote Park. His body had been brought to the nearest hospital, Calixto García. The man had died of a single shot to the chest fired at close range. A note crumpled in his hands said he was so depressed that he had decided to take his own life.

"But Juan was never depressed or suicidal!" Sharon said.

She felt a brief twinge of hope. Could it be someone else after all?

"We don't know if the letter is real," Agent Alicia answered. "Or if this man is actually your husband. He didn't have any identification papers, and we haven't located the weapon either."

Sharon looked out the window. They were now in a down-and-dirty neighborhood. She let out a long breath, fighting off the irrational fear that this was all a plot to kidnap her.

"What makes you think it's him?" she asked.

"A mortician who happened to be at the hospital recognized him as a former classmate," Agent Alicia said.

How surreal.

"You mean a musician?" Sharon asked.

"No, a mortician. She said they had gone to college together. She gave us his full name. We searched the records of newly arrived passengers and found his hotel on the list." Agent Alicia looked Sharon straight in the eye. "We also found out he had been questioned about the death of a Cuban transvestite killed two days ago. Do you know anything about that? Were you aware of any ties between your husband and any local gay groups?"

No, Sharon said, she knew Juan didn't belong to any groups. As the Seguridad woman continued to speak, Spanish sounded more foreign to Sharon than ever before. It had become cryptic, a puzzle of broken syllables and unintelligible phrases. Suicide? A mortician claiming to be Juan's old classmate? It was all absurd. Ridiculous. She was sure he was somewhere else, maybe in a motel with that damn Elsa. For a moment, she desperately wished he was. Better unfaithful than dead. *Let all this be a mistake*, she prayed silently.

They got to Calixto García Hospital. It wasn't just a hospital, as Sharon had expected, but a compound made up of over a dozen buildings. They had to wait at a gate while Agent Pedro showed his ID. After the car was allowed entry, he parked in an empty lot and guided them to a house with the words PATHOLOGY DEPARTMENT inked in Gothic characters on the facade.

The lobby had cracked marble floors. A single Cuban flag hung from the ceiling. A bulletin board displayed newspaper pages and printed notes. Two nurses noticed the trio of newcomers and started whispering. But that barely registered with Sharon. She followed the Seguridad agents to an office, making an effort to remain composed.

A hospital employee led the group to the end of a corridor. There, in a small tiled room that smelled strongly of disinfectant, a woman was bent over a stretcher where a nearly naked man lay. She didn't move when Sharon and her companions came in. Sharon ran to the stretcher. The other woman's hands rested on Juan's chest in a gesture that was both protective and rapacious, tender and fierce.

Next to the woman, as if reassuring her, was a man dressed completely in white aside from a series of colorful beaded necklaces. Sharon backed off, wanting to wake up from the tragic nightmare that her Cuban trip had become.

2

PADRINO'S FIRST MISTAKE

hen Padrino had visited the Savarria and Co. office, he'd encountered the same reception that Juan had. Only less warm, as he was clearly Cuban and didn't look like someone who could do business with a foreign company or even like he had a dollar to spare. But after being approached by the taller woman, he had also agreed to pay for Señora Dieguez's address. All he had been able to come up with was 50 CUCs and 300 Cuban pesos.

"I'm only giving you a discount because you're a fellow Cuban and *santero*," the woman had said with a wink. "Pray to Oshún for me, my friend, so I can find a wealthy foreigner to drain like my boss did."

"We can work on it," Padrino had joked. "So you think that Señora Dieguez . . . ?"

She shook her head. "Look, Señor Savarria is almost eighty years old, with white hair, a big belly, warts everywhere. Don't tell me a woman like Elsa is madly in love with him, or ever was." She laughed. "She was lucky; that's all."

Padrino found Elsa's house and stood outside, watching it.

He had parked his VW Beetle three blocks away, something he would refer to later as his first mistake. He had thought the old beaten-up car would attract too much attention in a neighborhood where most houses had newer and cleaner vehicles inside their garages or out on the curb.

It was a quarter to noon. He saw Elsa leave in a Lexus but didn't try to follow her. In fact, he didn't even think of her as a suspect. There was the remote possibility that she was the woman with the red umbrella that Magdala had seen, but he doubted it. He stayed because she was the only tangible link he had to the case, through the phone call Víctor had made shortly before his death. He was just thinking about the best way to approach her again. Then he would meet with Magdala. Ah, he would give her a piece of his mind for failing to mention the *maría* issue! He was almost tempted to drop the whole thing and let Pepito suffer the consequences of his actions. He didn't, because he was sure Pepito hadn't killed anyone and didn't want him taking the rap for it. Padrino had known the young man since he was fifteen. At least he thought he'd known him. And Padrino was also intrigued. Was that Cuban American that Marlene had mentioned the one whom Víctor had called? He wished he could tell her all he knew, but she wasn't in when he called the police headquarters. Maybe it was better to just wait.

The Lexus returned. Elsa went back in the house with two bags bearing the Habana Libre Hotel logo. Ten minutes later, a man arrived. He was of medium build and well dressed and looked very intent on where he was going. He went straight up to Elsa's door and, after a brief moment of hesitation, rang the bell. She came out, and Padrino managed to snap a picture of her with his cell phone. They appeared to be arguing at first, but finally the man went in, and Elsa closed the door.

Half an hour passed. Padrino thought of going to Magdala's apartment and showing her the picture. While he doubted that Elsa was the unidentified visitor, it wouldn't hurt to ask. But he didn't want to leave before the man did. He remembered what the woman at the office had said about Elsa's husband. Could she have a lover?

Quietly, Padrino sneaked onto the property and went around the house. There was an oval window that opened to the kitchen. Careful not to be spotted, he looked inside and saw Elsa and the man sitting at a table. They weren't too close, and there was no indication of intimacy. They were simply chatting.

Padrino retreated and waited a few minutes before peeking through two other windows. The blinds were half-shut on what looked like a kid's room with posters of baseball players on the wall. In the master bedroom, he made out a king-sized bed covered in a blue bedspread. He went back across the street.

Three hours later, Padrino was hungry and impatient. Was the guy going to spend all day there? What were he and Elsa doing? Padrino went around the house once more, but the kitchen curtains were closed.

By eight o'clock, he was almost ready to give up. His stomach was growling, he was thirsty, and the man still hadn't left. The bedroom blinds were closed too by then. He couldn't hear a peep. He called his wife and told her he would be late. "How late?" she asked. He wasn't sure. The lights in the house remained on the entire night. It had started to sprinkle, which only made the wait worse.

At 4 A.M., his efforts paid off. The main door was opened

slowly and he saw somebody, silhouetted against the darkness of the sky, coming out of the house and dragging—a suitcase? No, it looked like a big zippered bag. Was it the man? Padrino didn't move, afraid of the noise his footsteps might make in the quiet El Vedado night. He strained his eyes. It was Elsa.

The garage door went up and Elsa went in, dragging the bag. Padrino heard a heavy thump. He approached the garage but had to step back immediately as the Lexus sped out, drove down the driveway and got lost in the distance under the light rain. Watching as the taillights disappeared toward L street, Padrino cursed himself for having parked so far away. He had no chance of catching up with Elsa's car.

Was the man still in the house? Padrino returned to the kitchen window; its curtains remained closed, along with all the blinds. He rang the bell. If the man was there, he would question him. Padrino always carried his old National Revolutionary Police ID with him. Sometimes it got people to talk.

No one answered. Padrino tried to open the door. The house had an alarm installed, he realized, noticing the flashing red light, but it was what he called a *chapucería*, a "botched job." It took him less than ten minutes to disable it and open the door quietly. As he stepped in, the pungent smell of *creolina* hit him.

He walked through an elegant living room to a formal dining area and from there to the kitchen. There were crumbs on the white table.

"Hello?" he called out.

No one answered.

The lights were already on, so he began to explore the house. The room closest to the kitchen, the one with baseball pictures on the wall, looked the same as it had when he saw it for the first time through the window. The master bedroom, though, was a mess. The bed had been stripped of bedspread, sheets and pillows. There were small items scattered on the floor—soap, toothpaste, batteries, cheap sandals. Here, the *creolina* smell was stronger. The tiled floor, still wet, seemed to have been scrubbed recently.

Padrino snapped a few pictures. This was suspicious enough to warrant a formal investigation. He went on to an office and turned on the laptop there. He moved the mouse to the right side and looked at the "Recent" files. He saw only Excel spreadsheets and Savarria and Co. memos.

He returned to the living room. By the door was a piece of furniture he hadn't noticed before, a standing metal coatrack. There was a light gray coat on it, next to a red umbrella hung from one of the hooks.

He fought to contain his excitement. But this didn't necessarily prove a thing, did it? Surely there were more than a thousand red umbrellas in Havana. And yet, if Elsa happened to be the same woman who had entered Víctor's apartment the morning of his death, he would have something to tell Marlene Martínez. Something that could potentially help to exonerate Pepito.

A light went on in the house next door. It was almost five. Time to go. Padrino used his handkerchief to pick up the umbrella. Then he saw something that had escaped him when he'd come in—a photo with Elsa next to Raúl Castro. Padrino whistled softly. This wouldn't be easy.

It was still raining when he walked back to his car.

When Padrino got home, his wife, Gabriela, ran to the door to meet him.

"Where were you? I couldn't sleep all night; I was so worried about you!"

Padrino kissed her. "Sorry, *amor*. I'll tell you in a minute. But I'm starving. What's for breakfast, lunch and dinner combined?"

"I'll make you something right now. Ah, what a pretty umbrella!"

He placed it in the corner. "Please, don't touch it. It's the only clue I have for a case I'm working on."

"Does it have to do with that poor Pepito?" she asked, glancing at the umbrella.

"Not quite," he replied. "Or rather, yes, but I can't figure out how to put all the pieces together."

He devoured everything that Gabriela put in front of him: two fried eggs, a pork chop and half a loaf of bread.

"So, what's going on?" she asked.

He told her what had happened the previous night. She listened attentively across from him at the table, concern wrinkling her forehead.

"The guy just vanished," Padrino said. "And I may be a man of faith, but I don't believe in people disappearing into thin air."

"You think she killed him?"

"I do."

Gabriela cocked her head.

"If I were you, I wouldn't tangle with that woman," she said. "A photo with Raúl Castro, a house in El Vedado, owner of a foreign company—she's connected, eh!"

"I'll tell Marlene Martínez what I've found. We can work together on this."

"Please, let her handle it."

Padrino's cell phone rang. He recognized Rosita's number and answered. "What's up, *mija?*"

"Something horrible!" Rosita sobbed. "I need you to come to Calixto García Hospital right now."

"Why? Are you hurt?"

"No, not me. Juan's here, as Oyá promised. But—"

She paused.

"He's dead. I want to do a ceremony to . . . to get over this once and for all. It's too much for me, Padrino! You have to come and help me!"

Padrino closed the phone and sighed heavily.

"I'll be back by noon; I promise," he said to Gabriela.

"What? You're going out again? You look so beat!"

"I know, but Rosita's my goddaughter—you know how she is."

"She always has a fart trapped up her ass," Gabriela replied, annoyed.

"I know what you mean. But she said someone was dead."

"So? All she does is work with dead people!"

"I'll just stop by to see her for a bit."

Gabriela accompanied Padrino to the VW Beetle and, before he got in, said:

"Don't go back to El Vedado, *papi.* Above all, don't go alone. You don't want to bite off more than you can chew."

Padrino was transported back to his days in that Angolan hospital, when Balbina had taken care of him. He heard his nurse's melodic, deep voice again. "*Usted no sabe en lo que se está metiendo.*" Not wanting to admit that he might be getting into deep trouble here, he pushed the thought away.

3

DON'T LET ANYONE MESS WITH YOU

The kitchen phone had rung at 7 P.M. Elsa hadn't felt like talking, but she'd seen the 034 area code of her husband's number. It was 1 A.M. for him, Seville being six hours ahead of Havana. Why was he still awake? To check on her; that was why. He had called the house, not her cell phone, to make sure she was there.

"Hello, Savarria. How are you doing, *amor*?" She always softened the use of his last name with a term of endearment.

"Not well. You know I'm not doing well."

She didn't argue. The day had drained all her energy. "What's up?"

"The doctors"—he coughed—"are a bunch of *gilipollas*. They can't find anything wrong, they say. I don't buy that. They just don't care."

The doctors had found many things wrong with him, like sky-high blood pressure and cholesterol. Obesity. Risk of another heart attack unless he lost weight. But he wouldn't give up his heavy potages, his fried pork chops or his expensive rioja wine.

"What about you?" he asked. "Not screwing around with a Cuban stud, I hope."

It was supposed to be a joke. An old, trite joke. How many times had she bitten her tongue so as not to tell him that, had she wanted to cheat on him, he would be the last *cabrón* to find out? But truth be told, she hadn't felt even remote interest in any other man until she'd seen Juan again. And then that idiot had ruined everything.

"No Cuban stud for me, Savarria," she answered with a forced laugh. "Why would I need one when I have the most wonderful husband in the world? Or at least on the Guadalquivir River shore."

"Ah, the Guadalquivir misses you, my dear, and so do I."

No, he wasn't a total asshole, just an insecure old man. One who was conscious of his age. But she wasn't in the mood to humor him right then.

"Sorry, Savarria, I've got to go. I'm getting a call from the office."

"See if there's a way you can come back to Seville soon."

"I'll try."

"Ah, wait. Emilito sent me a . . . What do you call these messages that come through the phone?"

"A text?"

"Text, whatever. It had a picture of him in a bar with a girl. Drinking. That pissed me off. Aren't we paying too much money for him to hang out in American *bars*? Shouldn't he be studying?"

"He's getting good grades. Don't worry."

"I do worry. *Nena*, that fancy-schmancy college costs three times as much as Universidad Complutense de Madrid, which I bet is every bit as good. And here, we could at least keep an eye on him."

"I *am* keeping an eye on him."

"A mother's love is blind."

Elsa pretended to take the office call she'd invented and hung up.

If Savarria ever knew. . . She had lived in fear for the first two or three years. Emilito's features had always aroused suspicions among Emilio's uppity relatives, the ones who didn't approve of his marriage to a much-younger Cuban woman. Ah, the mean aunts and uncles who whispered among themselves how "oriental" the child had turned out! Thankfully, Emilio loved Emilito and didn't pay heed to the gossip. (*A father's love must be blind too, then.*) The boy was the light of his life. He had raised him from birth, and Emilito was, for all practical and emotional purposes, his son.

But how furious Savarria would be if he ever found out the truth. If Juan had contacted Emilito and Emilito, in turn, had told his father . . . Savarria was an old-fashioned Castilian man. People talked about Latinos being *machistas*, but that was because they hadn't dealt with the descendants of the *conquistadores*, Elsa used to tell her friends. The medieval concept of honor that had inspired plays like *La perfecta casada* and *El médico de su honra*—a golden-age drama by Calderón de la Barca about the honor killing of an innocent wife—remained very much alive in Emilio's generation. If he were to find out the truth, he would certainly demand a divorce, withdraw all financial support for Emilito, kick her out of the company she'd built. And her relationship with her son might be permanently damaged, even if he did forgive her for keeping such a secret from him his entire life. No, she couldn't have that.

She tiptoed to her bedroom, where Juan's body lay on the bed. A small puddle of blood had started to form around it.

She imagined Savarria's reaction to the scene. What would anger him more, that she had killed a man or that she had almost slept with him?

She retreated to the kitchen, sobbing. It all had happened so fast. When Juan had shown up at her house, she'd foolishly let him in because, even after all these years, she still loved him, and part of her had wanted to know if those feelings existed on his end too. But, of course, he had seen what Victoria had in those pictures, what anyone who knew their history could plainly see. How stupid of her to have left them out in the open.

Then she thought she had regained control. Juan seemed to accept her reasons for keeping quiet. Said he still loved her too. It seemed as if their relationship might actually have a chance—Savarria was nearing the end, wasn't he? She had given in to impulse and hurried to change into her most alluring lingerie, those pretty undies she hadn't worn in years, when she caught Juan copying her son's address. Sneaky *hijo de puta*. She lost it. Too bad the gun was right there in front of her, begging to be shot. Had she thought about it, she wouldn't have—

But it wasn't her fault! What had her father said? "Don't let anyone mess with you . . . Make them respect you." Well, Juan had been messing with her. Worse, messing with her son's life. No, it didn't matter that he was *Juan's* son too. Juan hadn't done a thing for the kid, hadn't even known he'd existed until that day. She had the right to protect Emilito. Her father, the *pincho*, would have approved. Juan had been betraying her. Again. Getting ready to ruin her life again, just as he had done twenty years before. She had been justified, had she not?

She closed her eyes, her memory, her heart. This wasn't about her. Her life, or at least the best part of it, had long been over. She had to think of Emilito. She would die for him, and she would kill for him. She had done it twice and would as many more times as she needed to.

Elsa lifted Juan's body and placed it, wrapped in the sheets and bedspread, inside the huge duffel bag that she had brought from Cambridge. *Coño*, he was heavy! Had she not been in such good shape, she would have never been able to carry it all by herself. Eduardo, her security guard, might have come to her rescue—for a price. But having an accomplice would have made the whole thing much more difficult and dangerous. It was safer to act alone.

She began to drag the bag outside. El Camino de Santiago had taught her the importance of keeping her strength up and using her body wisely. She thought it blasphemous to flashback to that supposedly sacred experience in such an unholy moment, but shrugged. If needed, she would walk El Camino once more as penance for her crime. But now she needed to focus on the task at hand.

She left the house at 4 A.M. with Juan's body in the trunk of her car, still inside the large duffel bag to avoid getting blood all over the car. She had changed into a brown sweat suit and comfortable shoes. She was shaking. As she sped out of her driveway, she thought she saw a shadow near the front entrance, but dismissed the idea. Someone out at that hour? It had to be nerves.

Her original plan had been to drop the body in Playas del Este, as far as possible from Havana. She had written a vague note suggesting it was suicide. But then she had turned onto Twenty-Third Street, seen the icy-blue light of a cruiser driving toward the Malecón and panicked. What if she was stopped for something or for no reason at all? *We need to look inside your trunk*, compañera.

A light rain was falling, and the streets were empty. She was passing by El Quijote Park, and the idea of leaving Juan's body there came as a sudden inspiration. It would look like a copycat of the suicide that had made people start calling the place El Parque del Suicida—including the note and the absence of the weapon. She stopped the car, took Juan's body out and left it there under the soft, cleansing rain. She got rid of the bloodstained duffel bag, sheets and bedspread in a dumpster in Marianao.

Before leaving the house, she had made sure to remove Juan's wallet from his pocket. She threw it into a different dumpster. In the same pocket, she had found a gold wedding ring, which she disposed of as well, wondering why he hadn't been wearing it. Then she spent a couple hours driving around the city in a haze, trying to soothe her frayed nerves.

At a quarter to eight, she proceeded to her office and took care of the most urgent affairs of Savarria and Co., trying to ignore Juan's and Victoria's faces, which seemed to peek gloomily at her from behind the assorted documents and from her computer screen.

Ay, Victoria! But that had been different. An accident. Besides, Elsa didn't even remember exactly what had happened. She had done her best to rid herself of the memory. Could she erase this one too?

Her thoughts were cut short by a call from her Villa Clara

manager. Had she authorized a new shipment of computers to the Universidad de Ciencias Médicas? No, not yet. She couldn't concentrate that day, though, and didn't want to make any rushed decisions.

"Let's hold off for now and discuss it tomorrow," she told him.

At least she was still a good businesswoman.

THE MEDAL OF SAN LÁZARO

When Padrino arrived at Calixto García Hospital, he saw a body lying on a stretcher. It was the very same man he'd seen going into Elsa's house the day before. But he didn't have time to ask questions. He had barely begun to comfort Rosita when a hospital employee came in followed by a man and two women. One was tall and clearly not a Cuban national.

"Yes, that's my husband," the foreign woman said in accented Spanish.

A nurse tapped Rosita on the shoulder. "*Compañera*, you have to go."

Padrino took his goddaughter out of the room and insisted on driving her home. Rosita was silent.

"Are you okay, *mija*?" Padrino asked several times.

She just stared at the streets and said nothing.

"The *orishas* work in strange ways," she mumbled at last. "When I was getting interested in someone else, Oyá sent Juan to me, as she had promised. But now he's dead."

"So that guy was—"

"The man I thought was my 'one and only' for twenty years. Funny that this happened right after I realized there's no such thing as a 'one and only.' Sort of tragic, you know?"

She didn't speak again until Padrino stopped in front of her house.

Her living and dining room were one large combined space inhabited by a green vinyl sofa with yellow patches, an oak table with three chairs that didn't match, a 1957 blue Frigidaire and a black-and-white Russian TV that didn't work. The kitchen was small, fully occupied by an iron stove and a collection of greasy pots on a cement counter. Ten steps led to the bedroom upstairs, a *barbacoa*.

A red ceramic bowl behind the door was a sign of respect to the *orisha* Elegguá. On a round glass table were statuettes of the Virgin of Charity and the Virgin of Regla. A framed print of Saint Thérèse of Lisieux represented Oyá. Marigolds, bananas, roses, oranges and peacock feathers were scattered around them. A copy of *El Monte* lay on the table.

Rosita sank down onto the sofa, staring straight ahead. Padrino went over to the kitchen and boiled water for chamomile tea. When he presented Rosita with a full glass, she took a sip of the sweet-smelling liquid and said, "I'm not even *that* sad. Can you believe it? I'm in shock but not sad." She leaned her head back. "Juan still loved Elsa, Padrino. He didn't come back for me. He came back for her."

Padrino sat next to his goddaughter. "*Mija*, tell me about Elsa. Have you known her a long time?"

"I never told you? I stole Juan from her. Well, not exactly, but I tried."

She told Padrino the story of her affair with Juan, most of

which Padrino already knew. And then she got to their run-in at the cemetery.

"After I told him what I'd done, he stormed off," she said. "He was so mad at me! I'm sure he went looking for her right away."

She was right on that front, Padrino thought.

"Do you think," he asked, "she had any reason to kill him?"

Rosita shook her head, surprised.

"Why, Padrino? No, I believe he committed suicide, like he wrote in his note. He probably tried to win her back and got rejected, so he went and shot himself."

"He was that crazy about her?"

"Yes. I saw it in his eyes. He loved her as much as I loved him all those years."

Padrino cleared his throat. He was hesitant to bring up Víctor, given her state. But it had to be done at some point.

"Do you happen to know a Victoria Sunrise?" he asked. "Her real name was Víctor."

She looked at him, startled. "Yes, she's a friend. Why?"

"Was he—she friends with Juan too?"

"They were close in college. Some people said they were more than friends. I wondered about it too, but then Juan showed me that he was a real man. Why?"

"Did Elsa know Víctor? I mean Victoria."

She had perked up. "We all took theater classes together, so I imagine she did. Yes, she must have, especially since she was dating Juan. Why do you ask?"

He didn't answer her question. "When was the last time you saw Victoria?"

"Last month, when she hired me to do makeup for a few

performers at Café Arabia. But what does she have to do with anything?"

"She was killed three days ago."

Rosita gasped. "What? Ay, no! Who did it?"

"I'm trying to figure that out."

She grabbed Padrino's hand so hard that it hurt.

"First Victoria, then Juan," she whispered. "It's weird."

"Do you know of anybody who might have wanted to harm Victoria?"

She began to rock herself on the sofa, her eyes closed.

"After I dropped out of college, we didn't see each other for several years. One day, I went to Café Arabia to ask if they wanted a stylist for their shows. The woman I talked to turned out to be Víctor. I wouldn't have recognized him. She insisted I call her Victoria and always wanted to have 'girl talks' with me. Poor Victoria. Poor Juan. This is a crazy world, isn't it?"

Padrino waited a few seconds before asking, "Is it possible that Elsa . . . could have killed Victoria?"

"No, Padrino, I don't think so." Rosita opened her eyes and looked at him with a baffled expression. "Elsa has everything—she has no reason to kill anyone. In all honesty, I hate that woman, but I can't imagine her doing that."

Padrino didn't press the issue. When Rosita complained of a headache, he suggested she take a nap.

"I need to go back to the office." She rubbed her eyes. "I had just arranged with the Pathology Department to deliver a body when I found out—"

"At least lie down for a bit. I'll give you a ride to the cemetery afterward."

"I appreciate it. The last thing I want is to get on a crowded bus today."

Rosita slowly climbed the wooden steps that led to the *barbacoa*. She slept in a single bed covered in a lacy pink bedspread. The nightstand was painted pink as well. On top of it was a heavy chain with an even heavier medal of Babalú Ayé. She buried her head in her pillow and sobbed for a while. A black cat jumped onto the bed, and she started scratching his ears.

"Elegguá, you're going to like those 'rice with everything' leftovers that I forgot to give you last night," she whispered.

The cat purred contentedly and curled up next to her.

Half an hour later, Padrino brought her more chamomile tea. He said a prayer with his hand on his goddaughter's forehead. When it was over, she smiled.

"I'm feeling better," she said.

"The *orishas* always help."

She handed him the medal. "That's for you, Padrino. A client gave it to me as part of her payment. It's her husband I'm taking care of today."

"Thanks."

He put it on. The medal knocked against his Santería necklaces, and its chain was so bulky that it hurt his neck. But he didn't want to offend Rosita, so he kept it.

She looked at her watch.

"It's getting late, Padrino. I need to start working on that poor guy. I also want to be available if they ask me for help with Juan."

"*Ay, mija.*"

"It's the least I can do. To close a chapter in my life, you know? In a way, his death has freed me."

After dropping off Rosita at the cemetery main gate, Padrino called Marlene Martínez, but was told that she was at a meeting with La Seguridad, which could take hours, for all he knew.

He remembered Gabriela's advice not to mess with Elsa but dismissed it. He was sure now that she had killed Juan and suspected she also had something to do with Víctor's death. If he could solve the case by himself, it would make things so much easier for Pepito! Besides, he didn't want to waste Marlene's time. And who was afraid of Elsa's connection with Raúl Castro? *Carajo*, not him! He drove back to El Vedado.

Much later, Padrino would say that his second mistake had been ignoring his wife's words.

5

THE SACRIFICES WE MAKE FOR OUR CHILDREN

Elsa got back home at five-thirty in the afternoon. She was wearing the same clothes she had put on early that morning, the brown sweat suit and Nike tennis shoes. Far from her usual executive-chic style, but the Lord—or *el diablo*—knew she had been too preoccupied to worry about looking fashionable.

She drove the car into the garage and went outside and across the porch to the main door. The garage had been built after Emilio had bought the house. She'd been meaning to add another entrance that connected the garage to the kitchen. Would she have the chance to do that or any of the other renovations she'd been planning recently? Would life be the same after this, or would someone discover the horrible things she'd done?

Her mind flashed back to the man who had called her, wanting to talk about Vic's death. She hadn't thought of him since. But he'd said he wasn't a cop and had probably been telling the truth. The Cuban police didn't call you politely in advance to find out what you knew about a case. They showed up at your house and arrested you.

She unlocked the door. The first thing she noticed was that the security system, which she had never trusted—why had they ever chosen to have it installed by a Cuban electrician?—was off. Had she left it like that? Every day before going to the office, she made sure to turn on the alarm. But she'd left in such a hurry that morning that she could easily have overlooked the detail.

She went back to the garage and retrieved the gun. She had considered disposing of it, but had decided to keep it just in case. She also took out her cell phone and thought of calling the nearest Unidad, but changed her mind about that as well. Given the circumstances, inviting the police for a visit wasn't a wise idea. She went into the house, gun ready in a lightly trembling hand.

The living room looked the same as usual. The TV was in its proper place, and nothing seemed to have been touched or moved. She walked carefully from the living room to the kitchen and found everything as she had left it. She went into the master bedroom, still tense. She saw the naked mattress—she had to replace the sheets. The former contents of the duffel bag remained on the floor where she had scattered them when she'd emptied it.

She inspected the closet. Her clothes, perfumes, shoes and purses were all there. The Rolex that Emilio had bought her for their fifteenth wedding anniversary was gleaming in its box. Even her diamond rings were there. Nobody had been in the house. She had forgotten to turn on the alarm, and that was that.

More confident now, she walked to what had been her son's bedroom when he was growing up. It looked as it had in the months since he'd left, from the photos of Industriales baseball players to his old DVD collection and the small TV.

She entered her home office. Her computer, a Dell laptop,

didn't appear to have been touched, but her mouse, which was always on the left side, had been moved to the right and placed too close to the keyboard.

If the alarm hadn't been off, she doubted she would have paid much attention to this. But she knew now that someone had been there. What if that shadow she thought she'd seen that morning hadn't been her imagination? What if that guy who had called her about Vic's death had shown up? Or sent someone to watch her? Had they broken into her house? She needed to move fast.

She called Iberia Airlines and asked for a ticket to Seville that night.

"I have an emergency at home," she told the office clerk, who knew her. "My husband is sick and needs me to be there as soon as I can."

"I'm sorry, Señora Elsa. Let me see what I can do. No, there are no more flights departing today. They all leave tomorrow afternoon."

"What time?"

"There's one for Madrid leaving at two P.M. That's the best we can do. And it will have to be first class."

"Of course."

"What date will the return ticket be for?"

Elsa massaged the back of her neck. "Let's make it just one way for now."

After buying the ticket, she hung up, went back to her bedroom, took a Louis Vuitton suitcase out of the closet and started filling it with her favorite pieces of clothing. In her handbag she placed the Rolex, her jewelry and her Spanish and Cuban passports. She returned to the office, turned on the computer and logged into her Gmail account. The e-ticket was already there.

She was getting ready to print it when the doorbell made her jump. She retrieved the handgun and placed it in the right back pocket of her sweat suit. She looked through the peephole and saw a man dressed in white with Santería beads and a big round medal around his neck. This seemed like the guy who had stopped by the office asking for her, based on her secretary's description. A mulatto *santero*. What did he want, and how the hell had he gotten her address? Ah, *las chismosas*, those gossips who worked for her! She would fire them both as soon as she got to Seville.

Then she glanced at the coatrack. Her coat was still there, but what about her red umbrella? The one she had taken when she'd gone to see Vic. It was gone. Or maybe she'd put it somewhere else. Where, *carajo*? She should've gotten rid of it before. But she didn't think like a killer. Because she wasn't one! At least, she hadn't been then . . . It had all been just an accident. God, or the *orishas* if they existed, knew that.

The doorbell rang again. She hesitated, but finally opened the door. "Yes, who are you?"

The question came out ruder than Elsa had intended, but she didn't attempt to soften it with even the hint of a smile.

"I'm the one who called and spoke with you earlier," the man said. "My name is Leonel Fábregas, but most of my friends and colleagues know me as Padrino. I just want to talk to you for a few minutes."

Elsa sized him up. She saw a tired older man who, judging by his attire, wasn't well off. Not the kind of person she would usually welcome into her house, but he possessed a certain self-assuredness and remotely military air that reminded her of her father and made her say, "Okay, you can come in for a couple minutes. But I don't have a lot of time. I'm leaving on a trip tomorrow."

She silently cursed herself for mentioning her plans. Damn if she didn't have reason to be nervous, but she needed to watch what she said.

The guy didn't look around the living room like most visitors, nor did he show any signs of being impressed by its luxury. In fact, he moved with the aplomb of someone who had been there before. She stared at him, a slow sense of rage building.

"I'm investigating Víctor Pérez Díaz's death, as I told you on the phone yesterday," he said.

"And I told you I hadn't seen her in ages," she replied. "So why are you here?"

"Because I'm now concerned about Juan Chiong's death as well. And I'm working with the police on it."

"You said you weren't affiliated with them earlier."

"I am now. Lieutenant Marlene Martínez, who's handling Víctor Pérez's case, brought me in after his friend was found dead."

Marlene Martínez. Juan had mentioned that name—the big-assed officer. Elsa remembered because the thought of Juan admiring another woman's butt had made her jealous. The *santero* wasn't bluffing.

"Juan Chiong entered this house yesterday afternoon and didn't come out," he said matter-of-factly. "You left today at four A.M. in your car. This morning, his body was discovered in El Quijote Park. I thought you might like to tell me something about this before I report my findings to Lieutenant Martínez."

Elsa let her features melt into calm. "Please, have a seat. I can explain everything. I don't want you getting the wrong idea about me."

She sat down on the sofa.

"I have nothing to hide," she went on. "Juan Chiong and I have a long history. We met in college. We were sweethearts, but he cheated on me." She paused for effect and added, "He ended up leaving without me for America with a friend of his and Víctor's."

She looked straight at the man, knowing she had him. The look in his eyes told her that he was absorbed in her story. That attentiveness made people vulnerable. She had captured her audience, the thing her old ISA instructors had always said she was so bad at doing. She didn't waste a second. Sporting a winning smile, she took the handgun from her pocket and shot him in the center of his chest. It was at such short range she didn't even need to aim. He fell as a red stain spread slowly over his white shirt, the beads of his broken Santería necklace lying scattered on the floor.

Hands on the wheel of her Lexus, Elsa drove through scarce traffic. In the back seat, Padrino's body lay wrapped in three sheets.

Would this nightmare ever end? How many more lives would a single lie, one she had told to protect her son, cost? She glanced behind her, fearing she had heard a soft sigh.

No, the man was dead. She'd checked for a pulse before dragging him to the car. It had been eight o'clock when she'd loaded his body into the Lexus. Had the neighbors noticed? She should've waited until it was darker out, but had been too scared to keep him in the house.

Elsa wondered if she'd been too impulsive. As usual. Even if the guy had told others what he'd seen, what concrete proof did he have? But he knew that officer, Martínez! He was working with the police, maybe even with La Seguridad. The revelations he could have made were more dangerous than what Juan could have revealed. Juan could have jeopardized her finances, but the *santero* could have had her sent to jail or, worse, the *paredón*, the firing squad the Cuban government didn't shy away from using.

Where to dispose of him . . . Leaving Juan's body in El Quijote Park had clearly been a mistake. She should've found a more distant, isolated place. But she reminded herself she wasn't a professional criminal, even if she was starting to feel like one.

She would be more careful this time. She thought of El Bosque de la Habana, a green area on the banks of the Almendares River. To the south of the Almendares Park, it wasn't really a forest, but looked like one with its magueys and hundred-year-old ceiba trees, huge vines hanging from them, lush tropical vegetation everywhere and the Almendares River meandering through. During the day, tourists arrived in their *almendrones* to take pictures of the river and walk around—she had once taken a couple of Spaniards who'd wanted to get lost in a "Cuban jungle" there—and *santeros* often used the area for ceremonies. But after dark, it was deserted.

She passed by the zoological garden, entered the *bosque* and parked under a big ceiba like the one outside her own house. The place was desolate. The sky was finally dark, and the crescent moon lit the trees. The perfect scene for a thriller movie, Elsa thought. She had always dreamt of acting in one, but not as the villain. She opened the back car door and dragged Padrino's body out. It wasn't rigid yet and seemed too warm. She felt for his heart, but a sticky, hot liquid bathed her right hand. Frightened and nauseated, she wiped her hand on her pants and used her foot to push the body under the ceiba, as far as possible from the road. Even if by some miracle he *was* still alive, he would be dead by the time anyone found him.

She thought of taking his wallet so he wouldn't be immediately identified and linked to her before she left. (Not that the tactic had worked with Juan. How had they figured out who he was so quickly?) Though she didn't believe in higher beings, the Santería clutter he had around his neck creeped her out, and she preferred not to touch it. A cursory inspection of his pockets revealed a cell phone, the ID card Cubans were required to carry at all times and an expired police badge. She took them with her.

How had it come to this? She kept asking herself the question. But as with Juan, she'd had no choice. The guy was in cahoots with the police. He knew the officer who had interrogated Juan. It had been within his power to have her arrested. She imagined the sorrow and disappointment her father, the *pincho*, and her young son would feel if she were to end up behind bars, accused of killing a man. Or two.

This had all been a series of mistakes and bad luck, starting with Vic's death. No point in trying to lock away the memories any longer. They came rushing back, as if a dam had been broken in Elsa's mind. Once again, she heard Vic's question, the one that had been replaying in her head for days: "Why won't you help a friend in need? All you have to do is make a quick call to Almodóvar and get me the audition."

They had been sitting in Vic's bedroom while the pork was

roasting in the oven. Elsa had looked distractedly at the old Avon bottles on the dresser. The entire apartment smelled of fat, which was making her nauseated. Vic chatted nonstop, but Elsa barely answered. The short walk from the *parqueadero* to the building had put her in a foul mood. The streets had been full of potholes and cracks. And why weren't there awnings, as there were in Seville, to protect people from the sun and the rain? She had left her umbrella in the hallway and draped her coat over the shower rod to let it drip-dry.

Vic had been looking for a wig she wanted to show Elsa. It was platinum blonde and longer than Vic's hair underneath. She put it on, walked into the little bathroom and admired herself in the mirror.

"What do you think?" she asked.

"Too flashy," Elsa said.

Vic took it off and left it on the wicker chair, carefully placing it on top of the towels.

"Didn't you say that Almodóvar offered you a role once?" she insisted. "He could do the same for me. I have talent."

Elsa rolled her eyes. "That was ages ago. The role offer, I mean. I haven't seen Almodóvar in years. He probably doesn't even remember me."

It wasn't true; they still exchanged Christmas postcards. But Vic was too old for the industry. Elsa wasn't going to tell her that, though. She wasn't *that* mean.

"Well, it's up to you," Vic said. "But you don't help me, see if I help you."

Annoyed, Elsa walked into the bathroom and grabbed her coat, ready to leave. What a mistake it had been to come here.

"When in the hell have you ever helped me?" she spat.

Vic put her hands on her hips. Her red nails looked to Elsa like drops of blood on her big fingers.

"This entire time, with my silence," Vic said.

"Don't be such a *cabrón!*"

"*Cabrona.*"

Vic chuckled. Was she making fun of her? Blinded by rage, Elsa slapped her. Vic slapped her back. Hard.

"Get out of my house!" Vic yelled. "You can't come in here to abuse me, *puta*. Who do you think you are?"

Elsa pushed her against the sink. Vic fell backward, the back of her head hitting the corner of the wall-mounted cabinet. She collapsed to the floor. The mirror that was attached to the cabinet door came unglued and crashed against the sink, shards scattering everywhere. Horrified, Elsa hurried to help Vic.

"I'm so sorry! I didn't mean to—"

Elsa thought of bringing her to the car, taking her to a hospital, but then realized it was too late. Vic's face was congealed in a sarcastic smile, and she wasn't moving. Her heavily made-up eyes were locked on to Elsa with a mix of surprise and reproach.

Elsa fled, the smell of pork roast chasing her all the way to the hallway. She retrieved her umbrella and hurried to the street. She got into the car and began to drive around, crying in disbelief. Had she really killed Vic? It hadn't been intentional. It had just been an accident. Why had she run away? She should have called a hospital, explained what had happened. But what if they blamed her?

By the time she returned to the neighborhood, she had had a change of heart. She would call a hospital, maybe say that she had simply found Victoria's body. But what if she *wasn't* dead, just unconscious? She parked a short distance from the building and got out of her car. Then she saw the throng of people gathered outside. They had already found Vic and were hauling off Juan and a younger man. It was too late . . .

But all of that was over. Nothing would bring Vic or Juan or this guy—she didn't even remember his name—back. *A lo hecho, pecho.* What was done was done.

On her way back to El Vedado, she took a detour to El Fanguito, one of Havana's poorest neighborhoods, and dropped the dead man's belongings in a rusty dumpster covered in flies. As she sped away from the slum, she thought of Emilito, poring over a science book in his MIT dorm.

"The sacrifices we make for our children," she whispered to the crescent moon.

6

THE UGLY *AMERICANA*

fter the woman who had been bent over Juan's body had been practically dragged out of the room by the man in white, Sharon had officially identified her husband's body. Juan was naked except for a white towel covering his privates. His chest was still stained from the blood he had lost. The hole left by the bullet was on his left side, as if the shooter had aimed to make sure the bullet went straight through his heart.

It didn't occur to her until later that she should find out who the woman was. An old classmate or acquaintance of Juan's? The mortician? In the meantime, Agent Alicia had gotten a call on her cell phone, and she and her partner left the room.

Alone with Juan, Sharon touched his face. He looked placid and happy. Happier, in fact, than he'd been while alive. At peace. She caressed his neck, his arms and hands but avoided his chest area. She was still afraid of hurting him. She noticed that he didn't have his wedding ring on. The nurses had probably removed it when they'd taken his clothes.

When the Seguridad agents came back, looking annoyed, she

told them everything she knew about Juan's activities, which was concrete up to the point when he had left the hotel.

"Do you have anything with his signature on it?" Agent Pedro asked. "A driver's license?"

"I have both his passports here," Sharon said, remembering she had put them in her purse to take them to Unidad 15.

She opened her purse and retrieved them. The agents looked at the signature pages, comparing them to the writing on a scrap of paper—his suicide note. Sharon stared at it. The handwriting didn't look identical to the signature on his passports, but it wasn't totally different either. It was so hard to tell from just a scribble.

"Do you think this is his handwriting?" Agent Alicia asked.

Sharon struggled to remember a time Juan had handwritten her a note. It was so rare nowadays, with texting and email.

"I—I don't know," she answered. "But I can't imagine a reason for him to—he wasn't depressed, for sure."

"You mentioned he was deeply affected by his friend's death," Agent Pedro said.

"Well, yes, but more so because he was there when the body was found, then arrested—"

"But he was treated properly, wasn't he?" he interrupted her.

"Yes," Sharon agreed nervously.

"We have to look at the whole picture," Agent Pedro said. "His friend's death, a night at the police station, being back in his beloved home country after so many years—all of these are emotional triggers."

Sharon frowned. Juan had never referred to Cuba as his "beloved" anything.

"It's a lot," Agent Pedro went on. "You also said that he had visited his grandmother, who was very sick."

"Yes. I think she has Alzheimer's."

"See? When you put it all together, *compañera*," Agent Pedro concluded, "it makes sense to believe that your husband, in a moment of grief, might take his own life."

Sharon had the impression that he was trying to lead her to that conclusion. What had changed when they'd left just a moment ago? Agent Alicia hadn't seemed convinced it was suicide during their ride from the hotel. Sharon remembered her last conversation with Juan, his joke about the *unidad* smell. No doubt he had been sad about Víctor, but not suicidal. She knew him at least that well.

"What about his friend?" she dared to ask. "Couldn't his death and Juan's be related?"

"No!" the Seguridad agents answered at once.

"Despite the efforts of our revolutionary government to integrate gay citizens into society, they still have their—issues," Agent Alicia said. "Citizen Pérez Díaz's killer has already been caught. That had nothing to do with your husband's suicide."

Sharon burst into tears. She recalled how emotional Juan had been about the trip, how he'd tried at first to travel alone. Would things have gone differently if she hadn't insisted on coming with him? Would he still be alive? The thought that she would never see him again, never hear *"amor"* in his Cuban accent again, sank in. She had lost him.

She couldn't stop crying. Agent Alicia left and came back with a nurse, who took Sharon to another aseptic little room. The nurse gave her a pill, and Sharon swallowed it without even asking what it was.

"I'm sorry you're going through this," Agent Alicia said.

"Would you like to talk to a counselor? We have some very good ones."

"No, thank you," Sharon whispered. "Please, just let me see my husband once more."

The Seguridad agents waited outside.

"Marlene Martínez is having a fit over the whole thing," Agent Alicia said to her partner. "I just talked to her."

"She thinks there's a connection, eh?"

"So do I." She shrugged. "And so do you."

Agent Pedro nodded.

"But the higher-ups were clear—go with the suicide theory, and keep things quiet. A couple years back we had that Canadian who fell off the balcony, now this. If tourists start to think it's not safe to come here, it'll kill the economy."

"Which is just starting to come back."

"Right. Now we need his wife out of here. I hope she doesn't stay long enough for the independent journalists to interview her."

"She'll probably want to take the body back home."

"Maybe not. Remember that woman who identified him, the mortician? She offered to take care of everything herself. Maybe she can convince the Yuma to leave before shit hits the fan."

"Here she comes. Let's take her back to the hotel."

When Sharon finally got a hold of an Interests Section officer, he assured her that he would prepare a Report of Death of an American Citizen Abroad, which she could use for legal purposes in Albuquerque. As for returning Juan's remains, the man, though sympathetic, wasn't encouraging.

"If an official investigation is still taking place, that's going to be lengthy," he said.

They were dealing with a similar case, he mentioned, an elderly Cuban American who had died in a car accident almost two months earlier while visiting his homeland, whom his family insisted on burying in Miami.

"It's been an ordeal," the man said. "They don't have the ten thousand dollars that the process costs and were asked to fill out so many papers that the body's still in Cuba. We've tried to help, but unless you feel very strongly about it, I recommend you find another way."

"Like what?"

"Cremation, perhaps?"

She might have agreed to it, but as soon as she lay on the bed, hoping to get some rest, she received a phone call from Necrological Services. The caller, a woman with a high-pitched voice, explained that the Chiong family had a mausoleum in Havana. Would Sharon like to bury her husband there?

"I'd rather cremate him," she said.

"Oh, are you sure? That's very much against Cuban tradition!" the woman said reprovingly. "We can do that if you want to, but it's going to take time."

"And how long will the burial take?"

There was a brief silence.

"In both cases, it may take several weeks, even months," the woman said. "There's an ongoing investigation. I just wanted to know in order to be ready when the time comes."

At this point, Sharon was too overwhelmed to make the decision. "Let me think about it."

The woman left a number and hung up. Sharon began to

connect loose threads. *Necrological Services?* Had that been the voice of the mortician who'd claimed to be Juan's classmate, the one who had first identified him?

Not a minute had passed before she got another call, this time from Agent Alicia. Was Sharon feeling better? Did she want to see a doctor, a psychologist, anyone? No? Well, then they would discuss what to do with the body, if she could handle it.

"Here, even when a death is ruled a suicide, we have to follow a lengthy protocol," Agent Alicia said. "Once it's over, if your husband has relatives who can help with the burial . . ."

"The only relative he has left is his grandmother," Sharon answered. "Based on what he told me, she's too old and sick to help. But a lady from the Necrological Services just called and said that his family had a mausoleum here."

"Ah, that's excellent! That will make things much easier for you. When are you leaving?"

"Our—my return ticket is for Tuesday."

"I imagine you might want to get home sooner."

Sharon froze. The woman was trying to get rid of her, get her off the island. Who did they think she was, some stupid American? She might've acted like one during this disastrous trip, trying to be kind and understanding, overly politically correct, and it hadn't helped her or Juan. It was time for a change. She would summon the ugly *americana* for the truly deserving.

"I won't be leaving Cuba until I find out *exactly* what happened to my husband," she said firmly and hung up on Agent Alicia.

Sharon made two more calls. One was to the Necrological Services employee.

"Let me know when the burial is taking place," Sharon said.

"I don't care if I have to wait a month or a year. I'm willing to spend as much time as needed here."

"Ah, well . . ." the woman stuttered, apparently surprised by the change in attitude. "As it happens, I've just heard from La Seguridad, and they've changed plans."

Aha, Sharon thought.

"They are going to bring me the body tomorrow morning."

"I want to be there."

The silence on the other side wasn't long.

"I understand," the Necrological Services person said in a kind tone. "It's your right, Señora. Do you know how to get to the Colón Cemetery? I can give you directions if you don't."

"I'll take a taxi."

"Okay. Be here at four tomorrow."

The second call was to Unidad 15. Lieutenant Martínez was in a meeting. Sharon gave her cell number to the clerk.

"I am Juan Chiong's wife," she said. "Actually, his widow. Tell Lieutenant Martínez that my husband has been murdered and I expect the Cuban Revolutionary Police to do something about it."

"Ah, uh . . . Okay, *compañera*. I mean, Señora. I will."

Sharon felt better. She would stick to her guns. Her return ticket could be changed. She would call Sonya if necessary. The Interests Section would have to back her up; that was what it was there for. She opened the bottle of Havana Club Siete Años and drank to Juan's memory. She refused to cry. She couldn't bring him back, but she would make sure that justice was done.

7

RED AND YELLOW

Gutiz el Guardabosque, the Bosque de la Habana's only ranger, started his day at 5 A.M. His first task was to collect the park's litter from the previous day. There was always plenty.

These dirty Habaneros, thought Gutiz, who was from Oriente. Hadn't anybody taught them that it was wrong to discard beer bottles, old newspapers, cigarette wrappings, empty cans, dirty condoms and worse in the forest, spoiling the sacred beauty of nature?

He also found sacrifices of chickens and goats and bananas tied with red ribbons but didn't mind the offerings to the *orishas*. As a San Lázaro devotee himself, he disposed of them with due respect. "But look at this," he grumbled, picking up a bloody sanitary towel with his work glove and dropping it into his metal cart. Was there no limit to Habaneros' *cochinerías*?

He thought he heard a faint noise coming from under a ceiba. Had someone abandoned another dog or cat? Unscrupulous people sometimes used the *bosque* to get rid of unwanted animals. He had already rescued three old mutts and a litter of kittens left to die in the forest. People who did that, he told himself as he walked toward the noise, had no soul.

But there was no house pet this time. Under the ceiba, a man dressed in white was clutching his chest. His shirt and pants were soaked in dried blood.

Gutiz knelt next to him. "Brother, what happened to you?"

"The police," the man whispered. "Call Unidad 15. This is—a life or death matter."

"It surely is for you!"

Gutiz helped the man sit up against the ceiba and noticed that a medal around his neck had been badly damaged. The ranger took off his own shirt and wrapped it around the man's chest to contain the hemorrhage.

"Stay put," Gutiz said. "I'm going to get you an ambulance right now."

The man couldn't hear him. He had fainted. Gutiz took one last look at him and ran to the *bosque* entrance, crying out for help.

Padrino's tongue felt swollen, like a wet sponge. Thirsty and dizzy, he found himself in a tight space moving unpredictably. He tried to turn around but couldn't. He realized he was on a stretcher.

"Don't move, *compañero*," said the nurse sitting next to him in the ambulance. "I don't want you losing more blood."

The memory of what had happened came back to him slowly. He had been shot. By Elsa, the woman with the red umbrella who had killed Rosita's boyfriend and possibly Víctor Pérez Díaz. That woman had cojones.

How right his wife had been. "You don't want to bite off more than you can chew," she had said. Well, *he* had been chewed and spit out. He needed to tell Marlene. Now. Was Elsa still in the country? What had she said about traveling the next day? That was . . . today.

Padrino managed a glimpse at the nurse's watch. Five to six. Marlene wouldn't be in her office yet. He felt a sting in his chest, closed his eyes and passed out.

When he came to, red and yellow lights flashed under his eyelids. The colors of fire, following Oyá's purple shades on the spirit's journey to the afterlife. Ah, this time he was dead for good, not like in Angola! He had missed passing through the Queen of Bones' domain. He wasn't sorry, though. Full of skeletons, worms and oozy things, it wasn't a restful place for traveling souls. But these bright, happy colors marked the advent of the new life that awaited him in the land of the other *orishas*. Would Yemayá, his patron saint and Santería mother, be waiting for him?

He opened his eyes. Yes, Yemayá was there! All those years as a faithful devotee of la Virgen de Regla hadn't been in vain. He didn't need to worry about worldly affairs anymore. Pepito, Elsa, Marlene, even his wife belonged to another realm now. He had arrived in a place with no crime, only peace. Yemayá herself, with her honey-caramel skin and big liquid eyes, was standing in front of him.

"*A gua wa o to, Omo Yemayá,*" he attempted to say.

She got closer. The *orisha* smelled of gardenia and, oddly, rubbing alcohol.

"Can you hear me, *compañero*?" she asked.

Compañero? That wasn't an *orisha*'s word. Then he noticed that Yemayá was wearing a starched medical gown. In one hand, she held the pencil-thin flashlight she had just shined in his eyes. In the other, she had what looked like a charred chip. He wasn't in Ile-Ife but on a hospital bed. He had survived. The wound on his chest, now bandaged, began to hurt again.

"You're stable now, but we'll need to monitor your vitals for at least a couple of days," the doctor said.

He exhaled heavily.

"Do you know what this is?" She showed him the round metal chip.

Padrino shook his head no.

"It saved your life," she said. "You were wearing this medal, and it absorbed enough impact from the bullet that it didn't kill you. You're a lucky man!"

The San Lázaro medal that Rosita had given him. He remembered it now—and how much he had disliked it at first because it was so huge. But the heavy alloy the metal was made of had provided just enough resistance to hinder the bullet from killing him. What had his goddaughter said? That the *orishas* worked in strange ways.

"You can thank your *santos*," the doctor said, lowering her voice.

Padrino thought he would need to arrange a special ceremony to honor Babalú Ayé as soon as possible. But he had to talk to Marlene first.

"What time is it?" he asked.

"Eleven o'clock," the doctor said. "You spent three hours in the operating room. But everything went well."

Was it too late? He hoped not. "I have to make a call, *Doctora*."

"You want us to call your family?"

"No, the police! Please, call Unidad 15, and ask for Lieutenant Martínez. Right now."

8

OYÁ'S PARTING GIFT

At the José Martí International Airport, Elsa waited for the passengers of the Havana-Seville flight to be called. It was 12:10. Her plane wasn't leaving until two o'clock, but she had been happy to arrive early. She had left the car keys with Eduardo, the security guard, and paid him to watch the house and take care of the Lexus in her absence. She had cleaned the back seat the best she could in the morning. In case of an investigation . . . Well, if it happened, she would be far away.

The smell of burned fat drifted from the airport cafeteria, which was selling *pan con chicharrón*, bread and pork cracklings. It was exactly how Victoria's apartment had smelled that time she . . . but soon all that would be behind her.

This was the right thing to do, move out of the damn country for good. Emilio had been talking about selling the company for a couple of years, since his heart attack. She had opposed it at first because she enjoyed managing the day-to-day operations of Savarria and Co. It gave her a pretext for going back to Cuba, where she was a woman of substance. In Spain she was still considered an immigrant, a *sudaca*, albeit with money and class. But she would spend more time in America, with Emilito. They could easily buy a house there, with the company worth at least 2 million euros. At last, she wouldn't have to deal with her lazy, gossipy, good-for-nothing Cuban employees anymore. She would be free to pursue something else. And above all, she would be safe.

Was there anything that could ever draw her back to Cuba? No, she was too afraid to ever return. The smell of the chicharrón became stronger. She walked away from it and sat on a plastic chair near the bathroom. How long until her flight? Still almost two hours! How she wished she were already nestled in her first-class seat.

A uniformed woman and a man in plain clothes entered the waiting room. Elsa's hands went cold. They looked around, then approached her with long, official strides. She wanted to run, but where would she go? She stayed put, though she knew they were coming for her.

Rosita gave the finishing touches to a discreet altar that she had built on the Formica table. It consisted of a purple cloth with a small print of Saint Thérèse of Lisieux on top and red rose petals scattered around.

La Seguridad wasn't pleased with her, but she didn't care. Following Agents Alicia and Pedro's orders, she had tried to convince Sharon to leave the country and let her take care of the burial and funeral procedures. But the American hadn't agreed. *Good for her*. Rosita wouldn't have either, had she been in her place. And Rosita had never sympathized with La Seguridad or wanted to do their dirty work.

On the floor was an oak casket with an engraved nameplate. Inside lay Juan in an elegant dark suit (the best she had in her funeral wardrobe) with a white rose pinned on his lapel. She placed his right hand on his chest, then crossed his left hand on top. It would have been nice to have had some ceremonial music—ideally, *batá* drums—to accompany him on his journey through Oyá's kingdom. Since that wasn't possible, she sang softly, "*A llorar a Papá Montero, zumba, canalla rumbero.*" That would have to suffice.

Yes, Juan was ready. But what about Victoria? In the middle of the turmoil, Rosita had forgotten her, but now recalled that she had died recently. "Killed," Padrino had said. *Siacará.* Her body hadn't been brought in, though. Rosita would have seen it. Maybe the investigation was still ongoing. She would have taken good care of Victoria too, given her a proper burial and made sure to tell all her friends.

Rosita looked at her watch. It was three-thirty. She planned to bury Juan in his family's mausoleum, though she hadn't asked permission. But who could she talk to? Abuela was too old, and the last thing she needed was to hear about her grandson's death. He didn't have other relatives, so nobody was going to complain.

Rosita had told Sharon to be there at four o'clock. That would give her time to process the paperwork. Ah, Sharon! Rosita hoped and prayed that the American had forgotten their initial encounter at the hospital, when she had come to identify her husband's body and found Rosita sobbing over it. They had been in the same room for barely a couple of minutes. She couldn't even remember Sharon's face. Oyá willing, Sharon wouldn't remember hers either. Meeting her again was a bit risky, but Rosita wanted to take a good look at the woman with whom Juan had shared the last years of his life. He hadn't loved her either, as his suicide proved. He had only ever cared for Elsa.

Rosita shrugged. Though she'd done this all out of respect for the love she'd once had for him, that love no longer existed. She was just fulfilling her duty, performing the last rites of death for him, and then she would put him out of her mind and life forever. Soon he, and the past they shared, would be six feet under. She wished she could talk to Padrino, but he hadn't answered her calls. Why did people have these expensive cell phones if they didn't bother to use them?

She surveyed the body, the casket, the wreath—the prettiest she could make in a time crunch. Everything was first-class, but she wouldn't charge Sharon a cent, even if she insisted on paying. Rosita felt sorry for the shortchanged American, having been shortchanged herself once. She still resented Elsa, who always came out on top in the battle for Juan's heart. A woman for whom things seemed to always work out, one who was never shortchanged.

But did any of that matter now? No. She and Armando had hit it off. He had invited her to dinner after Carlota had worked her magic on Rosita's hair with that Brazilian treatment, giving a beautiful shine to her tresses. The menu had featured his famous *arroz con todo*, which had turned out to be a scrumptious combination of rice, seafood, chicken, tiny meatballs, veggies and fruit in a curry-like sauce. The dessert was *arroz con leche* with raisins and small chunks of chocolate hiding under the creamy texture of the rice pudding. Armando was a master chef. They had kissed at the end of the date, and he'd tasted as delicious as his food.

She glanced at Juan's body, feeling embarrassed and triumphant at the same time. She had deprived herself of so much, waiting . . . for what?

She had wasted too many years but was off to a fresh start. Not only was she seeing Armando, but she had agreed to be Carlota's partner at Bellísima. This would be Rosita's last day at this job, though she had told Necrological Services that she would train her replacement if needed. She hoped they found one soon, because the business of death had no days off. She hoped her desertion wouldn't offend Oyá, but she had been in loyal service long enough, and there were other ways to worship. Armando was going to pick her up after Juan's burial in the Chrysler he had bought for his home-delivery venture. He was also planning to be an *almendrón* driver. What a resourceful guy he was!

A knock on the door cut her musings short. She hurried to open it, thinking it would be Sharon, but found two women dressed in gray uniforms followed by two men carrying an unpainted pinewood casket.

"I'm Rita Álvarez," the older woman said, "and this is Sister Yuleidi. We are from El Asilo de los Ancianos Desamparados. We've been trying to contact you for two days!"

"I'm sorry," Rosita answered. "I had a personal emergency."

El Asilo de los Ancianos Desamparados. . . was that a nursing home? She tried to remember where she had heard of it.

"We're having another burial in a few minutes, but I'll squeeze you in afterward, unless you want a mass or any special services," she added. "In that case, someone will take care of it tomorrow."

"*Compañera*, we're from a Catholic nursing home," Rita said sharply. "The deceased is a ninety-year-old woman and has gotten all the masses and services needed. We just need to bury the body before it starts to smell. Here is the property deed."

Rosita could have refused to handle it, as burials were supposed to be scheduled in advance, but didn't want to argue. After all, it was her last day there. She went out and gestured for the men to bring the casket in. She opened it and gasped at the old woman's emaciated, wrinkled face, which had begun to show the first signs of decomposition. Rosita's eyes clouded with tears. "Oh, Abuela!"

In the meantime, Rita, who had looked distractedly at the oak casket, exclaimed, "*Carajo!*"

Sister Yuleidi crossed herself. "Please, Rita, watch your mouth."

"But . . . that's the guy who came to see Tonita!" Rita said.

"You knew him?" Rosita asked, confused.

"He came to El Asilo to visit his grandmother," Rita said. "She's the one we are burying."

Rosita turned to the altar and crossed herself. Oyá didn't do things halfway. She quickly examined the property deed for the Lasalle mausoleum.

"Well, since you know Juan . . ." she said, tentatively. "I was planning to bury him in his family's grave. I hope you don't object, since you're the deed holders now."

"No, no problem at all," Sister Yuleidi answered. "What a strange coincidence, indeed! And how did this man die?"

Rosita sighed. Not a long explanation, with two bodies there waiting to be entombed! Thankfully, there was another knock on the door, and a woman came in. She was tall, slender and well dressed. Their eyes met, and Rosita had a vague feeling of recognition.

"I'm Sharon," the woman said. "Juan's wife."

Rosita shook her hand. "I'm so sorry for your loss, Señora."

Rosita made brief introductions all around.

"Oh, that's Juan's grandma!" Sharon said, peeking nervously at Abuela's casket. "He told me about her. I didn't know she was so sick."

Rita and Sister Yuleidi exchanged a perplexed look. An awkward pause ensued until Rosita broke it, saying in her most professional voice, "We are ready to proceed with the burials."

They all nodded, relieved. But then she turned to Sharon and added softly, "Unless you want to spend some time alone with him?"

"Yes, thank you," Sharon whispered. "Just a moment. I would like that very much."

The men carried Abuela's coffin outside. Rosita, Rita and Sister Yuleidi followed them while Sharon said her last goodbye to Juan's corpse.

Rosita thought that Juan had not taken care of Abuela as he should have. Victoria had told her that he had phoned the nursing home only a few times over the last twenty years. Even if he had been living in La Yuma, he could have been more present in her life. Now he would spend a long time near her, atoning for his neglect. Yes, Oyá, the wise Queen of Bones, knew what she was doing. She always did.

Rita touched Rosita's arm. "Are you two related?"

"Excuse me?" Rosita blushed, thinking she was talking about Juan.

"You and that lady," Rita said. "You look a lot alike."

Rosita then realized why Juan's widow had seemed familiar. They were the same height, had the same auburn eyes. Even their hair looked similar, especially with hers more lustrous thanks to Carlota. Related, huh? Well, maybe in a way, they were.

"We've only just met," Rosita said.

Sharon came out. She was pale but calm. Four cemetery workers arrived soon and carried the two caskets to the Lasalle mausoleum. The Asilo de los Ancianos Desamparados crowd walked behind them, followed by Rosita and Sharon.

"I understand that you identified my husband in the hospital," Sharon said suddenly.

Rosita's ears burned hot. "I was so . . . so surprised when I saw him again in . . . that hospital," she stammered. "It was the last thing I expected. I'd heard he had left Cuba a long time ago."

"How did you know him?"

"We took some college classes together, back in the day."

"Did you study at the ISA too?" Sharon gave her a side-glance.

"Yes, for a while, when I was very young. Everybody knew everybody there. Juan was part of a tight-knit group."

"The Three Musketeers, right?"

Rosita coughed. She was getting antsy. How much did this woman know? Rosita then noticed Sharon was wearing a black coral necklace. Black coral, a favorite of Oyá's. That had to be a good omen.

"Yes, that's what people called them," Rosita said, trying to sound casual. "I had forgotten all about it."

She thought of adding that she and Juan had barely known each other, having had different majors, but decided against it. She didn't want to lie lest it offend Oyá—again.

"He told me a bit about his college years and the Special

Period," Sharon said. "It was one of our last conversations. He sounded . . . fine. You know, I don't believe for a second he committed suicide."

Rosita didn't answer. She did believe Juan had offed himself, but she couldn't explain the reasons to his widow. She walked faster, wishing that the whole thing was over.

Sharon's cell phone rang. She excused herself and answered. Rosita couldn't help but listen to the exchange.

"Lieutenant Martínez? Yes, thanks for calling. What? You caught *her*? It was . . . a woman?" Sharon turned completely white. "Yes, Lieutenant, I know who Elsa Dieguez is."

Rosita watched the emotions pass over Sharon's face: disbelief, horror, anger and then quiet understanding. The same feelings boiled inside her, but she willed her face to be like stone. When the call ended, Sharon was shaking. Instinctively, Rosita held her arm. They continued walking in silence and stopped by the Lasalle mausoleum.

Sister Yuleidi said a prayer. Rita and the nursing home men repeated it. Sharon mumbled something in English that Rosita couldn't understand. She wouldn't have heard properly even if the words had been uttered in perfect Spanish. As the prayers went on, she stood there in stunned silence. She remembered Padrino's questions about Elsa, which had sounded so absurd to her. But it turned out he'd been on to something. He had, after all, been a cop once.

She relived her encounter with Juan at the cemetery. He had rejected her to meet death. At his old lover's hands, no less. And now Elsa had been caught and would have to pay. Was that Oyá's parting gift to her faithful handmaid?

Once the two caskets had been placed in the grave, Sister

Yuleidi tipped the cemetery employees. The Asilo de los Ancianos Desamparados crew left.

"I need to go to Unidad 15," Sharon said. "They found Juan's killer. Oh, that damn woman! The moment I saw her picture, I had a bad feeling about her. I knew."

She couldn't go on. Rosita took her hand and walked with her to the parking lot. A fifties-era orange Chrysler with a sign that read RICE ON WHEELS on the door was the only vehicle there.

"Would you like a ride to the police station?" Rosita asked. "My boyfriend can take you."

"If you don't mind . . ."

"Come with me."

Armando got out of the car and kissed Rosita on the cheek.

"Free at last, *amor*!" he said.

She kissed him back, then told him that they needed to take Sharon, "the widow of a former classmate," to Unidad 15 in El Vedado.

"No problem at all," Armando said. "But I have to make a delivery first, unless this is an urgent matter."

"Nothing's urgent anymore," Sharon replied in a tired voice.

Rosita snuggled next to Armando in the narrow front seat. Sharon sat in the back seat. It was sweltering, and she tried to open the window but couldn't.

"Sorry, Señora, it's broken," Armando said apologetically. "I've just gotten this baby and need to restore it."

He turned on the ignition. After some huffing and puffing, the car finally started, and they drove off.

Rosita remembered Oyá's party on the day of Candlemas. She remembered the dance, her prayers, the *orisha*'s promise and the twisted way it had come true. *Goodbye, Juan*, she thought. Ashes to ashes, a sad pile of bones for their queen.

Armando turned onto Malecón Avenue, and the indigo expanse of the ocean appeared in front of them, rimmed by the seawall. The horizon blossomed in shades of gold and ruby. Rosita closed her eyes and smiled, bathed in the sunlight.

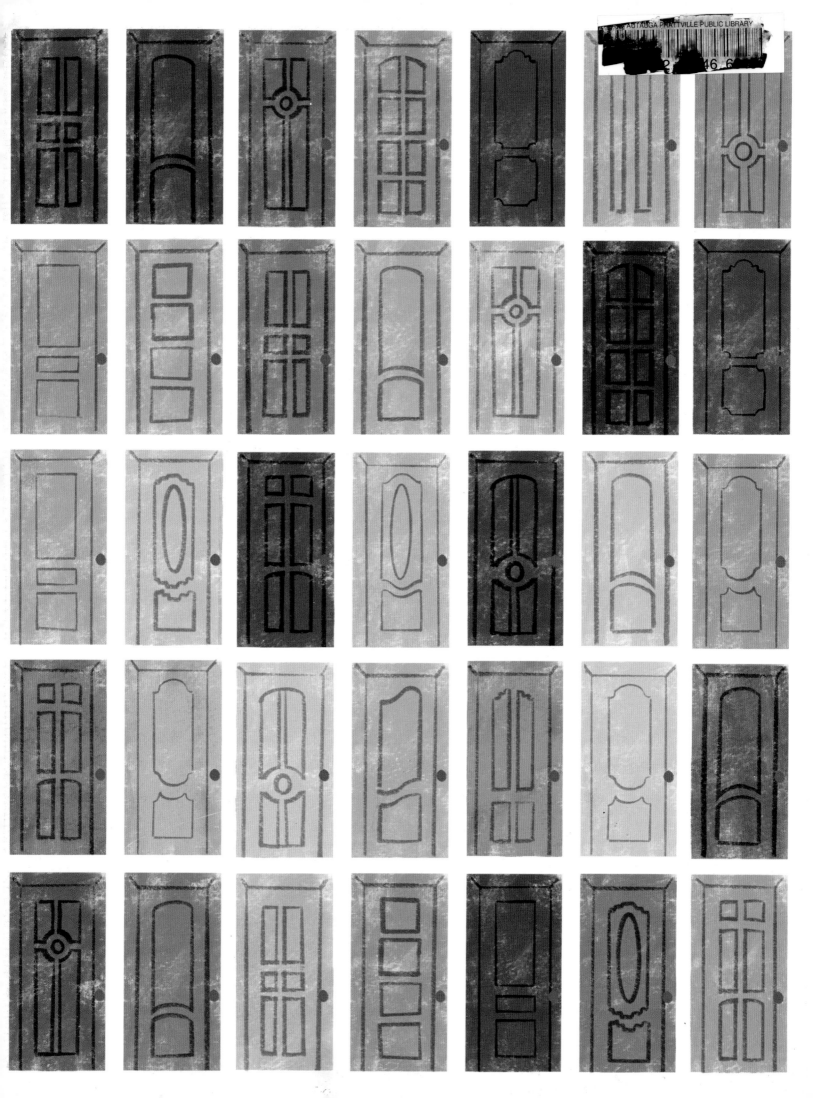

To my dear one, for changing the world just by being yourself. And to N, K, J, and all the tireless trans-rights advocates, for making the world better for everyone. —M.P.

For the kids who see themselves in this book. So glad you are you. —M.M.G.

Visit us on the Web! rhcbooks.com

Educators and librarians, for a variety of teaching tools, visit us at RHTeachersLibrarians.com

Library of Congress Cataloging-in-Publication Data
Names: Pincus, Meeg, author. | Gimbel, Meridth McKean, illustrator.
Title: Door by door: how Sarah McBride became America's first openly transgender senator / Meeg Pincus; illustrated by Meridth McKean Gimbel.
Other titles: How Sarah McBride became America's first openly transgender senator
Description: First edition. | New York: Crown Books for Young Readers, an imprint of Random House Children's Books, a division of Penguin Random House LLC, [2023] | Includes bibliographical references. | Audience: Ages 4–7 | Audience: Grades K–1 | Summary: "A picture book biography of Delaware State Senator Sarah McBride"—Provided by publisher.
Identifiers: LCCN 2021027914 (print) | LCCN 2021027915 (ebook) | ISBN 978-0-593-48465-4 (hardcover) | ISBN 978-0-593-48466-1 (library binding) | ISBN 978-0-593-48467-8 (ebook)
Subjects: LCSH: McBride, Sarah—Juvenile literature. | Delaware. General Assembly. Senate—Biography—Juvenile literature. | Transgender legislators—Delaware—Biography—Juvenile literature. | Legislators—Delaware—Biography—Juvenile literature.
Classification: LCC F170.4.M33 P56 2023 (print) | LCC F170.4.M33 (ebook) | DDC 328.73/092 [B]—dc23/eng/20220310

The text of this book is set in 16-point Fairfield LT Std.
The illustrations were created using pencil, watercolor, and Procreate.
Book design by Elizabeth Tardiff

MANUFACTURED IN CHINA
10 9 8 7 6 5 4 3 2 1
First Edition